The boy next door is...

M000199868

all
grown
up

#1 *NEW YORK TIMES* BESTSELLING AUTHOR

VI KEELAND

All Grown Up
Edited by: Jessica Royer Ocken
Proofreading by: Elaine York, Eda Price
Cover model: Christian Hogue www.imdmodeling.com
Cover designer: Sommer Stein, Perfect Pear Creative, www.perfectpearcreative.com
Formatting by: Elaine York, Allusion Graphics, LLC, www.allusiongraphics.com

all grown up

Age is an issue of mind over matter.

If you don't mind, it doesn't matter.

-Mark Twain

chapter one

Valentina

B *uy a thong.*
I rubbed my eyes and leaned in to re-read the Post-it Note stuck on the lampshade beside the couch where I'd fallen asleep. I had to be reading that wrong.

Nope. It read *buy a thong*, alright. Only it wasn't in my handwriting. Smiling, I pulled the yellow square from the girly looking tasseled lampshade, which tilted as I unstuck the note. I automatically reached to right it, then pulled back. A tilted shade or crooked painting made Ryan nuts. Leaving it gave me a renewed sense of joy about my divorce.

Come to think of it, my ex-husband had hated this lamp set when I'd brought it home. Like the dutiful wife I was, I'd hidden them away in the guest bedroom. The day after Ryan moved out, I'd dusted them off and carried them out to the living room. I'd since bought some coordinating fringed throw pillows he'd hate, too.

I stood, and my dull headache began to throb. *Ugh.* Wine hangover. I padded to the kitchen for some much-needed coffee and two Tylenol. On my way, I found another sticky note—this one on the front door.

Join Match.com

I pulled the yellow square off and crumpled it up, along with the thong note. Last night had been movie night with my best friend, Eve. Once a month, we shared a bottle of wine (or two) and watched movies. We'd been doing it since senior year in high school—more years than I wanted to compute so early in the morning.

It was no secret to anyone who knew me that I had a slight obsession with sticky notes. On most days, you could find to-do squares stuck to my front door, bathroom mirror, the dashboard of my car...just about anywhere. Wadding up the individual papers as I finished each task made me feel like I was getting things accomplished. These days, the squares were all over the place—quadruple the amount I normally had—because I'd been using them to study for the Italian language teaching certification test. Post-its with translated phrases were all over the house.

Apparently, my best friend had gotten in on the action before she left me passed out on the couch last night.

Get laid was stuck to the refrigerator. At least I was reading her to-do list in order—I needed the thong and Match.com to get my celibate self some action.

It wasn't until hours later that I came across the last of Eve's sticky notes. The one stuck to the bathroom mirror read: *Brunch with my amazing best friend. Noon Sunday, Capital Grille on 72nd.*

"You should go out with Liam."

Every other Sunday, Eve and I went to a different restaurant to check out the competition. She owned a French bistro on the Upper East Side and liked to sample the menus and check out the pricing of new places—though today she seemed to be checking out more things than usual.

"Liam? As in our waiter?"

"Yup."

"How old is he, like twenty?"

Eve lifted a martini glass filled with pink liquid to her lips. "I have vibrators older than him." She sipped. "But he's over the age of consent. And I'm guessing I could throw those things out if I took him home. I bet he can get an erection on command." Eve snapped her fingers, demonstrating how it might work. "*Hard*, Liam."

I chuckled. "You'd probably need to throw *Tom* out if you brought that young man home."

"Don't tempt me. He fell asleep in the chair at eight o'clock last night. What kind of a friend lets her best friend marry an old man?"

"Like any of us could've stopped you, even if we'd thought marrying Tom was a mistake. Which it wasn't. Besides, who the hell else would put up with you? We all were just grateful you weren't going to die an old maid."

"Speaking of old maids..."

"Don't even go there."

"Have you gone out with Mark yet?"

"Mark and I are just friends."

"And he wants to jump your bones."

"The ink on my divorce papers is barely dry."

"It's been eighteen months."

Really? January, February, March, April... Oh my. It has been. Where does the time go these days?

"Eighteen months isn't a long time."

"You were separated for *two years* before that. How long has it been since you've had good sex?"

"How did we get from talking about you to my sex life? Or lack thereof? *Again.*"

Eve had started lobbying for me to date while Ryan was still packing his shit into the moving truck. She meant well. But lately she'd amped up her normal nudge to a full-blown push.

She ignored my attempt to change the subject. "How long? Two-and-a-half years, Val?"

"Actually." I pushed the pasta on my plate around with my fork. "If we're talking *good* sex, sadly, it's more like ten years. Ryan wasn't exactly passionate toward the end."

The very handsome (and very young) waiter came back to our table. "Can I get you ladies anything else?"

When he spoke, he looked directly at me. I might not be up on the dating scene, but I could swear that was flirting.

"Some dessert? Something sweet, maybe?"

He really is adorable. "Umm...I'm pretty full, actually. But thank you."

"It's on me. Can't I tempt you even a little? Let me surprise you. You never know, sometimes a little taste is all you need to get your appetite going again."

I looked at his forearms—corded and tattooed. *You can say that again.* "Umm...sure. Maybe I'll take one home for Ryan."

The waiter's smile disappeared right before he did.

"What the hell did you do that for?" Eve scolded.

"What?"

"Mention a man's name to a guy who was hitting on you."

"I meant Ryan, my son—he might be coming home from college this weekend—not my asshole ex-husband. "

"I knew that. But hot-ass waiter didn't."

"So? You don't seriously think I'm going to hook up with a twenty-year-old, do you?"

"Why not? You don't have to marry him. You just need to get back out there, Val."

"I am out there. I just haven't met anyone."

Eve's face screamed *bullshit*. And she was right. Since my divorce, I hadn't even attempted to meet anyone. Honestly, the thought terrified me. The last date I had was in eighth grade when Jimmy Marcum took me to the middle school graduation dance. My ex-husband Ryan and I had been together since high school.

"I'm nervous about dating. I never really did it." I grabbed the napkin from my lap, feeling a sneeze coming on. "*Achoo!*"

"God bless you." She leaned forward and covered my hand with hers. "I know, sweetheart. But the longer you wait to get back out there, the harder it gets. You're over-thinking it."

We paid the bill and walked to our cars with our arms linked. When we arrived at my Volkswagen Routan, Eve shook her head.

"You need to get a different car."

"What? Why?" My silver SUV was in great shape. "Volkswagens are cool."

"Yes. The one Lara Meyer's older brother drove to high school was cool. A hippie bus or a little bug convertible, maybe. That thing...is a minivan. It looks like you're driving around a car full of kids to soccer practice before going home to make your husband dinner."

"That's exactly what I used it for."

"*Used* it for. You've had that thing for ten years. Your kid started driving his own car almost three years ago, for God's sake. I don't think you need the minivan to take him to practice anymore."

"Whatever. It's just a car."

"Want to catch a movie tomorrow?"

"I can't, actually. I have study group. The test is coming up soon."

"See you next Saturday, then?"

I squinted.

"You're coming to our Memorial Day barbeque."

"Wow, is it the end of May already? I think my calendar is filled through June."

Eve kissed my cheek. "Wiseass."

She walked to her car parked a few spots away and yelled over her shoulder as she unlocked her BMW.

"By the way, I wrote your telephone number on the back of the check for the hot waiter. Goodnight, Valentina. Enjoy."

Based on the grin she gave me as she rolled past me and waved, I had no idea if she was kidding or serious.

Jesus, I hope she was kidding.

⁓

The next morning when I powered my phone on, I had two missed calls from an unknown number and a text from Mark.

Mark: *Chinese or Italian tonight?*

It was Mark's turn to host our Saturday evening study group, and the host supplied dinner. He lived in Edgewater like me. Desiree and Allison, the other two in our foursome, lived on the other side of the river in Manhattan.

6

Valentina: You do know my maiden name is Di Giovanni, right? I'm never picking moo shu over meatballs. ☺

Mark: Di Giovanni, huh? That's much more sexy than Davis. You should use it. It suits you better. Italian, it is. See you at five.

He really was a nice guy. Moving things from friendship to more wouldn't be that difficult. We had a lot in common—both divorced, kids around the same age, and decided on a late-in-life career change to teaching. But I just didn't see him in that light. Not that I'd actually put any effort into *trying*, even though I was pretty certain he saw me that way. As was Eve.

My phone buzzed as I poured my morning coffee. *Unknown caller.* Hmm...the third one since last night. I swiped ignore and thumbed off a text to Eve.

Valentina: Did you really give that waiter my number last night?

She responded by the time I'd finished my first dose of caffeine.

Eve: No. But I might have accidentally given your phone number to someone else.

Valentina: Accidentally? How do you accidentally give a phone number to someone?

Eve: Promise you won't be mad.

I hit *Call* rather than texting again. "What did you do?"

"Let's start out with what I *didn't* do."

"Okay..."

"I didn't give your number to that waiter."

"You already told me that."

"I know. But I could have, and I want to make sure you know I would never give out your phone number *on purpose.*"

For Eve to sound worried about telling me something, I knew it wasn't small. "*What did you do*?"

"I accidentally put your phone number on Match. com."

"You *WHAT*?"

"I didn't mean to make it public. I thought it was private, but the setting was wrong. Green means go. Red means stop. Who the hell makes a website where the red button means yes?"

"What are you talking about? I don't even have a Match.com account."

"Umm...you do now."

My stomach sank. "Please tell me you didn't."

"I didn't." She paused, and for a second I felt a little relief. Then she continued. "I didn't...*mean to.*"

"What did you do?"

"I signed you up for a Match.com account last night when I got home. I set it all up, but didn't intend for it to be public. At least not right away. I thought if I set it up and made it easy for you, you might be willing to give it a shot. I was going to talk to you about it at the barbeque."

"You *intended* for it to be private. Meaning it isn't private?"

"That's not the worst part."

"What could be worse?"

"Since I *thought* it was set to private. I set up the account with a joke status to show you."

Oh God.

I ran to my laptop and flipped it open. "What does it say?"

8

"Relax. It's down now. I took it down within an hour. But not before it got a lot of attention. I realized what had happened when the email I set up to use with the account started pinging every two minutes."

"What did it say?" I screeched.

"It said, *Thirty-seven-year-old, divorced mother of one seeks casual fuck to get primed for dating again.*"

"Please tell me you're joking!"

"I wish I was."

A week later, my phone seemed to have calmed down. One night, sitting on the couch with a glass of wine, I even summoned the courage to look at the page Eve had set up for me.

Something you've always wanted to do: Go to Italy.

Favorite color: Hot pink. Not cotton candy or strawberry ice cream pink. Fuchsia. The bolder the better.

I sipped my wine and smiled. That was totally something I would say. Eve had done a good job being me.

Favorite quote: *Una cena senza vino e come un giorno senza sole.*

My smile widened. She had actually spelled it right. *A meal without wine is a day without sunshine.* It was my father's favorite quote. When he passed, I had two wooden signs custom made—one for my kitchen and one for my mother's.

Physical description: Five foot five, slim waist with curves north and south. Olive skin, long, dark, curly hair that I obsessively straighten, even though my curls kick ass, and blue eyes that are my only genetic gift from my mom. My best friend said to tell you, "You'll look twice. I promise."

Age: Twenty-nine (plus eight, but who's counting).

Who I'm looking for: Mr. Right, of course.

My ideal match is: Between the ages of twenty-eight and thirty-eight. Tall. Smart. Funny. Loves to travel. Can dance (because I can't). Takes the scenic route when driving. Has a distinguished palate. Is not named Ryan. Has a fun nickname. (Nicknames of Cunnilingus King go to the top of the pile.)

She had posted a few pictures of me. Each one was captioned. The first was a shot of me in a bikini cannon-balling off the diving board into Eve's inground pool. My hair was flying in the air, knees tucked, and I held my nose. You couldn't see my full face, but from the profile, you could tell I was smiling and laughing. The picture was funny. It wasn't one I would have picked, but it had a lot of personality, and I liked it. Underneath it, she'd captioned: *Not afraid to fly.*

The second picture was taken at Ryan's high school graduation. I was wearing a black and white floral sundress with a halter top that made my boobs look bigger than they are. I had on a wide-brimmed, white sun hat. It had been windy that day, so I was holding the rim of the hat down, and it covered almost all of my face—except my lips. The only thing you could see was bright red lipstick on an ear-to-ear smile. The caption on that one read: *This is me being a proud mom.*

The last shot was a picture of Eve and me in high school. It must have been taken in 9th or 10th grade, seeing as I wasn't pregnant yet. We had our arms around each other and wore matching outfits. Underneath that one she had written: *Same best friend for more than twenty years.*

After editing out some of the crazy Eve had imparted into my profile, I left it set to private. I walked to the fridge and poured myself a third glass of wine. As I shut the door, a magnet tumbled to the floor. The piece of paper it had been holding floated through the air and landed at my feet. I picked it up and read a little. Eve had made the list during one of our movie nights a few weeks ago. The title was written in bold strokes and underlined: **Val's My Turn List.** The first few entries were in her handwriting. They started innocently enough...

Become a teacher
Visit Rome
Plant a giant garden with only flowers
Take dance lessons
Go to prom
Learn to surf
Go to a music festival
Leave my Christmas tree up until March
Get a pug

These were all things I'd wanted to do, but Ryan had been against—going back to school, traveling to Europe, planting a garden for no reason other than to smell flowers, getting a dog. We'd had a garden in our yard, but my ex-husband had filled it with vegetables. He'd thought planting flowers where no one could see them was a waste. And the tree—I *loved* having my Christmas tree up. There's just something about coming down the stairs in the morning when it's still dark, and the tree lighting up the living room. But Ryan hated decorations—he called them clutter and always insisted our tree come down on December 26th. If it were my choice, I'd keep it up year-round. I'd also wanted a dog, a pug, to be specific. But Ryan claimed they made him sneeze, even though we had plenty of friends with dogs, and he seemed fine at their houses.

Over the years of my marriage, I'd let my wants take a backseat to everything else. And that had been the point of the list Eve had started for me—it *was* my choice now. *My turn.*

While the first nine or so items on the list were harmless, things had become much more interesting as the evening went on—and we finished the second bottle of wine.

Wear sexy lingerie under my clothes for no reason
Date seven men in seven nights
Have sex in a public place where I might get caught
One-night stand—no names exchanged
Anal sex

Threesome had been crossed out after Eve and I debated the merits for a while.

I folded the piece of paper and tucked it into my purse. This was the last thing I wanted my son to find when he finally came home this summer. Taking my filled wine glass back to the couch with my laptop, I sat staring at the screen for a while. *Match.com.* I sipped and flipped through the photos Eve had posted. You really couldn't see my face in any of them—no one would have to know if I just went online and checked things out. And I suppose if half of the things on my My Turn list were going to get done, I'd need to start with a date.

I wasn't sure if it was the reminder from the list of all the things I hadn't done, or maybe the wine. Or maybe...just maybe, it was time. But I did something I never thought I would do...I hit *public* on my profile.

Screw it. It's my turn.

chapter
two

Ford

My assistant had a mighty fine ass.

"How the fuck do you get any work done around here?" Logan's head turned to follow Esmée as she walked out of my office. Her hips swayed from side to side, and my friend's head synchronized perfectly.

I couldn't blame him. The damn thing was a work of art. Full and curvy—currently wrapped in tight red fabric that molded to her body—a perfect upside-down heart. When Logan's head craned to the right and nearly touched his shoulder, I knew he was mentally flipping that heart right-side up.

Esmée reached the door and looked back over her shoulder with a flirtatious smile. "Is there anything else I can do for you, Mr. Donovan? *Mr. Beck?*"

"We're good. Thanks, Esmée."

Of course, Logan being Logan, he couldn't keep his mouth shut.

"Do I have to work here to hear you say *Mr. Beck* with that accent every morning?"

Esmée was a recent transplant from Paris to New York. Her heavy French accent escalated her sexiness from an easy ten to an overflowing eleven-plus. I should have known better than to ask her to bring us coffee with Logan anywhere in the vicinity.

"Ignore my friend. He doesn't get out in public much. Would you mind shutting the door behind you?"

When the door closed, I wadded up a paper from my desk and whizzed it at him. "Stop ogling my staff, douchebag. You're going to get me sued for workplace harassment."

"Don't tell me you haven't made a play for that."

"I don't dip my pen in the company ink."

"Since when? Last time I stopped by your office, you were banging that redhead from accounting with the sexy-as-shit shoes. And if I'm not mistaken, her cousin, too—at the same time, you lucky fuck."

"That was a long time ago. I've matured since then."

Logan tipped his chair back and smirked. "I forgot. That's right. The receptionist—*Ms. Mature.* What was her name again? Misty? Marsha? Magdalene?"

"Maggie. And don't remind me. That cost me a small fortune."

"I would have paid a small fortune for what that woman gave you."

"Except you don't *have* a small fortune, asswipe."

A few years ago I was going through a rough patch and not thinking with the right head. My receptionist videoed herself while giving me a blow job under my desk. I had no idea the whole thing was a setup. She'd positioned cameras from two different angles and told me to act like a pissed-off boss giving his secretary a job to do. I'd never been into role play before, but it turned out to be pretty damn hot.

Until she showed me a copy of the video and threatened to sue me for sexual harassment in the workplace. My attorney made me settle before it went to court. That was a business lesson in growing up they hadn't taught me in college.

"So what's our plan for next week?" Logan asked.

"My place at six. The C train is a block north on Eighty-first."

Every year my college buddies got together for a weekend pub-crawl. We started early and hit a different bar within walking distance of each stop on a train line. One hour per bar. Ten stops on the train, ten different bars. Most years, guys started dropping by the fifth stop. But Logan and I always made it to the end. I paced myself, alternating waters between my drinks. Logan, well, he didn't do the conservative approach. But the fucker could put away more drinks than anyone I'd ever met.

"What do you say we go warm up? Hit O'Malley's?"

I looked at the time on my phone. "It's ten thirty in the morning."

Logan shrugged. "So?"

"I have actual work to do. In fact, you need to get the hell out of here. I have a meeting in ten minutes."

"I still can't believe you get to call sitting in this place and having that Persian kitten fetch you coffee, work."

"A person from Paris is Parisian, not Persian, dumbass. And not everything is as simple as it looks."

He shrugged and stood. "Whatever. Drinks tonight?"

"Can't. Picking up Bella."

"*Annabella*. How is your little sister?"

"Not so little anymore. Spent a semester abroad in Madrid. She's flying home tonight. I told her I'd pick her up at the airport."

"She's in college already?"

"Going to start her second year. Nineteen."

"Damn. She was always a cute little thing. Bet she's a hot number now that she's legal."

"Don't even think about it, asshole."

Logan chuckled and held out his hand for a shake. We clasped. "Next week, then, pretty boy?"

The intercom buzzed, and Esmée's voice came through. "Ford, you have Mrs. Peabody on the line."

Logan's forehead wrinkled. "Peabody? You still talk to that nutjob?"

"She's not a nutjob... She's just eccentric."

"Eccentric is just the polite way of saying nutjob." Logan shook his head. "I worry about you sometimes. I think you might be as nuts as her."

"Get out, jackass. And don't harass my receptionist on the way out."

It made no sense to leave the office and go all the way uptown to my place, only to head back downtown to shoot over to the airport at ten. I had enough shit to do here to keep me busy for days anyway. By the time seven o'clock rolled around, the floor was pretty empty—just me and the night cleaning crew. I'd ordered in some Thai food and decided to go sit in the seating area in front of the windows, rather than behind my desk with my back facing the city.

I sank into the leather couch, slipped off my shoes, and propped my feet up on the glass table in front of me. Still a few hours to kill, so I started to sort through my email while eating with chopsticks out of a cardboard container. My inbox was a damn disaster. At any given moment, there were always three-hundred unread and follow-up items to manage. I sorted them oldest first and opened one I'd been avoiding for nearly a week. The director of marketing wanted me to consider a half-million-dollar investment in an advertising campaign with Match.com.

I normally didn't question his judgment—he'd been with my dad for twenty-five years. But I wasn't so sure a dating website was the right place to market high-end Manhattan shared workspace. And that was a damn big chunk of change. Part of the problem was, I had no experience with how the online dating scene worked or the buying habits of its users.

After reading the PowerPoint proposal, I clicked on the link on the last slide, deciding to give the site a test drive. It took me about ten minutes to set up an account. When it prompted me to begin a search, I felt like I was shopping at the supermarket for the ingredients to make my favorite meal—interests, background, height, body type. I started to get into it and added shit like my favorite slogans and my *happy place* so the site could match me with women with similar ideals.

My search returned more than a thousand profiles. I clicked on a few, and within minutes, one face began to blur into the next. Every woman I saw at the popular bar of the month must have also had a profile on this damn site.

I clicked around a little more and noticed some ads starting to appear. Within minutes, they knew enough about me to target exactly the type of product I'd buy. I'd listed one of my hobbies as hiking and checked the box for income over two-hundred-and-fifty grand a year.

An ad popped up on the left of my screen showing a Patagonia brand, top of the line, all-weather backpack for four-hundred bucks. This site knew their users—probably gathered more intimate details than anywhere else.

After I finished buying the blue Mountain Elite bag, I clicked back to my email and told the director of marketing to move forward. *Sold.*

With no desire to continue my email cleanup and hours before I had to leave to pick up Bella, I narrowed my Match.com search criteria and updated my profile. The age category took me about ten minutes of staring at the screen.

Eighteen to twenty-four?
Twenty-five to thirty-one?
Thirty-two to thirty-eight?

At the ripe old age of twenty-five, I was done dating the eighteen-to-twenty-four crowd. Been there, done that. I had no patience for games. I wanted a woman who knew who she was, rather than one who tried to be the woman she thought I wanted. *Unclick. Later, eighteen to twenty-four.*

Leaving the box on the twenty-five to thirty-one age group checked, my pointer then hovered over the next box. Why was I excluding an awesome thirty-two-year-old? That's more experience. And likely less bullshit. *Click.*

After all my modifications, I now had only a dozen or so women who were my supposed ideal match. One through five seemed interesting, definitely worth a second look. Then I clicked on number six—a woman from New Jersey. Her profile writeup actually had me laughing out loud.

Intrigued, I clicked over to her pictures. There were only a few, but one in particular caught my attention. It was a photo taken from the side as she cannonballed into a pool. Her dark hair flew high above her, and the portion of her face I could see was scrunched up in a smile. And while I couldn't get a good look at her body, since it was all folded up, I could see she had the curves to rock the bikini she wore. Even better, she looked like the type of woman who cared more about having fun than her hair and makeup getting ruined in the pool. And lately, the latter was the type of woman I seemed to attract when I went out.

By the time my phone buzzed, reminding me it was time to leave to pick up Bella, I'd wasted almost two hours on a dating site I never thought I'd visit. I started to shut down my laptop, but the last open window had the photo of the woman cannonballing. It made me smile again before I clicked it closed.

My finger hovered over the power button to turn off my Mac, but then I thought better of it and went back to the dating site one more time.

I scanned through my matches, looking for one in particular. Finding Val44, I took one more peek.

What the hell? Why not?

Plenty of people used sites like this.

I clicked the button beneath her profile to let her know I was interested.

———

"This place is so boring."

I dragged the last of my sister's bags into my apartment and grabbed a bottle of water from the fridge. It was pretty damn humid for almost the end of May.

"Manhattan? Is boring? That's one I haven't heard."

Bella rolled her eyes. "I don't mean Manhattan. I mean your apartment. What fun can I have staying with my brother?"

"Where else would you stay? Besides, you're here for the summer, not forever." *Thank God for small things.* Bella had been fourteen when our parents died five years ago. I'd never thought about *not* taking her in and becoming her guardian, even though I was only twenty at the time. But I'll admit I was relieved when she'd decided to go away for college. Raising a fourteen-year-old was sure as hell easier than a nineteen-year-old.

"The summer house. I'll go out to Montauk for the summer."

"I can't commute from there every day."

"So? Who asked you to commute? I meant *I* would spend the summer out there, and *you* would spend the summer here."

"Not happening."

"Why not?"

"Because you'd be all alone, and there's no security out there."

"*It's Montauk.* No one even locks their doors. We spent every summer out there growing up. Montauk is safer than Manhattan."

"How do I know you aren't going to have wild parties?"

"So what if I do?"

"You're nineteen, not twenty-one."

She arched a brow. "And you never had a drink or threw a party until you were twenty-one?"

"That's different."

"How?"

"It just is."

"God, Ford. When did you turn into *Dad*?"

Even if I had security installed at the beach house out east, I wasn't sure it was a good place for Bella to be. Neither of us had been there since we lost Mom and Dad, and if there was anyplace in the world that was filled with memories of them, it was Montauk—Mom hosing down our feet in the outdoor shower, having breakfast with Dad on the back deck. Dad leaning in the doorway quietly, watching Mom dance to music in the kitchen. The way he smiled when he looked at her—that thought picked at a wound that had only just begun to heal.

When our accountant had suggested we rent out the place, I didn't even entertain the idea. I'd rather take the loss on maintaining the property than let strangers into the house.

Bella would never be able to handle the stir of all those memories. Honestly, I wasn't sure I could either. I should probably just put the place up for sale.

"Come on, Ford. You know, I don't actually need your permission to go. I can grab the Jitney while you're at work."

Of course she was right. Bella was over eighteen and could go anywhere she wanted now. The only thing I held over her was the purse strings. I was her financial trustee until she was twenty-one.

"Maybe we can spend a weekend out there or something?" I said.

"You mean the two of us? Gee, how romantic. Sounds like a blast."

I sighed. This was going to be one long-ass summer.

chapter three

Valentina

At first, scrolling through the responses I received had been entertaining. I'd sift through the dating profiles while having a glass of wine and read the endless stream of messages. But after a few days, it became apparent that even though some of the guys seemed nice, I wasn't going to respond to any of them.

I had no idea what to say. *I'm totally not ready.*

Just as I was about to sign off and go to bed, an instant message popped up on the bottom of my screen. I didn't even know you could send those. Donovan620 from New York City wrote: *Ryan is my middle name. Am I disqualified?*

I'd forgotten to change the part of my profile that said my ideal match was not named Ryan, having been too focused on removing the part about favoritism shown to those nicknamed Cunnilingus King. Although, it was probably just as well since the thought of calling another man *Ryan* after so many years with my husband was just too odd to me. Plus, it was also my son's name.

When I didn't respond in a few minutes, another message popped up.

Donovan620: Really? I'm vetoed because of a middle name? I can probably get it legally changed if it works out. Although, my grandfather might be upset.

His message made me laugh, so I typed back.

Val44: I actually think Ryan as a middle name would be fine, so long as you would stipulate to abbreviate it in your signature and not introduce yourself utilizing it.

Donovan620: If anyone you meet on here introduces himself using his first, middle, and last name, you should delete him immediately. That's just weird.

Val44: You're probably right.

Donovan620: I get that a lot. So...why so anti-Ryan, Valentina D?

He'd used my full name, which meant he must have checked out my profile. Curiously, I clicked on his. There was only one picture, although it definitely caught my attention. He was mid air, jumping off a high-dive board, and the photo was taken from the ground. His knees were tucked and his arms wrapped around them as he cannonballed into a pool. It was almost the same profile pic as my photo, except he was, of course, a man. I looked closer—Donovan620 was definitely a man, with some amazing muscular arms wrapped around his knees. Even his calf muscles bulged in the shot.

Another message popped up. I hadn't responded to his question about the name Ryan.

Donovan620: Are you busy checking out my profile or ignoring me?

Val44: Ignoring you.

Donovan620: Well, you're not very good at it seeing as you just responded.

He made me smile again. So I 'fessed up.

Val44: I might have been checking out your profile. Did you notice anything interesting about our profile pictures?

Donovan620: That's what caught my attention. Any woman who cannonballs is worth changing my middle name for.

Donovan was witty. I liked him. And maybe, just maybe, his muscles were nice, too. I refilled my wine glass.

Donovan620: That wasn't the only coincidence. Go ahead, check me out fully.

Clicking back to his profile, I continued to read.

Age: 25

My ideal match: Old enough to know better, young enough to not give a fuck. Smart. Loves the outdoors and simple things in life—like taking the scenic route when driving.

Val44: Did you just add that to your ideal match?

Donovan620: Nope.

Val44: Well, it seems as though we have a few things in common. It's too bad I don't meet the rest of your criteria.

Donovan620: What part?

Val44: While I'm definitely old enough to know better, it seems I do give a fuck.

Donovan620: I'll overlook your sensibility, seeing as you've dealt with my unfortunate middle name.

Val44: That's very kind of you. But we have another problem—one I'm afraid we won't be able to get past.

Donovan620: And that is...

Val44: You're too young for me. You're twenty-five. I'm thirty-seven.

Donovan620: Your profile states that your ideal match is between the ages of twenty-five and thirty-eight.

Val44: My friend wrote that. I've recently updated it to over 35.

Donovan620: Is she a good friend?

Val44: Yes. Why?

Donovan620: Then you should listen to her. She knows you and probably knows what she's talking about.

Val44: Yes, but—

His next message popped up before I could finish.

Donovan620: Age is only a number. What's important is you're obviously young at heart since you still cannonball, and you'd choose the scenic route over the faster freeway. Don't say no just yet. Talk to me for a while. See if we connect. Then decide.

Val44: I don't know, Donovan. I had a child at a young age. My son is not that much younger than you.

Donovan620: A week. Come on. This is my first experience on Match, and you don't want to ruin that for me. The outcome of this could scar me for life if it goes sideways.

I thought about it for a while. I wasn't planning on meeting him in person during that time.

Val44: Is it really your first experience on here?

Donovan620: I swear. You can check the join date on my profile.

I figured he didn't have a reason to lie about something so insignificant, so I took his word for it. Maybe taking the plunge and talking to someone on here for the first time, when it was also his first time, wouldn't be too bad. I mean, neither of us would have any preconceived notion of how it was supposed to go, which would probably alleviate the stress of feeling like I had no idea what I was doing.

Val44: And we would just chat online for the next week? Not meet in person?

Donovan620: If that's what you want, yes.

I knew I had to eventually dip my toe back in the water. Why not take a baby step and chat online? *Practice.* Since it wouldn't lead to anything at the end of the week, how could it hurt to agree?

Val44: Okay. A week.

"You didn't tell me you were turning your Memorial Day barbeque into a bash." I handed Eve a glass cake dish filled with my homemade tiramisu. It was her favorite.

"Just a few extra."

The backyard was visible from the kitchen through a double set of French doors. There had to be fifty people outside, and inside there were a few milling around, too.

Normally, the Monroe Memorial Day barbeque capped at twenty.

"A few? Who are all those people? I would have made two desserts."

Eve waved off my comment with her hand, then dug into the utensil drawer. She pulled out a huge serving spoon and, before I could stop her, scooped a heaping spoonful from the delectable dessert I'd just handed her.

"That took me hours to make!"

"I wasn't going to share it anyway. Haven't you ever noticed that every year I hide it in the back of the fridge and accidentally forget to put it out?"

My phone buzzed in my pocket. It had been doing that a lot lately. Donovan and I had spent hours messaging back and forth the last four days. We'd even progressed from chatting within the dating app to texting—probably not the smartest move, but at least now I got a text notification when he messaged and didn't have to open the app every five minutes to see if I'd missed something.

Donovan: Did you leave any of that tiramisu at home?

Valentina: I can't leave any at home, or I'll eat it. That stuff is my weakness. I might as well glue some ladyfingers to my ass with the calories in there.

Donovan: Now those sound like delicious ladyfingers...

I felt a little tingle reading that last sentence. He'd been polite in our exchanges, for the most part. But sometimes he'd throw in sexy one-liners like that, and I really sort of liked it.

"Who are you texting?" Eve asked.

"No one."

She squinted. "No one, huh?"

Tom Monroe saved me from further interrogation. Walking inside from the yard, he wrapped one arm around his wife's waist from behind, pulled her flush against him, and stole the serving spoon out of her hand. He shoveled a heaping bite of my beautiful tiramisu between his lips and spoke with a full mouth.

"This stuff is better than sex."

Eve arched an eyebrow at me. "Told you. Old."

Her husband, used to her playful jabs, ignored her. "Did you meet Jonathon yet?"

Eve elbowed him. "She just got here. I haven't mentioned Jonathon yet."

Tom snorted. "Or Will. Or Jack. Or Mike, Adam, or Timmy. Although, I think my wife is wrong and Timmy is gay."

I fixed my stare on my friend. "What is he talking about?"

Eve took the spoon back from her husband and filled her mouth with more dessert. Pointing at her cheeks, she made garbled sounds to relay her inability to speak.

I looked over her shoulder. "Tom, what did your wife do?"

"She made me invite every single man in my office. I'm guessing you had no idea."

"Good guess." I turned to Eve. "*Please* tell me you didn't tell them I was single and looking to meet someone."

"Of course not."

"Thank God."

"I told them you were single and looking to get laid."

My eyes widened to saucers.

Eve reached out and put her hand on my arm. "Kidding."

"You better be."

She wriggled out of her husband's hold and slung her arm around my neck. "Come on, let me introduce you to some people."

Jonathon turned out to be a really nice guy, although not my personal taste. He was good looking enough. The problem was more his abundant spirituality. I like a man who has strong beliefs, don't get me wrong. But when someone spends fifteen minutes preaching to me about his church and religion during the first twenty minutes we meet, I think he may be a little too reverent for me and my frequent potty mouth.

Will lived with his mother and had not ever been married—a warning sign even to a non-dater such as myself.

Mike told me about his ex-wife for a half an hour. Clearly, he was still hung up on her.

Timmy, well...Tom called that one. He was more interested in Mike than me.

That left me with Adam. Six-feet tall, clean shaven, broad shoulders under a navy polo with a little horse on it and Ferragamo loafers. My interest was sparked.

"So you work with Tom at Dunn and Monroe?"

"Been there about a year now."

"What do you do?"

"I'm the VP of Finance."

For the next half hour, Adam and I got to know each other. He was as funny and smart as he was handsome and polite. He certainly checked all the boxes for a man I should date. Yet...no butterflies swarmed in my belly. But maybe my expectations were off. Maybe I'd watched too many sappy romance movies. I'd felt that excitement when I'd first met Ryan, though I was a teenager back then. Perhaps things were more subdued and pleasant when dating a man in your late thirties. That made sense.

Though when he excused himself to take a call, I realized I was wrong.

My phone vibrated in my pocket, so I dug it out. Donovan's name flashed on the screen...causing a flutter in my chest and a swarm of bees in my belly. *Damn it.*

Donovan: How's the party you didn't invite me to go to with you?

Valentina: It's nice. Although, calmer than most years. It has a very different vibe. No one is even in the pool.

Donovan: No one in the pool? See, you should have invited me. I'd be in the pool and so would you.

I looked around. The usual Monroe pool party barbeque was more like a cocktail party this year. People were dressed a little nicer, and the air was stiffer. It was nice, just not the usual carefree, anything-goes party Eve normally threw.

Valentina: It's a different crowd than usual. More of Eve's husband's colleagues from work.

Donovan: What does he do?

Valentina: He's a mutual fund manager.

Donovan: Sounds boring. Definitely should have brought me.

Valentina: Oh really? And what do you do that is so exciting?

Donovan: I told you, I'm self-employed.

Valentina: Yes, but you haven't elaborated.

Donovan: You haven't asked.

He had a point. I'd been hesitant to delve too deeply into who Donovan was over the last few days. The more we chatted, the more I liked him. And I had no intention of getting involved with a boy of his age. Finding things in common would make it even more difficult to cut this tie at the end of the week. Before I could respond, my phone buzzed again.

Donovan: Not even a little curious?

Valentina: Of course. I just didn't want to be too intrusive.

Donovan: Intrusive = Afraid to get to know you for fear I might actually like you.

Valentina: That's not it at all.

That's totally it!

Donovan: Well, then, I'm good with intrusive. So ask away.

I sighed. Looking around the yard, I realized I had met a ton of very nice people today. But I was more interested in talking to Donovan. I took a seat and bit the bullet.

Valentina: Dearest Donovan, might I ask what it is you do for a living?

Donovan: Sure thing, Val. I'm glad you asked. I'm in real estate.

Totally not what I expected him to say. I had this picture of Donovan riding a bike with a messenger bag slung over his shoulder or working as a first-year fireman. Definitely not a suit-wearing, Manhattan real estate wheeler-dealer.

Valentina: Wow. That wasn't what I thought you were going to say.

Donovan: What did you think I did?

I didn't want to insult him and say I thought he might be a messenger, so I went with fireman, thinking it was harmless.

Valentina: I don't know. Fireman might have been my guess.

Or fantasy. Whatever.

Donovan: Women tend to think firemen are hot, correct?

Valentina: Don't get ahead of yourself now.

Donovan: Okay, then. What, exactly, made you think I might have been a fireman?

Shit. I was drawing a blank.

Just then, Adam returned.

"Sorry about that. It was my daughter. She's sixteen, and it was a crisis. Her mother took away her flat iron for leaving it on, and she thought calling me and demanding I tell her mother to give it back was a good idea."

I smiled. "I take it she wasn't happy when she hung up."

"You can say that again. My ex and I don't agree on much, but we've done well at supporting each other's parental decisions."

"How long have you been divorced?"

"Nine years. You?"

"How did you know I was divorced?"

"Eve might have mentioned it."

I forced a smile. "Sorry about that. She means well. But she insists I need to get back into the dating world even though it's only been eighteen months."

"Would I be overstepping if I asked how long things weren't great before the divorce? For me it was at least five years. So when we finally split up, it had been a long time since either of us was happy, and we were both ready to move on."

"I suppose you're right. We were separated for two years before the divorce, and things hadn't been great in a while." My phone buzzed in my hand, and I looked down.

"Do you want to take that? I can go grab us some drinks. How about a refill for that margarita?"

"I'd love that. Thank you, Adam."

Returning to my phone, there were three successive texts from Donovan, a minute apart.

Donovan: Got nothing, huh?

Donovan: Admit it. You think I'm hot.

Donovan: Got a buddy who's on NYFD. I can borrow his uniform if you go out with me.

Valentina: Sorry. I was talking with someone.

Donovan: Man or woman?

Valentina: Why do you ask?

Donovan: Because if it's a man, I want to know if you think he's hot, too.

Valentina: You're pretty full of yourself, aren't you?

Donovan: Me? You're the one having hot and sweaty fireman dreams about me.

Valentina: I never said...

My texting was interrupted by another from him. He had fast fingers.

Donovan: Admit it.

Valentina: Why is it so important to you?

Donovan: Because I like you. And if you're fantasizing about me, there's a better chance I can talk you into going out with me.

I really wished he were a bit older—even just a few years and into his early thirties would be more appropriate.

Valentina: I like you, too, Donovan. I don't want to lead you on. I've enjoyed this time chatting with you...I really have. But you're just too young for me.

Donovan: I'm actually not that young. I did some serious thinking about this yesterday. The average life expectancy of a man is 68.5 and for a woman it's 73.5. That means you're probably going to live five years longer than me. Therefore, I have a 5 handicap.

Valentina: A handicap?

Donovan: Yeah. Like in golf. I get to add five years to my age. So we're really only seven years apart, and you can certainly get past that.

I chuckled and shook my head.

Valentina: Nice try. But your logic is flawed. We measure life by how long we've been here. Therefore, you receive no handicap.

Donovan: It's time you changed that outlook, Val. Age shouldn't be counted by the time we've been alive. It should be counted by the years we have left. Look forward, not back.

It was just a funny exchange. I didn't think it was meant to be profound or anything of the sort. Yet his words hit me. I *had* been looking back, for a long time now. Donovan was right.

I gulped back the rest of the margarita in my glass and stared at my phone for a long moment. The party was going on all around me, yet everything was suddenly quiet.

I was single.

I hadn't been happy in a long time.

My son was a grown man and no longer needed me.

Pretty soon, I'd be making a major career change.

Why was I constantly looking back at my failed marriage?

Valentina: I might have daydreamed a little about how you would look in a fireman's uniform. And...

I took a deep breath.

Valentina: If you still want to go out on a date, let's do it.

Donovan: You just feel bad for me because I'm going to die five years earlier, don't you?

I laughed out loud. It felt good. Like taking in a deep breath on the first day of spring.

Valentina: I just had an epiphany. I'm looking forward now. And forgetting all my self-imposed rules of the past.

Donovan: Now you're talking. When do I get to see you in person?

Adam was heading back my way with a filled margarita glass.

Valentina: Can we talk tomorrow? I've been rude to the gentleman who just fetched me a drink.

Donovan: Gentleman?

Valentina: Yes...Adam.

My face brightened at yet another forward-thinking thought. Only this one, I probably shouldn't have shared with Donovan. I was just so damn excited, though.

Valentina: Maybe I'll go out with Adam, too! Chat tomorrow! Have a good night.

After that, I tucked my phone into my pocket and gave Adam my full attention. The world was suddenly brighter.

chapter four

Valentina

"**W**hat the hell do I wear for a date? I haven't been on one in twenty years."

I frantically tore through my closet. Everything I owned suddenly seemed to scream *soccer mom*. I pulled out a new outfit I'd worn a few weeks ago and held it up against me, showing it to Eve.

"Is he taking you to a funeral?"

I actually *had* bought it for a funeral. *Oh my God.* I had nothing to wear.

I tossed the hangers on the floor of my closet and joined Eve on the bed. Covering my face with my hands, I grumbled, "I can't do this. I can't go."

"You have a closet full of clothes and a kick-ass figure. There's something in there you can wear. Besides, all you really need is nice underwear. That's all he'll care about."

My eyes widened. "He's going to see my underwear tonight? On the first date?"

Eve took pity on me, letting me off the hook easier than she normally did when she screwed with me. "Relax. I'm joking."

I reached for a tissue on my end table. "*Achoo!*" My other hand covered my rapidly beating heart. "Thank God. Honestly, I have no idea what he's expecting. What I'm expecting. What the hell I'm even doing."

"You're taking your life back. *It's your turn*, Val. That's what you're doing. And it's about damn time." Eve got up from the bed and walked into the closet. "And if you want to show this young hottie your underwear tonight on the first date, you do that. You do whatever makes you happy. It's time you put your own needs first."

"But what does he expect to happen?"

"If he *expects* anything to happen, he's an asshole and not worth your time."

"Maybe it's too soon."

Eve popped her head out from my walk-in closet and spoke to me sternly, not unlike how I might've warned my son at times. "You're going."

My shoulders slumped. "Yes, Mom."

"And don't sneeze on the poor guy!"

Oh God. What if I do sneeze on him? I hadn't thought of that. Ever since I was a little girl, I sneezed when I got nervous. It had been in check for years—probably because my mundane life didn't have anything going on in it to get excited or nervous about—but lately I'd noticed it happening again.

Eve had disappeared into the closet, but she came back out. "And stop worrying about sneezing on him now!"

She knew me so well.

It took another forty-five minutes for us to agree on what I should wear, and in the end, almost the entire contents of my closet were in a heap on my bed. I had on a red skirt, cute, strappy, high-heeled sandals that I'd bought but never had occasion to wear, and a form-fitting black top that showed off a hint of my cleavage.

"You don't think this top is too tight?"

"You look sexy, yet classy."

I reached for a sweater, even though it was a warm evening. Eve swiped it from my hand. "You don't need a sweater. You just want to cover up."

She was absolutely right. I sighed, pushing out a nervous breath. "Fine." We left the bedroom a disaster and walked to the kitchen.

"What time is he picking you up?"

"He's not. I'm meeting him."

"He didn't offer to pick you up? Wait, let me guess. He did. But you told him you would rather meet him somewhere instead."

"It's safer that way."

"And you can't chicken out if you give him your address."

That, too.

"I'm not chickening out."

Eve opened the fridge and pulled out a bottle of water. Uncapping it, she pondered something before speaking. "Why don't I drive you and pick you up? I can wait outside and make sure he isn't a serial killer or anything."

"You just want to make sure I go and check him out in person."

She guzzled half her water. "Where did you say you were meeting him? Tom and I were talking about going out to eat. Maybe I will come spy on you, tell you if he's worthy of seeing your panties on the first date."

I arrived at the restaurant ten minutes early, and yet I was still sitting in my car fifteen minutes after the time I was supposed to meet Donovan. I'd never had a panic attack, but I was pretty certain that's what was happening. My palms were sweaty, my heart was racing, and I had the uncontrollable urge to flee to the safety of my home—although there was no way I could possibly drive in this condition.

When my phone buzzed with an incoming text, I hesitated to look at it, knowing there was a good chance whoever it was would make me deal with my current situation. By ignoring it, I could buy more time. So that's what I did for another five minutes.

The next time my phone buzzed, it was a phone call instead of a text. I peeked at the caller ID. It was Donovan, and I was twenty minutes late. He had been such a nice guy so far. He didn't deserve me standing him up. Taking a deep breath, I swiped and answered.

"Hello."

"Valentina? Is everything okay?" His voice was deep and raspy. Really manly and *really* sexy. Something else I didn't expect.

"Yes. No. Yes. I mean, no. I'm sorry, Donovan. I'm not going to be able to make it tonight."

"What's going on? Are you okay?"

"I am. It's...it's...I didn't realize I wasn't ready until now." Just then, a horn blared off in the distance. I had my car window cracked open to get fresh air.

"Where are you?"

"I'm...I'm...sort of in the parking lot."

"Of the restaurant?"

"Yes." I felt like an idiot admitting it.

"Nervous?"

"You might say that."

"Want me to come outside?"

"Not really."

"What can I do to help?"

"Nothing. I'm sorry. I know this is ridiculous. I'm acting like a teenager, and I'm so embarrassed."

"What kind of car do you drive?"

"Please don't come out and get me. It'll make my humiliation even worse."

"I won't come out unless you want me to. I just want to make sure you're safe."

"I drive a silver Routan. But I'm fine. I just need to sit here for a while."

"Okay. Stay on the phone with me. Maybe it will help you relax. You shouldn't drive if you're nervous anyway."

Here I am jerking this poor guy around, and he's offering to keep me company on the phone while I stand him up. "Thank you."

"So I probably shouldn't tell you this if you're already nervous about meeting me, but it's too odd of a coincidence to keep to myself."

"What?"

"You need to come inside because an old lady I know had a dream that I met my future wife today."

"What are you talking about?"

"Mrs. Peabody. It's a long story, but I sort of have a friend who's older, and she sometimes has these premonitions and weird dreams. This morning she randomly called me and said she woke up at two in the morning knowing I was going to meet my future wife today."

"Oh really?" I chuckled. "Did she say anything else?"

"No. Well, except that she smelled cinnamon buns in the oven and then vomited right after."

"She what?"

"She threw up. But that's normal. She always throws up after her premonitions."

I shook my head. "I think you're right."

"So you'll come inside?"

"No..." I laughed. "I meant you shouldn't have told me, because now I'm afraid you might be a little crazy."

"We're all a little crazy, Val. What fun would it be if we only filled our life with normal things?"

That was a question I could answer, since my life had been boring as hell the last few years: no fun at all. Maybe I needed a Mrs. Peabody in my life.

"You're right."

"What's your favorite drink, Val?"

"I usually drink wine, but my favorite mixed drink is a dirty martini."

Donovan sounded amused. "Not what I was expecting."

"What were you expecting?"

"Some frou-frou drink."

"They're a waste of calories."

"Well, I'm going to sit at the bar and order two dirty martinis. If you decide to come in, yours will be waiting for you. I'm in no rush. Why don't you take a few minutes, put your seat back, shut your eyes, and relax. I'll call back in a bit to check on you."

"Okay. Thank you."

A few minutes later, a knock at my window startled me. I nearly froze, expecting it to be Donovan. But it wasn't. Instead, it was an older man wearing a white dress shirt, black vest, and black slacks—a waiter and not my date. In one hand, he held a dirty martini, and in the other he had an antipasto plate.

I rolled the window down the rest of the way. "Hi."

"From the gentleman at the bar."

Smiling, I accepted the delivery, took a healthy gulp of the martini, and hit *Call* on my phone.

Donovan answered without saying hello. "This counts as a first date now. We're having a drink together. Mine's delicious. How's yours?"

I settled back into my seat. "It's yummy. Very dirty. I like a lot of olive juice."

"As long as you brought it up, I like it dirty, too."

I chuckled. "Is that so?"

"It is. I'm sorry. Hang on a second. I have someone beeping in, and I need to take it."

"Go right ahead. I'll just sit here and enjoy my cocktail." The line went quiet for a moment, and then he came back.

"Sorry about that. I should tell you that there's another woman in my life, a very demanding one."

"Oh?"

"She's a giant pain in the ass, but I can't seem to figure out how to ignore her calls."

"Your ex-wife?"

"Worse. Little sister. I'm always afraid it will be that one time something is really wrong and I don't pick up."

"Did something happen?"

"She's upset at the painter who's working in my apartment at the moment."

"What did he do?"

"He arrived at 9 a.m. this morning...on a Saturday."

"Okay..."

"She doesn't get up until at least one."

43

I chuckled.

"By the way, your drink only has one shot of alcohol. It's mostly olive juice. But maybe you should only drink half, in case you decide not to come in and want to drive in the near future."

God, this man was so damn thoughtful. The way he made everything easy for me made it harder at the same time. We stayed on the phone talking for another half hour. Considering our current predicament, the conversation focused on bad first dates. Since I hadn't really had any in twenty years, Donovan did most of the talking. He told me he despised when people ate off of his plate, yet it seemed to be a frequent occurrence. His last three first dates had all ordered salad, drank too much, and then proceeded to pick at his plate of food.

"I wanted to stab my last date's hand with my fork every time she reached over. I don't get it. Order your own food if you're hungry."

"They're probably self conscious about ordering a big meal in front of their date."

"Why?"

"Because almost all women are self-conscious about their weight."

"Are you?"

"I used to be. But as I came into my thirties, I learned to accept that I was never going to be stick thin, and instead, now I love my curves."

"I love your curves, too."

"You haven't even seen my curves yet."

Donovan went quiet.

"Did I lose you?"

"Nope. I'm still here."

Then he was quiet again. We'd never had an awkward moment before, and I wasn't sure what he was thinking.

If he was half as smart as he seemed, he was probably thinking *What the hell am I doing talking on the phone with this nutcase?*

I spoke quietly. "I'm sorry about tonight."

"Nothing to be sorry about, Val."

"That's not true. But thank you for saying that."

Again, he went quiet. He was probably regretting the day he messaged me, and I couldn't blame him.

After a full minute of dead silence, we both went to speak at the same time. Oddly, we said the same words. I said, "Listen, Donovan," just as he said, "Listen, Val."

"You go first," I offered.

"Ladies first."

"I—" When I opened my mouth to begin to thank him and say goodbye, I noticed the waiter again walking to my car. This time, he was carrying a piece of cake. "The waiter is walking my way with a huge piece of chocolate cake. Is that for me, too?"

"I had to buy you dessert. Can't have your first date in twenty years suck now, can I?"

The waiter smiled as he approached. I began to roll down my window to accept what looked to be a delicious slice of molten chocolate lava cake, then realized just how insane I was being. "Can you hang on one second?" I asked Donovan.

I pressed mute before getting out of the car. I thanked the waiter and stood outside with my cake in hand. After a minute, I took a deep breath and headed to the restaurant door to have dessert with my date. *In person.*

Inside, the bar was almost empty. Even though his back was to me, it wasn't too hard to figure out which man was Donovan. There was an older couple sitting at one end of the bar and two girls who looked barely legal sitting a few stools away from a man holding his phone to his ear.

I unmuted my phone and spoke quietly. "The cake looks delicious. Thank you."

"You're welcome."

My feet felt heavy, like my shoes were made of concrete blocks. Staring at Donovan's back, I was quiet for a moment as I watched him.

"Listen, Val, I would absolutely love to see you in person. But if you're not ready, you're not ready. I don't want to make things more difficult for you."

I swallowed. "I think I'm ready."

"You do?"

I nodded. "I better do this before I change my mind. Turn around. I'm standing about twenty feet behind you." I held my breath as I watched Donovan turn. Even though his head whipped around, it seemed to happen in slow motion.

My eyes locked with his. He was even more gorgeous than I had imagined after seeing his profile. His dark blond hair was tousled in that sexy *I don't give a shit* way, but still looked perfect. Strong masculine features—a rugged jaw coated in day-old stubble on sun-kissed skin, a straight, prominent nose, and eyes the color of honey. His deep blue tie was loosened at the collar, and his wide shoulders filled out his dress shirt, pulling slightly over the muscles of his pecs.

Gorgeous. Yet there was something very familiar about him. I just couldn't put my finger on it. Donovan took a few tentative steps toward me. If I didn't know better, I would have thought he was as nervous as I was.

The waiter who had been visiting my car interrupted Donovan's approach, extending a credit card. "Your card, Mr. Donovan."

Mr. Donovan?

Donovan is his last name, not his first?

Donovan...Donovan? I knew a Donovan.

My eyes widened.

Oh my God.

Everything clicked into place at rocket speed.

His profile said his happy place was Montauk.

He has a sister about five years younger.

Donovan. *Ford.*

Ford Donovan.

The boy next door at our summer home.

The one who used to keep an eye on Ryan for me years ago. His little sister had played with my son.

Donovan saw the look on my face.

And then I saw the look of recognition hit him.

"*Mrs. Davis?*"

My hand flew up to cover my mouth. "*Achoo!*"

chapter five

Valentina

When morning finally rolled around, I thought I'd get an early start on the day. I'd tossed and turned all night, unable to sleep. Thoughts about Donovan—Ford—kept infiltrating my brain, even though I tried my hardest to forget the entire nightmare had ever happened.

I vacuumed the house, unloaded the dishwasher, and had started sorting through a pile of mail when my cell rang. Eve's face flashed on the screen.

"Give me all the details."

I shook my head repeatedly, even though she couldn't see me. "It was horrible."

"What happened? What did the bastard do to you? I'll cut his balls off."

Eve's response made me smile for the first time since I'd laid eyes on my date. "No. It wasn't that kind of horrible. He was a perfect gentleman."

"Okay..."

"Very sweet and funny, too."

"Sounds awful," she said sarcastically.

"And gorgeous."

"The balls on him."

"That's not the worst part."

"Let's see...he's young, gorgeous, sweet, and funny. What could be worse than that? He's hung like a horse?"

"I wouldn't know. And you know why I don't know that?"

"Because you're an uptight prude who hasn't been laid in years?"

"That might be true. But the larger problem is that he is one of Ryan's friends."

Eve cackled. "That's not a problem, *that's fantastic!* Bang his brains out and send him to play golf with your ex. Let him eat his heart out when he realizes what he lost."

"Ummm...Eve, I wasn't talking about my ex, Ryan. I was talking about *my son.*"

"I'll be over in twenty minutes."

The minute I opened the door, Eve hurried past me without saying a word, whipped up a batch of mimosas, and downed an entire flute before even attempting to start our conversation.

"So he didn't recognize you online either?" she said as she refilled her glass.

"There really isn't a clear picture of my face on the dating site, remember? You loaded the pics. Besides, I haven't seen him in years. And his name is Ford Donovan. I just assumed Donovan620 meant his first name was Donovan, and I didn't connect the two...at all."

"Why haven't you seen him in so many years? You're always out in Montauk in the summer. Do they rent out his house or something?"

"No." I swallowed hard. "His parents were killed in a car accident five or six years ago. A tractor-trailer lost control on the LIE during an ice storm. I didn't find out about it until quite a while after. But the house has sat unused for years now."

"Oh God. That's awful."

"Yeah. His parents were older than Ryan and me. But most people who have kids my son's age are older. They were a really happy couple—very much in love. High school sweethearts like us, too. I actually remember watching them on the beach the last summer they spent out in Montauk. Ford's dad would lie on the blanket with his head on his wife's lap and sunglasses on, and she would read to him. It was really sweet, and it made me realize just how much Ryan and I had grown apart."

"What did Ford say when he realized who you were?"

"He said it didn't matter to him. He actually tried to convince me to stay and go through with the date. Can you believe that?"

"Why didn't you?

I looked at Eve like she had two heads. "Did you miss everything I just said? He's not only twenty-five, but he used to babysit *my son*."

Eve sighed. "Did you have a drink, at least?"

"No. Well, sort of. I had a little meltdown before we even met, and he had a waiter deliver a martini to my car while I was freaking out about going inside."

She interrupted. "Your minivan, you mean."

"Yes. My old-lady minivan. That I belong driving. He, on the other hand, belongs behind the wheel of that little sports car he has."

"What kind of a car is it?"

"I have no idea. Why does that even matter?"

"Because you deserve a boyfriend with a hot little car."

"He's not going to be my boyfriend."

"Why not?"

"Eve, did you drink the first batch of these things on the way over here?"

"Let's break this down. Stick to the details. What's the real issue? Is it his age or the fact that he knows Ryan that bothers you?"

"Both."

"So if he had never met Ryan you'd go out with him?"

"No. He's too young."

Eve grinned. I really thought she might be losing it. "I can't wait to meet him."

"What? You won't be meeting him."

"But I'm coming to spend the weekend with you in two weeks out in Montauk."

"So? He hasn't been there in years. I'm hoping that won't be changing anytime soon. I just want to put the entire bizarre incident behind me."

She smiled. "Well, that makes one of us."

After our study session that evening, Allison started to clean up Mark's dining room table. "I have to run. I didn't realize it was so late. My husband's car is in the shop, and he works the night shift so he needs to take mine."

"Go. I'll help Mark clean up," I said.

"You sure?"

"Of course. My son is away at college. He was supposed to come home two weeks ago, but he got a last-minute summer internship. So he's staying in North Carolina. Sadly, I sort of miss cleaning up after someone."

Allison gave me a hug. "You're the best."

"Hey, what about me?" Mark said. "I cooked all this Italian food."

Allison laughed. "The Salpino's delivery guy held the door open for me when I came in." She plucked a cookie out of the white bakery box on the dining room table and shut the top. She pointed to the gold sticker on top. "Did you make the cookies from scratch, too?"

Tonight it had been just the three of us, since Desiree couldn't make it. So when Allison left, it was just me and Mark.

I picked up the plates and brought them to the sink. The kitchen and living room were an open floor plan with just a step down from one room to the other.

"How do you feel about the test?" I asked. "You ready?"

"*Sta arrivando se sono pronto o no,*" he said. *It's coming whether I'm ready or not.*

I smiled. *"Stai andando alla grande."* *You're going to do great.*

Mark collected the rest of the dinner and dessert mess while I loaded the dishwasher. When he was done, he leaned a hip against the island.

"What?"

He was looking at me funny.

He shrugged. "Nothing. I was just thinking we should celebrate after we pass the exam."

"That's an excellent idea. And I like your confidence— *after* we pass not *if* we all pass."

"Maybe we could go out to dinner. Italian, of course."

"That sounds perfect. I think Desiree is going away the week after the exam, but maybe the week after that."

Mark's face told me I'd misunderstood before he said anything. "Oh. I meant just the two of us celebrating."

I loaded the last dish into the dishwasher and dried off my hands. "Sorry. I thought you meant all four of us."

A moment of awkward silence passed. Eventually, Mark said, "And here I thought I was being so smooth."

"Oh, you were smooth. I'm just totally out of practice. Honestly, a date could smack me in the head, and I wouldn't recognize it. It's been a long time."

He looked hopeful. "Well, then it sounds like you're due for one."

I didn't want to lead him on. I liked him. I really did. He'd become a good friend. I just didn't think I liked him in that way. Which was too bad, because if he were my boyfriend we could spend the entire summer out in Montauk. Yet he didn't give me that flutter—the type of flutter the guy who was perfectly wrong for me caused. *Damn you, Ford.*

"Would you mind if I took a rain check on a date until after the test? I want to focus on that for now." Plus, I wasn't sure.

He forced a smile. "Sure."

I left feeling kind of down. I *wanted* to want to go out with Mark. But it felt like the right decision putting it off. Maybe after a few weeks of not seeing him in class and our study group, I'd start to miss him and realize I'd been wrong.

My phone had been in my purse all night, and when I pulled it out at home to put it on the charger, I saw I had a few missed texts. I felt that familiar flutter low in my belly seeing they were from Donovan—or rather, *Ford.*

Donovan: I had drinks with a woman tonight.

The flutter suddenly died. As screwed up as it was, I felt a pang of jealousy. Ridiculous, I know. A guy I couldn't go out with, wouldn't go out with, and had no claim to. Yet it didn't make what I felt any less real.

Donovan: I ended it early. Would have rather have had cocktails with you, even from the parking lot.

God, why did he have to be so sweet? And so damn young. I probably shouldn't have responded, but...

Valentina: If it makes you feel any better, a man asked me out tonight, and I sort of blew him off, too.

The little dots jumped around as he started to type back immediately.

Donovan: Is it wrong that just hearing a man asked you out makes me jealous?

I smiled sadly. *I feel your pain, buddy.* Before I could respond again, another text came in.

Donovan: Why didn't you say yes?

Valentina: Mark and I are good friends. I just don't see him like that.

The texting stopped for a few minutes, and I grew anxious waiting for his response.

Donovan: Have coffee with me.

Coffee. It sounded so innocent.

Valentina: I can't.

Donovan: Why not? It's just coffee. There's nothing devious about two adults sharing a cup of coffee. I wasn't asking to make it for you in my apartment the morning after while you're wearing my T-shirt.

An image flashed through my head of me standing in front of a coffee pot wearing just Ford's T-shirt and a satisfied, goofy smile. My hair was a wild mess from the night before, and he wore nothing but a pair of gray, low-hanging sweats. He walked up behind me and slinked his arms around my waist, pulling me flush as he brushed my hair to the side and kissed my neck.

"*Morning,*" he growled against my skin.

I reached up and touched the area he'd kissed. Blinking a few times, I realized I'd been daydreaming. *Oh my. Vivid. Think maybe I should take a quick shower and put down the phone.* I plugged my cell into the charger on my nightstand and forced myself to walk away.

The shower proved to be more difficult. Without any mental stimulation except the neutral color of the tumbled stone tile, my mind tended to wander. And tonight my hand wanted to join in while my brain put on a show. My effort to clear my mind of all things Ford did just the opposite, and I had to cut the shower short.

After my bedtime ritual of moisturizing and primping, I got into bed and turned off the light. I had every intention of ignoring my phone and going to sleep, I really did, but a half hour later it was eating at me, and I realized I'd never get any rest without knowing if there were more texts waiting for me from Ford.

So I unhappily pulled my phone from the charger on my nightstand. Sure enough, a few new texts had arrived while I was attempting to clear him from my mind.

Donovan: Did I lose you?

Donovan: If you're going to ignore me, there's no reason to hold back. Nothing to lose....

Ten minutes later...

Donovan: Okay, so I lied. I want to have coffee with you because I can't stop pic-

turing you wearing my T-shirt the morn-ing after.

Donovan: You look really sexy in it, by the way.

Donovan: One cup of coffee.

Donovan: I'll be on my best behavior.

Donovan: I swear.

That had been his last text, but the minute I finished catching up on them, a new one arrived.

Donovan: You're reading my texts now. I can see they just changed to Read. So I know you're not sleeping...

I smiled sadly and sighed.

Valentina: No, I'm not sleeping. Although, I should be. You know why? Because I'll be up a five a.m. tomorrow morning, no matter what time I go to bed. I bet you can sleep until noon, like most young people.

Donovan: Actually, I'm at the gym by 5:30 and the office by 6:45 every morning. Nice try. How about coffee at 6 a.m., if you're up anyway?

I chuckled to myself.

Valentina: You're persistent. I'll give you that. But I'm sorry, I just can't, Ford.

I'd started to type: *I just can't—no matter how much I want to.* But I erased it. I needed to put an end to this craziness, for both of our sakes.

Instead of responding, I went to my contacts and ed-ited *Donovan* to *Ford*—a gentle reminder that Donovan wasn't a man I could ever be attracted to; he was simply Ford, *the boy next door.*

chapter six

Valentina – Two weeks later

The air smelled better in Montauk. The salt seemed to open my lungs and wash away the stresses of life. It had long been dark by the time I arrived. After Memorial Day, Friday night East Hampton traffic became a war zone of designer-clad people. It was why I'd always preferred Montauk. For most men there, a fancy dinner outfit meant changing out of your fishing boots.

Standing on the back deck at almost midnight, I shut my eyes and listened to the waves crashing as I inhaled deeply. After a few more exhales, my shoulders began to relax.

Until a voice startled me.

"Mrs. Davis?"

I jumped and let out a very girly sounding scream.

"I'm sorry. I didn't mean to scare you. It's Bella—Annabella Donovan from next door."

"Oh." My hand held my chest. "Hi, Bella. I didn't see you there."

Our beachy neighborhood didn't have fences, just a sand pathway between the elevated houses. Bella stood on the beach at the bottom of the stairs leading up to my deck.

"I didn't know anyone else was out here," she said. "I wasn't even sure if you owned the house anymore. I haven't been out here in years. But I'm glad you guys are still around. It's so quiet at night out here."

"Actually, it's just me now. Ryan and I divorced, and my son Ryan is staying at college for the summer to do an internship." I held my breath for a moment before asking the next question. "Are you...out here alone?"

"Yep. I drove my brother crazy enough that he let me come out for a long weekend. I wanted to stay the entire summer, but God forbid he trust me out here alone."

A confusing mix of relief and disappointment hit me. I'd be lying if I said I hadn't thought about Ford often over the last couple of weeks—he'd made sure of it with a text or two each day. But I hadn't answered since the night I'd come home from study group.

"So it's just us girls then," Bella said.

"I guess so." I smiled.

"Until my pain-in-the-ass brother shows up."

My skin prickled, and it wasn't because of any chill in the air. "Are you...expecting him?"

"He's not supposed to come out, but he doesn't trust me. He's away on a business trip right now, although I get the feeling he might show up when he gets back. He called me five times today and had an alarm system installed at the house."

"Well, I suppose that's what big brothers are supposed to do, watch out for their sisters."

She shrugged. "Hey. Would you want to do a sunrise yoga class on the beach with me? It's only a few houses down. I've been getting up a half hour before and walking to warm up. I have a free pass for a friend if you want to try it tomorrow."

I felt rather out of sorts from the surprise of Bella being next door, not to mention the prospect of her brother coming out to check on her. So I failed to think of a quick excuse why I couldn't do sunrise yoga.

"Umm... Sure. I'd love that."

"Awesome. I'll meet you back here at six?"

"That sounds good."

"Okay, then, I'm going to go shower. I have sand in places there shouldn't be sand. 'Night, Mrs. Davis."

She smiled and had begun to walk toward her house when I called after her. "Bella?"

She turned back.

"Call me Valentina or Val, please."

"Okay, Val. See you in the morning."

I walked out onto the deck with my morning coffee and found Bella stretching on the sand behind our houses.

"Am I late?" I called down, checking the time on my phone.

"Nope. I'm early." She bent to the right and stretched her left arm over her head. "I woke up an hour ago hearing what I thought was the sound of rain hitting my window. But when I came out, it wasn't raining."

"Do you want some coffee?"

"I'd actually love some. I ran out and had to make decaf this morning, which is like taking a shower with a raincoat on. What's the point?"

"I couldn't agree more." I nodded my head in the direction of the house. "Come on, let's get you properly caffeinated."

Inside, Bella looked at the small picture frames lined up on the kitchen windowsill while I poured her a steaming mug of coffee.

"So you and Mr. Davis are divorced now?"

She focused on an old picture of my ex-husband and our son. I'd eradicated the house of all other traces of Ryan Sr., but it didn't seem right to get rid of that picture. My son wore his Little League baseball uniform and looked up at his father in admiration. A part of me hoped keeping that photo around might someday remind my son that he was missing out by pushing his father away since our divorce. The things that happened between Ryan and me shouldn't have to ruin the relationship of father and son—but my son was protective of his mother.

"It'll be two years this fall that our divorce was finalized."

She crinkled up her nose. "He wasn't very friendly, was he?"

I chuckled. Ryan had never been a fan of the Donovans next door. He'd complained that they played their music too loud and let their kids run wild. He'd rolled his eyes when Bella's parents danced on the back deck together, while I often secretly wished I had that type of marriage.

"No. He wasn't the most friendly neighbor, was he?"

We shared a smile as I handed Bella cream for her coffee.

"I mean, I haven't seen him in years. But I remember he always looked like he just finished sucking a lemon."

That *was* a perfect description of Ryan the last ten years. *Bitter.*

After Bella fixed her coffee with cream and enough sugar to induce a diabetic coma, we sat on the chaise lounges on my back deck. The morning dawn was magical out over the beach.

"So what are you studying in college?"

"I'm not sure. I'd love to go into something like acting. I was originally a business major, but my brother took all the brains when he was born and left me none."

"I'm sure you're plenty smart."

"Business majors have to take Accounting 101 the first year of school. The professor told us before the first test that if we didn't get at least a sixty, we might want to drop the class because it only got harder from there. I got a twenty-eight."

My eyebrows shot up. "Out of a hundred?"

"And I studied." She sipped her coffee. "I dropped the class the next day. I don't even know why I picked business for a major. I think I just felt like I was supposed to *have* a major, know what I want to be when I grow up. Like Ford."

"Not everyone knows what they're supposed to do right away. I was a CAT-scan technician for fifteen years. It was a good job because it allowed me to work part time around Ryan's school schedule, although it was never something I was passionate about. I actually went back to school to become an Italian language teacher, and I'm taking the licensing test in a few weeks. My grandparents are from Italy, and I always loved the language. I'm really excited about it now. Took me almost twenty years to figure it out, though."

"That's really cool. I'd do that, but I sort of suck at foreign languages. It's part of the reason I'm thinking acting might be for me. You really don't have to be good at English or math. Plus..." She smirked. "My parents always said I was a drama queen."

"You'll figure it out. Just take your time."

Since Bella had brought them up, I figured it was okay to talk about her parents. "By the way, I'm really sorry about your parents, Bella. I didn't hear about it until a few weeks after it happened, or I would have come to the service. I didn't even have your home address to send a card. I always liked your parents and admired their relationship."

"Thank you." She smiled sadly. "It's weird being out here without them. Every time I open the back door or look out to the beach, I feel like I should see them making out. It used to gross me out, but now I think it's kinda cool how much they were into each other. In a weird way, it was good they died together. One wouldn't have made it without the other."

Wow. What a beautiful, yet sad, thought. We sipped our coffee in comfortable silence for a while after that, enjoying the sunrise. When a crowd started to form down the beach, we figured it was time to get going.

Bella and I laid our mats on the sand next to each other and spent a few minutes stretching. I was bent over, dangling my fingers into the sand as I reached past my toes, when I felt a hand on my back. Startled, my immediate reaction was to pop up quickly—so quickly that I caught the instructor off guard and smashed my head right into his jaw.

"Oh my God. I'm so sorry!" I rubbed the top of my head as his hand reached for his jaw. *His very sexy jaw. Oh God. Figures.*

"It's okay. That was my fault. I thought you saw me walking around. I was trying to guide you to bend straight. You're dipping to your right."

I definitely would have noticed him. Our instructor was tall, with dark hair pulled back in a ponytail, tanned skin, and dark eyes. *Tall, dark, and handsome.* Definitely handsome. Although that wasn't the part that was so distracting. No, that I could deal with. But the loose, gray sweatpants and no shirt—that was exactly what I'd imagined Ford wearing in my fantasy a few weeks ago. That thought, along with the ridiculously amazing carved chest standing before me, turned me into a bumbling idiot.

"Oh. Jeez. Yeah. Sorry. To the right? Okay. Yeah. Sorry again."

The instructor's brows rose, and he grinned knowingly.

The heat rose on my cheeks and wouldn't let up. "Umm. Sorry again."

"Not a problem. Why don't we try that again? This time without the beat down." Hot Instructor winked, then put his warm hand on the exposed skin of my back. "Bend at the waist."

I was thrilled to hide my face and have an excuse for the color that had already rushed to my cheeks. When my fingertips reached the sand, the instructor stepped behind me and gripped my hips with both hands, guiding me to shift to the left. "There, you're aligned now. When you stretch into your bend, there's less chance you'll injure your back."

I stayed down long enough that he moved on to someone else. When I eventually rose, Bella leaned toward me, failing at her attempted whispering.

"He's hot and was totally checking you out."

The sunrise morning yoga class turned out to be the best exercise class I'd ever taken. Not only was the instructor amazing at poses and helping all of the students ease into positions, but he guided us to use those moments in pose to appreciate the beauty around us. The sunrise, the light shining on the unusually calm ocean, streaks of orange and gold shimmering on the water—it was absolutely breathtaking.

As we moved through our vinyasa, coming into up-ward-facing dog, my eyes, which had been closed for the last few minutes, suddenly opened. I had that sensation you get when someone is watching, a prickly awareness I felt all over my skin. Looking to the left and right, I could find no one in my peripheral vision, and the instructor was busy helping a woman a few rows ahead of me. Yet that strange feeling stayed with me through the end of the class.

After our hour was up, the yoga instructor came over to introduce himself. "We didn't actually get to meet before." He extended his hand. "I'm Ty. I haven't seen you in class before. Are you vacationing in Montauk this week?"

"Actually, I live a few houses away. Well, I have a summer home here. It's my first week out, and Bella invited me to the class. We're neighbors."

Ty smiled at Bella and returned his attention to me. "Did you enjoy the class? We're out here five days a week."

"The class was amazing. You'll definitely be seeing me again."

"I'm looking forward to it."

Something about the way he said that, or maybe it was the gleam in his eye, made me feel good. I might have been thirty-seven, but I liked to think I'd begun to grow old gracefully.

Bella and I shook the sand from our mats and rolled them up. I stared out at the ocean as she tied hers closed. "Remind me not to have coffee right before yoga," she said. "I've had to go to the bathroom for the last seven poses."

My skin had a layer of sweat on it from the workout, and a warm breeze floated by, leaving my arms with goosebumps. I should have felt grimy, but instead I reveled in the chills, feeling more alive than I had in a long time.

"Thanks so much for inviting me. Let me make you some breakfast after I wash up."

Bella groaned in response to my invitation. Not exactly the answer I'd expected.

"What's the matter? Please don't tell me you're on a diet. You're so thin."

I was still facing the ocean, but I turned toward our houses just as she filled me in on her problem.

"My pain-in-the-ass brother's here."

chapter seven

Ford

I stood on the back deck watching the yoga class for nearly a half hour before it ended. For the last two days, I'd been telling myself I needed to come out to Montauk to check on Bella, make sure everything was okay—that was the reason I was coming. The *only* reason. But seeing Valentina walk up wearing tight, black yoga pants and a cropped exercise top that showed off her flat stomach, I realized I wouldn't have even known if my sister had a giant hole in her face.

"I told you, I'm fine," Bella whined as she approached, still thirty feet away.

Valentina stared at me, looking nervous. I assumed she hadn't shared our little Match.com chat and almost-date with my sister, and she was anxious that I might let on. Of course I wouldn't. I kept my sex life far away from my Bella—not that there was any sex to talk about when it came to Val anyway. Unfortunately.

Reaching the deck, my sister kissed my cheek chastely and then jogged to the back door. "I have to go to the bathroom. I'll be back in a minute. Do you remember Mrs. Davis?"

"I do."

Val had been looking anywhere but at me until I began to speak.

"How are you, Mrs. Davis?" I arched an eyebrow and sipped my coffee. Once I heard the back door close and my sister was out of earshot, I took a step closer to Valentina. "You haven't answered any of my messages."

"I...I didn't know what else to say."

"But yet you read them all. You could have blocked me or just ignored them."

She looked flustered. "I didn't want to be rude."

"Uh-huh. Just rude enough to ghost me, got it." I took another step closer. "Can I ask you something?"

"What?" She spoke to my shoulder, and I wasn't sure if she was avoiding eye contact or watching for Bella. Probably both.

"Valentina?" I waited until she looked at me. "Have you thought about me since the night at the restaurant?"

She closed her eyes. "It doesn't matter."

"To me, it does."

"Let's not make it any more difficult than it needs to be, Ford."

It was the first time I'd heard her say my first name. And I liked the sound of it... I liked it a lot.

"Why don't I go first? I thought about you. *A lot*."

"Why does it matter if I thought about you if nothing is going to come of it?"

"It just does," I said.

The sliding glass back door to our house made a high-pitched screech as it slid open. Salt air rusted everything out here.

I lowered my voice. "Tell me the truth, and I'll keep pretending you're only Mrs. Davis."

Valentina's eyes flared. The door squeaked again as my sister closed it behind her.

I lowered my voice even more. "Come on. Tell me. Did you think about me?"

Her eyes flitted between my sister and me a few times. I leaned in and whispered, "Say it."

"No."

Without taking my eyes off of Val, I spoke to my sister. "Hey, sis. I've been meaning to tell you something."

Valentina looked like she was about to freak out. I smiled and mouthed *Say it*. The panic on her face was adorable.

"Fine," she gritted through her teeth. "I did. Are you happy now?"

I grinned from ear to ear. "You hear that, Bell? Even *Mrs. Davis* says I'm right."

Bella had no clue what we were talking about, yet rolled her eyes. "Whatever it is, don't encourage him."

"I'll try to remember that."

"What are you doing here?" my sister asked. "And why are you here so damn early? You had to leave the city at four in the morning to get out here at this time."

I shrugged. "Figured I'd beat traffic." I locked eyes with Val. "Lately, I haven't been sleeping well anyway. Something's been on my mind. Keeps me up at night."

My sister assumed I was talking about work. "Well, just do what you always do. Go after it like it's nobody's business, and you'll get it."

"Very good advice." I grinned.

"We were just going to have some breakfast. Valentina was going to cook. But since you're here, you can take us out, Mr. Moneybags."

"I can do that." I looked to Val. "John's Pancake House?"

"Ummm...I don't mind cooking. You're welcome to join us."

No way was I passing up an opportunity to get inside her house. "Even better."

"Well, why don't you give me a little bit, and I'll wash up and get breakfast started."

She disappeared into her house. I impatiently waited fifteen minutes, and then Bella finally came downstairs.

"You didn't even change yet?" I said.

"My roommate from school called while I was upstairs. It's impossible to get Brooke off the phone." She tossed her cell on the couch and pulled the hair tie from her hair. "Think Val will mind if I take a quick shower?"

"Why don't I go over and let her know before she starts cooking. Then you can take your time."

"Perfect. Thanks, Ford."

Yeah. Perfect.

"Hey." Val opened the screen door and looked over my shoulder for Bella.

"She'll be over in a bit. She wanted to give us some alone time."

Val's eyes bulged. She was cute when she freaked out, but I let her off the hook, leaning in close as I passed. "Joking. Relax."

I hadn't been inside her house in years...probably since I was seventeen and kept an eye on Ryan the last time. The layout was exactly the same as ours, only hers was painted brighter colors. I headed straight to the kitchen, my nose leading the way.

"Our chaperone is in the shower. What smells so good?"

"I'm making spinach and feta frittatas, with bacon on the side."

A bunch of yellow sticky notes on the refrigerator caught my attention. A few had obvious errands written on them, but one just said *Oil*.

Val noticed me reading. "The back door squeaks."

"You want WD-40, not actual oil then."

"Oh yeah. Okay. Thanks."

"I have some lube that can take care of you."

She glanced sideways at me, unsure if I was being a wiseass or not. I managed to keep a straight face and turned back to the fridge.

Pointing to another sticky, I asked, "VS?"

"Oh. I...uh...need to pick up..." She shook her head. "It stands for Victoria's Secret."

"I can help you with that, too. The mirrors in dressing rooms can't be trusted. I'll come so you can model for me."

Valentina laughed, and that sound was freaking awesome—right up there with my other favorites like the ocean and a crackling fire. It drew me closer to where she stood in front of the stove. Three burners were going at once.

"Wow. That looks delicious."

"I only have three small pans, so I can only make two frittatas at a time."

I shrugged. "Works for me. Bella doesn't need to eat anyway."

"How thoughtful of you." She walked to the refrigerator, took out the feta, and began to sprinkle it into the pan with the eggs.

I moved behind Val, definitely closer than was neighborly, and took a deep breath in. "Smells delicious."

She ignored me. The burner she wasn't cooking on had a paper-towel-lined plate filled with crispy bacon. I reached around her to swipe a piece, and my chest brushed lightly against her back. I heard the hitch in her breath, even over the sizzle of the bacon.

Good to know.

She didn't budge as I leaned in to steal a second piece.

This time, I purposely brushed against her back. "You smell good."

Her hair was pulled up into a ponytail, allowing me to see the nape of her neck, skin that was pebbling with tiny goosebumps—so I didn't back up.

"I love knowing you thought about me this week. Are you curious what I was doing when I thought about you? Because I can't stop wondering what you were doing when you were thinking about me."

Valentina's breathing grew more labored. I wanted to turn her around and press my body against hers, make her gasp into my mouth. But even though I could see her reaction to me on her skin, her body language was still rigid. I'd managed to crack the door open, but she wasn't inviting me in.

Hesitantly, I touched her arm.

"*Ford.*" Her voice strained in warning—like her head and body were in conflict and her head was only barely winning the fight.

"I'll go first. I thought of you during the day when I was at work, staring at the computer where we'd first messaged back and forth online. I thought of you as I was at a lunch business meeting yesterday, wondering what wine you would order. But my favorite time to think about you was at night. I'd take off all my clothes, get into bed, shut my eyes, and reach down and grab my—"

"Anybody home?" My sister's voice interrupted.

Shit. Instinctively, I stepped back. Val shook her head a few times before rushing to the door.

Bella still had wet hair from her shower. Figures she'd pick today to not spend an hour getting herself ready. "Mmmm...it smells good in here. That workout made me so hungry."

I caught Val's eye. "Watching it made me *hungry*, too."

Val walked back to the stove, not glancing in my direction again. I stood a few feet away, leaning against the kitchen sink with my arms folded over my chest, just watching her.

"There's coffee in the pot and creamer in the fridge," she said to Bella. "Help yourself."

"I haven't had a frittata in forever. Our mom used to make them. You sort of remind me of her. Doesn't she remind you of Mom, Ford?"

My eyes shut, and I shook my head. "She definitely does not remind me of Mom."

Val plated the two frittatas and set them on the table. "You two eat."

"We'll wait for you," I said.

"Yours will get cold while I make mine. *Eat.*"

Bella caught my eye and smirked as she sat down at the table. She pointed her fork at me before digging in. "See? *Mom.*"

I was definitely waiting for Val to eat after that comment. I wasn't really that hungry anyway. She finally sat a few minutes later.

"The class this morning was amazing, right?" my sister said.

"It was. I really enjoyed it. It's been a while since I did yoga, so I might be sore later, though."

"And that instructor was totally into you. I bet he asks you out next time."

Valentina gave my sister a polite smile, and then our eyes caught briefly. My sister was totally oblivious, so of course she continued.

"He couldn't keep his eyes off of you. We should take the class again tomorrow. He's totally worth getting up so early for."

I had a momentary lapse in sanity. "Maybe I'll take the class, too."

"*You?*" My sister snorted.

"Sure. Why not?"

"You've never done yoga."

I stood and put my plate in the sink. "I'm all about trying new things."

"Well, I'm all about getting a job today."

"A job? You're only out here for the weekend."

Bella's lips pursed. "I have an interview for a summer waitressing gig at a restaurant in town. I figured if I got a job, you might start to see that I'm responsible enough to stay out here for the summer. Plus, I need to save some money. I sort of blew through my savings during my semester abroad." She looked down at her phone. "Shoot. My interview is in twenty minutes. I'm going to be late. Let me help you clean up before I go, Val."

Valentina waved Bella off. "I got it. Go to your interview. You don't want to be late."

"Go," I added. "I'll help Val clean up."

"Okay. I owe you one."

"I'll add it to the pile of ones you owe me."

Val and I were both quiet after the screen door slammed closed. It felt like small talk was needed.

"She's supposed to be out here for a four-day week-end, and she's interviewing for a job."

"Well, at least she took some initiative. You could have arrived to a house full of knocked-over, red Solo cups and passed-out teenagers."

"I suppose."

Val stood and picked up her plate and Bella's. But I took them from her hands. "I got it. Sit. You cooked."

"I can't just sit here and let you clean up."

"Why not?"

"I don't know. I just can't."

"I tell you what, if you don't let me clean up, I'm going to continue my story about what I was doing when I was thinking about you this week."

She started to speak, but then closed her mouth and sat back down, a light blush on her cheeks.

I mumbled to myself, though loud enough that she could hear, "Shame. It's a phenomenal story."

After I had all the dishes rinsed and loaded into the dishwasher, I noticed a puddle of water forming at my feet. "I think you have a leak?"

"Crap. Ryan was supposed to fix that when he was out here last summer. I told him to call a plumber, but since we share expenses on the house, he never wants to spend on a repairman."

"I can take a look."

"No. It's okay."

"I'm good at fixing things." I grinned. "Don't let my pretty face fool you into thinking I'm a wuss."

"Really, it's fine. I can call someone."

I put my hand on her shoulder. "I'm going to fix it. Do you have a bucket and a toolbox somewhere with a wrench?"

"I think Ryan has some things in the closet."

On second thought, I didn't want to use her ex's shit for some reason. "I'll just run next door and grab what I'll need to take the drain apart and see what's going on."

"Oh. Okay."

I got to the front door and turned back to make an obnoxious joke about getting to take care of her pipes after all, but when I did, I found her eyes firmly attached to my ass. Caught, her eyes jumped to meet mine, and a guilty look washed over her face.

I winked. "The feeling's mutual. I admired your ass for most of your yoga class, so we're even." I wiggled my brows. "Be back to take care of your pipes."

chapter eight

Valentina

Ryan certainly didn't look like *that* anymore.

I bit my lip, staring down at the lower half of Ford sprawled out on my kitchen floor. He'd taken apart my sink, found a crack in the drainpipe, and went to three different plumbing supply stores to find the right part—one all the way in East Hampton. Now he was shoulder-deep inside my cabinet, installing the new drain. I stood nearby, handing him the occasional tool and ogling his body. I couldn't help myself. His dark T-shirt had ridden up, giving me a personal peep show starring rock-hard abs, a deep-set V, a tattoo that ran up his side, and a sexy-as-all-hell thin line of hair that ran down into his Calvin Klein underwear band. The view had my fingers itching to trace that happy trail all the way down to the end.

He twisted his body as he used the wrench to tighten something, and the V of his abs deepened. *Jesus*. On second thought, I was pretty sure Ryan *never* looked like that. I sighed, quietly mourning the loss of what was right in front of me—mere inches away—yet I'd never have.

Ford slid out from the cabinet, and I quickly averted my eyes, hoping I wouldn't get caught checking him out a second time today.

"Go ahead. Give it a test run. Turn the water on."

I leaned forward and lifted the handle on the faucet while Ford watched from beneath. After a minute, he smiled. "Good as new."

"Wow. Thank you so much. I owe you big time. You'll have to let me make you a nice dinner, at least."

"How about you let me take you out to dinner instead?"

"That's not repaying you the favor. It's just adding to my debt."

He raised a brow. "You can square up after our date."

"Ford..."

"Relax. I'm joking. Sort of. How about a beer on the back deck instead?"

I smiled. "That sounds amazing, actually. Let me just clean up in here, and I'll join you. There's plenty of beer in the fridge."

"Actually, I'm going to run next door and take a quick shower." He held up his hands.

They were greasy and dirty. *And manly.* There's something so sexy about a guy whose hands look like he isn't afraid to do physical labor. Rugged hands had always been a turn-on for me. Then there were the tattoos on his muscular forearms. I really needed to stop finding things sexy about this man.

Boy...I mean boy.

He's not a man, Valentina.

I looked at his broad shoulders. *God, he really does look like one, though.*

Needing a distraction, I started to clean up. "Okay. Sounds good. I'll see you in a bit, then."

Somehow I managed to not stare at his ass as he walked to the door this time.

After I cleaned up the mess in the kitchen, I went to the bedroom to get changed. The afternoon sun had started to heat up the house, and I knew the back deck would be scorching hot.

Picking an outfit proved more difficult than I thought. Normally, I'd just throw on my bathing suit with shorts or a cover up in the afternoon, but I didn't want to look like I was trying to attract attention. My C-cups were difficult to hide under the best circumstances. I wound up changing three times and finally settled on a plain white T-shirt and a pair of old, ripped denim shorts. The shorts were a tad young for me, but Eve might've mentioned that my ass looked good in them. Plus, they were sort of messy looking, so it wouldn't seem like I'd been trying too hard.

I came down the stairs just as Ford knocked on the front screen door.

"Hey." He eyed my legs and grinned. "You look good."

His hair was slicked back, still wet from the shower, and he had on nothing but a pair of board shorts and aviator sunglasses. I cleared my throat and tried to ignore the eight-pack and tattoos now on full display.

"Umm... Thanks. Do you want some sunscreen? The sun is roasting on the back deck at this time."

God, I sound like his mother.

"Nah. I'm good. I don't burn."

I started to mentally prepare my *UV rays are dangerous even if your skin doesn't turn red* speech, but I stopped myself. A twenty-five-year-old man doesn't need a lecture.

Boy.

He's a boy, Valentina.

I grabbed two beers from the fridge, and we went out on the back deck and sat side by side on two lounge chairs. Ford held out his beer to me. "To being back in Montauk."

I clinked my bottle with his. "To being back in Montauk."

The icy cold beer really tasted delicious. Ford must've agreed, since he made a loud *ahhh* sound when he'd finished guzzling half the bottle.

"I missed it out here," he said. "I forgot how much I love it."

"When was the last time you were out here? I know I haven't seen you guys in years. But Ryan and I split use of the house, and I let him use it the last two seasons, so I could have missed you."

"I haven't been out since the summer before my parents died. I was definitely avoiding coming. This place is filled with so many memories. But so far I feel at peace being here. I guess enough time has passed now that I can remember the good times and appreciate them, rather than be bitter that they're gone."

"Your parents really loved Montauk. I'm sure they'd be happy you feel that way and can make new memories of your own."

We were quiet for a while, taking in the waves crashing against the shore and the sun glistening along the water. Even though it was a warm, almost-summer day, the beach was pretty empty. The tourist season didn't really start to peak until the kids got out of school, which was another week or two away.

"Yeah. They really loved their summer time at the house." He brought the beer bottle to his lips and kept looking at the ocean as he spoke. "Life was busy when we were home in the city—they worked a lot. Time seemed to slow down out here, though."

"I used to watch them together and envy their relationship. They were so sweet to each other, and it reminded me how far apart Ryan and I had grown."

Ford looked over at me and smiled sadly. "They used to have Mason jars on the nightstands in their bedroom next door. During the summer, they'd write these short little love notes on slips of paper and put them in each other's jars—one or two lines saying random things they liked that the other did that day. Then on Valentine's Day every year, they'd come out by themselves to check on the house. They'd stay for one night and exchange jars."

"Wow. That's so romantic."

"Yeah. And we always teased my dad that he was just too cheap to buy a Valentine's Day present." Ford chugged the rest of his beer and caught my eyes. "You know, my mom was a year older than my dad."

"Is that so?"

He nodded. "Being attracted to an older woman must run in the family."

I laughed. "I don't think that's a genetic trait, and one year is a lot smaller than twelve."

"I did some Googling last week. Jay-Z is twelve years older than Beyoncé. Ryan Reynolds is eleven years older than Blake Lively."

"Men have liked younger women throughout history."

He wagged his finger at me. "I thought you might say that. So I'm prepared. Hugh Jackman's wife is thirteen years older than him. Allison Janney's boyfriend is twenty years younger. And Sarah Paulson is thirty-two years older than Holland Taylor."

He definitely got credit for ingenuity. Luckily, I was let off the hook from having to respond by the sound of someone knocking at my front door.

"Valentina?" Bella yelled.

I went to let her in, while Ford stayed on the back deck.

"Hey." I opened the screen door. "How did your interview go?"

"It went great. They offered me the job. But I need your help. I was hoping you could help me convince my brother to let me stay out here for the summer."

Ford bellowed from the back deck. "Still can't fight your own battles, huh, Bella?"

Her shoulders slumped. "Shit. I didn't know he was here."

I offered a sympathetic smile. "Sorry. But come on out back. And congratulations on getting the job."

On my way out to the deck, I grabbed Ford another beer. Handing it to him, I took my seat without thinking anything of it.

Bella looked back and forth between us. "Well, don't you two look cozy?"

I felt compelled to explain, even though we weren't doing anything wrong. It wasn't unusual for two neighbors to sit together and share an afternoon beer.

"My kitchen sink was leaking, and Ford fixed it for me. It took him hours. He just finished up."

Ford looked over at me and shook his head. He knew what I was doing.

"What do you want, Bella?" he said.

She put her hand on her hips. "I want to stay. Your apartment is boring, and I love it out here. The restaurant hired me to work their busy shift—Thursday, Friday, Saturday, and Sundays—so I'll be working all the time and won't be able to get out of control."

Ford sat up and scratched his chin. Bella took the opportunity to keep selling.

"Plus, Valentina will be out here all summer, so she can keep an eye on me."

He looked over at me and pushed his sunglasses down his nose to meet my eyes. "You're staying out here all summer? Not just weekends?"

I nodded. "I have to go into the city to take my teaching exam next week, but other than that, I don't have any plans to leave."

Ford squinted. I could see the wheels in his head turning. He rubbed his chin. "The *entire* summer, huh?"

I nodded hesitantly.

He looked at his sister. "You know what? Go ahead. Stay. I think it might be good for you to spend time out here this summer after all." He flashed a mischievous smile. "In fact, I'm looking forward to spending as much time out here as I can, too."

Well, that most certainly backfired.

Later that night, I was studying on the couch when Ford knocked on the door. "Hey. I have to head back into the city early tomorrow morning before traffic. I just wanted to talk to you about Bella."

"Sure, come in."

He looked at the books strewn all over and my pile of homemade flashcards. "Cramming for your exam next week?"

"Yeah. It's on Thursday."

"You know, I speak some Italian. Maybe I can give you a hand, if you need it."

"You do?"

"I did a semester abroad in Rome my second year of college. Actually, I was only there about seven weeks." He looked away. "That's where I was when I got the call about my parents' accident."

"Oh God. I'm sorry. That must've been awful—getting a call like that when you're so far away."

He nodded. "Say something in Italian."

"Like what?"

"I don't know. Anything."

I thought for a moment, then said, "*Spero davvero di non bombardare questo test.*" *I really hope I don't bomb this test.*

Ford grinned. "I have no idea what you said, but it sounded sexy as fuck."

I laughed. "Let me hear you say something."

He cocked his head to one side. "*Mi piace molto il tuo aspetto senza un reggiseno.*" *I really like the way you look without a bra on.*

My eyes widened, and I looked down. Sure enough, my nipples were practically piercing through my shirt. I hadn't been expecting company. I folded my arms across my chest. "It's cold in here."

"Really? I'm kind of warm."

So damn cocky.

"You said you wanted to talk to me about Bella?"

He chuckled. "Yeah. If the house starts shaking from a party, will you let me know? I won't be able to get back out here until next weekend."

"I'm sure she'll be fine. But if it makes you feel better, I'll keep an eye out for her."

"Thanks. She's a pain in my ass. But I want to keep her out of trouble."

I smiled. "You have a soft side, Ford."

He leaned in and kissed me on the cheek before moving his mouth to my ear. "I have a *hard* side I'd like to show you, too."

My entire body joined my nipples in zinging to life.

Ford pulled his head back. He took one look at my face and a wicked grin spread across his. "The *entire* summer. I can't wait."

chapter nine

Valentina

"I'm so happy that's over." I breathed out a long sigh of relief.

Mark and Allison were already outside waiting for Desiree and me to finish the test. They'd gotten done early, but I'd wanted to take every last available minute to review my answers a third time.

"What did you think?" Mark asked.

It was easier than I'd thought it would be, yet I was afraid to jinx myself and say that out loud. "I felt prepared."

Desiree smiled. "Me, too. Although, I'm not sure I have the best judgment on how things are going. I also thought my ex, Travis, was going to propose the night he dumped me."

We all laughed. "So what is everyone doing for the summer? It's going to feel like we have a lot of free time without classes and studying," Mark said.

"I'm going to Minneapolis for a few weeks to watch my nephew because my sister needs to have a hysterectomy," Allison said.

"I'm sorry to hear that, but what a great sister you are to help out. I'm spending the summer in Montauk. We have a house out there. If you get back early, you should come out and relax a little." I looked at all three of my study partners. "You all should."

"We? You're doing a summer share?" Allison asked.

I shook my head. "No. Sorry. *We* is me and my ex-husband. I have the house this summer, but we take turns. It's been almost two years, yet I still slip up and say *we* sometimes. But we do own it together, so I guess, technically, it's okay in this instance."

"I've never been to Montauk," Mark said.

"And you've lived in New Jersey your entire life?"

Mark laughed. "Yup. Born and raised right in Edgewater. I've never been to the Hamptons either. Guess I should rectify that sometime soon."

"You really should. I personally could do without the Hamptons. In the summer it's mostly just upscale shops and mobbed with polished people. Montauk is way more laid back, for the most part—an old fishing village and more casual. I love it out there."

"Well, then, I'll have to make a point of coming out this summer. Maybe you can give me a tour if I do."

"Sure." I looked at Allison and Desiree. "Really, guys. Let's keep in touch. You're all welcome if you come out."

We hugged and promised to call soon, and then I headed to my car. I'd had to turn off my phone before the test started, so I powered it back on. As soon as the screen illuminated, Ford's name popped up with a new text message.

Ford: Well, how'd it go? Don't keep me hanging...

I smiled. Ford and I had been texting all week. Initially, the texts had been about Bella—he'd asked if I'd seen her and how things were going. But the last few days they'd had nothing to do with his sister. It felt like we were back to when we'd first started texting, before I knew Donovan620 was Ford—the *boy* next door.

I'd be lying if I said I didn't enjoy our communications. He was witty, and, though I shouldn't have, I looked forward to hearing from him. I might've even been checking my phone like a teenage girl the last few days. I knew it was wrong, but I could justify it in my head as keeping in contact because of Bella. It was the right thing to do. And now, he was just being cordial—asking how my test had gone. That was it. He was being neighborly... I couldn't *not* respond.

I sighed, knowing full well that I was full of shit, yet texted back anyway.

Valentina: I feel like I did okay.

He texted back immediately.

Ford: Excellent. We'll need to celebrate this weekend.

I hated that I got a flutter in my belly reading that he'd be in Montauk again soon.

Valentina: You'll be out this weekend?

Ford: Already here. Got back about an hour ago.

I masked how I really felt.

Valentina: Oh. That's nice. I'm sure Bella must be happy with some company.

Ford: Forget her. Hoping you'll be happy with some company, too...

I didn't want to answer truthfully, so I decided against responding at all. The man made me flustered to begin with, and I needed to drive. I'd see him tomorrow. So I tossed my phone into my purse and started the car.

The *man* made me flustered.

Boy.

Think of him as a boy, Valentina.

I wanted to so badly.

But it was becoming harder and harder to remember his age.

———

"Hey," I yelled over to Ford as I walked out onto my back deck. He blinked a few times and looked up from his laptop. I thought he'd seen me come out, but apparently he hadn't.

"You're back."

"Just got in a few minutes ago. How's Bella?"

"She's good. Just left for work. The house is still standing, so I guess things went okay."

I smiled. I'd planned to sit on the back deck and enjoy the late-afternoon sun, but it felt weird now since we were both alone. Our houses stood so close together that we could probably jump from one deck to the other if we had to.

"Glad it worked out. You look busy. I'll let you get back to work." I waved and turned to go back into the house.

Ford's voice stopped me as my hand hit the handle to the sliding glass door. "Wait," he called. "What are you up to now?"

"Umm. I...uh...I was going to go for a walk," I lied. "It took me almost four hours to get here with all the traffic. Figured my legs could use a good stretch."

"Mind if I join you? I need to stop staring at this computer."

"Uh. sure. That'd be great. I'm going to go change. I'll be back in a few minutes."

Changing turned into fixing my hair, brushing my teeth, and touching up my makeup. I was really disappointed in myself for putting in so much extra effort.

When I walked back out to the deck, I found Ford waiting at the bottom of my stairs with two glasses of wine. I had two beers in my hand. "Guess we both had the same idea."

"Great minds. Do you want to leave one here or double-fist it for our walk?"

"Why don't we sit for a few minutes before we start walking? I'm not sure I'm capable of maneuvering through the sand without spilling both."

"Good idea." We sat side by side on the third stair from the sand. I chose to drink the wine first, while Ford picked up the beer.

"Did you bring beer because you know I like it?" he asked.

I smiled. "Did you bring the wine because it's what I drink?"

He smiled back. "Only because we don't have any olive juice in the house. I'll have to remedy that."

Our legs brushed against each other, and arousal shot through me. Seriously, it was just a leg. What the hell was wrong with me? My libido had been dead for so long, and it had to pick a totally inopportune time to wake up? *Nothing like a smidge of alcohol to put it back to sleep.* I swallowed half my glass of wine and tried to be myself.

"You looked like you were stressed sitting in front of your laptop. Everything okay at work?"

"Nah, it wasn't work. I was weeding through the mountains of women on Match.com who messaged me."

The burn of jealousy crept through my body, making me feel warm.

"Oh. That's nice."

Ford bumped my shoulder with his. "Kidding. I haven't been on Match since we started talking. You?"

I shook my head. Not wanting to analyze *why* either of us hadn't gone back to the dating site, I moved our conversation along. "I must've misread concentration for stress."

He shook his head. "You actually didn't. I have some big decisions to make at work that are weighing on my mind."

"You said you work in real estate, right?"

"Yeah. My family owned a commercial storage business, and my dad and I had started to move into temporary office space, too. The commercial storage side of things doesn't do as well anymore, so we'd begun transitioning the buildings we own into something new. The storage facilities convert into pretty nice temporary office suites—high ceilings, exposed ductwork, and brick. We converted one before the accident, and it's done really well. People love the idea of having a place to go work with everything available to them—receptionist, printers, Wi-Fi, furniture—but without the long-term lease commitment and expense. Most people only work from an office a few days a week, so sharing the cost and space with others works out."

"Wow. That's amazing. Were you a business major in college?"

He shook his head. "Architecture."

"Well, I guess converting the space goes with that, then, right?"

"Yeah. My dad was the business side of things. I just saw the potential in the old buildings. It was something we were doing together." He pushed around the sand with his foot and grew quiet.

"It must've been a lot to step into everything after your parents..."

He nodded. "My parents were smart about contingency planning, though. They had a trust in place so if anything happened to them, the stock in their corporation went to me and my sister, but their CFO became the president until I graduated college and turned twenty-one. Once I did those things, I had the option of becoming co-president, which I did. Then at twenty-five, I became the sole president."

"So you've had help the last few years, but now you're on your own?"

"Technically, yeah. But Devin, the CFO, is still there for me whenever I need him. We have a few more commercial storage buildings with leases coming due, so I'm struggling to decide whether to convert them into more temporary office space. Now would be the time. That's the stress you read on my face while I was on my laptop."

"I take it that's not an easy decision."

"It is and it isn't. The storage business still makes a profit, but the office space is a much higher return on investment. One of the buildings that could be available to convert soon is the first one my parents bought twenty-five years ago. It was special to them, so it feels wrong to change things... They worked so hard to build what they had."

I might not be a business mogul, but I knew adding emotion to any business decision made it so much harder. "Let me ask you something. If your father was still here, and he saw the numbers for the office space compared to the storage business, what would he do?"

Ford smiled. "He'd convert them all except for the building they started with. He'd keep that one for my mom."

I shrugged. "Well, maybe that's your answer, then."

He thought about that for a minute and then nodded. "You know what? You're right. I'm looking at it wrong. I should be honoring my father by doing what I think he would do, not by freezing his business in time."

I bumped my shoulder to his playfully. "Boy, that was easy. Your job seems like a piece of cake."

Ford chuckled and finished off his beer. He stood and offered his hand to help me up. "Come on. It's your turn. We'll solve all your problems during our walk."

"What if I don't have any problems?"

He smirked. "Oh, but you do. Your head and your body are at odds on a certain issue. That's one we should discuss in detail."

―――――

"So when do you get your results from the test you took?"

Ford and I had walked about forty-five minutes down the beach. Behind us, the sun was beginning to go down, and the sky lit up with gorgeous shades of orange and purple, so we turned around to head back and enjoy the view.

"Seventeen days."

"That's not too bad."

"No, not at all. I did my student teaching with an older woman who said it took two months to get her results years ago."

Ford smirked.

"What?"

"I was just thinking how you're going to be *that teacher*—the one who gives all the high school boys wet dreams."

I wrinkled my nose. "Ugh. Don't even say that."

"What? I totally would have been fantasizing about you if you were my teacher." Ford chuckled. "In all seriousness, I think it's cool you went back to school and got your degree—decided to become a teacher. Did you always want to be one?"

"Yeah. Ever since third grade, when I had Mrs. Moynihan. I loved to read, but I had a weird obsession with outer space at the time. Every Monday and Friday, we would go to the school library and pick out books to read during quiet time. All the other kids picked out books like *Harold and the Purple Crayon*, while I wanted to read books about Pluto and space asteroids. Some of my classmates had begun to make fun of me—calling me Valentina from Venus, so I switched to books similar to the other kids', even though I didn't really enjoy them. Anyway, Mrs. Moynihan noticed, and one day at the library she handed me a book she said she thought I'd like. The outside was a regular, popular kids book, but inside was a book about the solar system. She'd taken the paper cover off a book and put it on what I really wanted to read so I could read in private."

"That's awesome."

"I kept changing out the covers until two weeks after we got back from Christmas break, when we had a guest speaker—a retired astronaut. He brought an old space suit, and all the kids went crazy. The next week, they all started taking out books about astronauts on library days. Mrs. Moynihan was always special to me. I kept in touch with her for years. When I was in tenth grade, she died, and my mom took me to her wake. We walked over to Mr. Moynihan to give condolences, and he recognized my name. Turned out, the reason he remembered my name was because his wife had spent an entire Christmas break hand-writing letters to a hundred-and-fifty astronauts begging them to come speak at the school because she had a student who needed the others to see how cool space could be."

"Wow. A hundred-and-fifty, hand-written letters. That's dedication."

I nodded. "What did you want to be when you were little?"

Ford grinned. "Well, it changed as I got older, but in kindergarten my teacher had us draw pictures of what we wanted to be. I drew Santa Claus."

"You wanted to be Santa?"

"Don't laugh. It's a damn good job. You only work one night a year, you get to fly around on a sleigh pulled by kick-ass reindeers, and everyone leaves you cookies on the table when you stop by."

"Uhhh, Santa works all year making the toys."

He shrugged. "I thought the elves did all that."

"What happened after you found out Santa wasn't real?"

Ford abruptly stopped in place, and his eyes bulged. "Santa's not real?"

The two of us cracked up. When we started walking again, Ford said, "You're going to think I'm full of shit, but after I realized the Santa thing wasn't going to work out, I wanted to be an astronaut."

I shoved his arm. "You're just saying that because I told you I was obsessed with space."

Ford drew an X across his chest. "I swear. But it does make sense why our connection is so strong. We're both space nerds at heart."

He was teasing me, but he wasn't wrong. Our connection *was* strong. Even before I knew his personality came attached to a gorgeous face and ridiculously hard body, I'd felt it, too. Ford made me laugh and feel good about myself.

I tamped down that thought and steered our conversation to safer territory. "So how did you wind up going to school for architecture if you were such a space nerd?"

"I was actually a dual applied science and architecture major in college the first two years. But dropped the science in my third."

"What made you focus on architecture?"

He looked over at me, and it seemed like he was debating how to answer. Finally, he shrugged. "Life. I'd been living away in Boston at college, and after the accident, I wanted Annabella to stay in New York and finish school with her friends. We have a pretty small family—my dad was an only child, and my mom has one sister. My Aunt Margaret lives in Ohio and offered to take us both in, but we'd just lost our parents and experienced enough change to last a lifetime. So I moved back home, and Bella and I stayed together in our parents' apartment while I finished my degree and started to work full time in the company. The change to one major just seemed more practical. I didn't have as much free time to do the work for two difficult majors."

Oh. Wow. I hadn't thought about the logistics of them losing their parents—what had happened immediately after his parents died. Naturally, I'd assumed it had been a life-changing event—to lose both young parents unexpectedly in one day. But Ford had sacrificed so much for his little sister. He'd become a parent with a teenage daughter and an inherited business to run overnight. The choices he'd made were noble and mature.

I reached out and touched his arm. "Not every person would have given up what you did."

"Trust me, I had my moments where I didn't do the right thing. A few years back, my aunt had to step in and set me straight. One morning I walked into the office and sat at my desk, and it hit me that I was a forty-five-year-old man at twenty-two. I had a sixteen-year-old kid, lived in my parents' house, and was even sitting in my father's chair. I felt like my own life had disappeared, and I'd literally become my father."

I understood some of how he felt. Getting pregnant at seventeen meant the abrupt end of my youth in a lot of ways. "I get it. I vividly remember being home one Friday night when I was twenty. My husband was sleeping on the couch at eight thirty, and I had a two-year-old sleeping in the other room. I flicked on the TV, put my feet up, and started to watch *Family Feud*. My mom used to watch it all the time, but with a different guy hosting the show. I looked down, realized I was in my pajamas at eight thirty on a Friday night, and it hit me that I'd turned into my mother."

Ford looked over at me. "What did you do?"

"I got dressed in clothes that no longer felt right to wear, put the baby monitor next to my sleeping husband, and went out with Eve."

I smiled, remembering that weekend. I'd stayed out for almost two days, but in the end, Eve had to practically carry me home because I was drunk and crying so hard because I missed my son.

"I partied for two days, then was in bed sick for three. But I definitely wondered if I'd made the right choices a few times."

"Yeah, I did something similar—except my rampage lasted almost a year. I'd started to screw up at work, was bringing women home while I lived with my little sister, and I blew through a boatload of money from my parents' life insurance. My aunt finally called me on it. She told me to get over myself, because while being my father might not be what I'd planned, I should be honored to stand in the man's shoes at all." He nodded. "She was right. Plus, Mrs. Peabody called me about fifteen minutes after my aunt finished reading me the riot act and told me to get my head out of my ass."

My brows drew together. "Mrs. Peabody? The woman you mentioned that has premonitions or something, right?"

"Yeah. She sometimes wakes up in the middle of the night with these strong feelings. She's had them since she was a kid. But that day, she called me right after my aunt left and said she had a feeling something bad was going to happen to me." He chuckled. "Then she told me to sober up and pull my head out of my ass. Right before she hung up on me."

"Who is she?"

"It's a long story, but I dialed her by accident a few years ago. At least, I think it's an accident. She doesn't. One night, back when I was in a shitty place, I'd been attempting to drunk dial some woman I'd met. I dialed wrong and reached Mrs. Peabody. We started talking, and I rambled on and told her my life story. She said she'd been up late, expecting a call because of a dream she had that a stranger needed her help."

"Oh, wow. That's crazy."

He laughed. "Yeah. That's the tip of the iceberg with Mrs. Peabody. She's seventy-six and lives in an assisted living facility out in Wyoming."

"And you kept in touch with this woman after that?"

"I still keep in touch with her. It's been about three years now. The day after my drunk dial, I woke up and vaguely remembered talking to someone. So I looked through my missed calls and dialed the last number. Mrs. Peabody answered, and we got to talking again. She had just left the podiatrist's office and found out she needed to have her toe amputated the next day. She's diabetic and has circulation issues. Anyway, we talked for a while, and I wasn't sure if she was crazy, clairvoyant, lonely, or just eccentric. I'm still not entirely sure. But she sounded nervous about the surgery, and it was obvious she just needed to talk. So we spent a few hours on the phone again, only that time, she did most of the talking. I figured I owed her one. After that, I reverse-searched her telephone number and got an address to send some flowers for her recovery." He shrugged. "We've been talking a few times a month ever since."

"That's a little bizarre, yet also oddly sweet. Though I do believe some people have special gifts like that."

"Oh yeah?" He smirked. "Then I feel inclined to tell you Mrs. Peabody called this morning and said if my neighbor didn't sleep with me, something bad might happen to me."

I squinted. "You're so full of shit."

He chuckled. "Okay...but if I break a leg tomorrow, that's all on you."

We stopped as we reached my house and stood at the bottom of the stairs. We had to have walked five or six miles, yet I could have kept walking for another five talking to him—it was just so easy to do.

"For what it's worth, you should be proud of how you've handled things since the accident—especially your sister. You might not have done everything perfectly, but she seems like a regular nineteen-year-old who's pretty well adjusted."

"Yeah. I had a lot of help, and it wasn't always pretty. But I wound up in the right place, even taking a different path than I'd expected."

Modesty was another quality I found attractive in a man. Why couldn't Ford be an egomaniac?

"Even though I'm divorced and starting over at thirty-seven, I wouldn't change a thing either."

"You see? We're not as different as you think."

Maybe not in values, but an entire generation gap stretched between us. "Oh yeah? Who's your favorite musician?"

"I listen to everything. But I'm into Jack Johnson right now."

"Never heard of him. My favorite band growing up was The Backstreet Boys."

Ford shrugged. "That's not a difference. That's an opportunity to share new things with each other."

"I don't have an Instagram or SnapFace."

"You mean SnapChat."

"Whatever. I just proved my own point. I don't even know what social media is called anymore. Are you on Facebook?"

"No."

"Let me guess, because Facebook is for old people?"

"No. Because we don't know my mother's passwords, and when I had an account, it kept sending me reminders of stuff with her tagged after the accident."

Shit. Now I felt awful. "Sorry. I didn't realize."

It had grown dark, and Ford and I lingered at the bottom of my stairs for a while longer, but eventually it felt like I needed to call it a night. I thanked him for joining me on my walk.

"Hey!" he yelled up as I reached the top step. "Have dinner with me tonight?"

I frowned. Not because he'd asked, but because I wanted to. I *really, really* wanted to.

"I can't."

"Have plans already?"

I shook my head.

"Too tired from your drive out and our walk?"

I shook my head again. "I'm sorry, Ford."

He gave me a sad smile. "It's okay. I'll wear you down. I don't give up easily. Goodnight, beautiful."

chapter
ten

Valentina

I heard the music from my kitchen and assumed people must've come to the beach early today. Stirring my coffee, I found myself singing along as I went to enjoy the morning view with my cup of caffeine on the back deck.

A shirtless Ford held up a mug as I walked out. "Morning, neighbor."

What a view, alright. I could get used to seeing that every morning.

"Good morning." I forced my eyes back to the screen door to slide it closed and then turned to look out at the beach, shielding my eyes. It took me a minute to realize no one was out there yet, and the music was coming from next door. I squinted at Ford. "Backstreet Boys just *happens* to be playing this morning at your house?"

He grinned and waved for me to join him over on his deck. "Come have your coffee with me and listen to my new favorite band."

I rolled my eyes.

"Come on. I downloaded *two full albums*."

I laughed, but went to join the crazy man on his deck anyway.

Boy.

Crazy boy.

I walked down my stairs, took a few steps on the sand, and went back up his stairs to the deck. When I reached where Ford was sitting, he stood and took my mug from my hand, setting it down on the table.

"What was your favorite song? Wait...let me try to guess... 'I Want it That Way'?"

"Nope. But I think that was their most popular song."

The song 'Everybody' was currently playing—it had a disco dance rhythm to it, and Ford took my hand and led me into a twirl. I giggled when he then took a turn at twirling under our arms.

"I'm not a great dancer," I said.

"No one's watching, I promise."

We fooled around dancing for the rest of the song. It felt really good. When the next one came on, he still had my hand.

My eyes lit up after the first few bars. "This is it! This was my favorite song. It's called 'Incomplete'."

"Yeah? Well, then we definitely can't stop dancing yet." Ford tugged my hand, and I practically tripped into his arms.

Before I could give it any thought, he'd wrapped his other arm around my waist and pulled me flush against him. God, it felt good. It had been a long time since I'd been in a man's arms, especially one with a body so firm—*so, so firm.* And he smelled incredible, too—woodsy, but clean, very masculine.

I took a deep breath in, and Ford pressed his hand against my back. Every muscle in his body felt so hard against my soft. He knew how to slow dance and was confident in his lead, which made my mind wonder if that skill might carry through to the bedroom.

Stop it, Val. Don't go there...

Ford's head ducked down, and he rested his cheek against mine. He sang some of the chorus—about being sexual and rocking your body, and I fully gave in to enjoying the moment. I knew it was dumb, but...did I mention *how good* his hard body felt? This was as close as I would likely get to feeling it pressed up against mine, so, hey... why not? I let myself get lost in him.

Which was why I didn't hear anyone coming until the squeaky screen door of his house slid closed.

"Thought we had a *no overnight guest rule*," Bella quipped.

I jumped out of Ford's arms and stumbled back, almost falling on my ass.

Bella's eyes widened as she caught sight of me. "Oh. Val, I didn't realize it was you. It's so early. I assumed he'd had a girl overnight."

I was so flustered. "No. Just me." I reached for my coffee on the table. "It was...Backstreet Boys...and... yeah....my favorite old band...and so...I should be going." I practically ran from their deck. "*Achoo!*"

God damn it. Bella probably thought I was nuts, but I didn't stop to look back to check.

Inside the safety of my own house, I leaned my head against the door. I was breathless from, well, everything— the way it had felt to be in Ford's arms, getting caught red handed, running up the stairs to my house. What the hell had I been doing, allowing that to happen? I'd been so deprived of human contact, contact from a man, that I'd let myself get caught up in a touch that felt good.

Eve was right. I really needed to get laid.

But at the moment, I really needed a cold shower.

"Knock, knock," Bella called from my back door.

I got nervous, thinking she might've been coming over to bawl me out—tell me what a dirty old lady I was for what she'd walked out to see earlier.

I took a deep breath and slid the door open. "Hey."

"What are you up to today?"

"Ummm. Nothing."

"Wanna go to the art show in town? It's outdoors under tents in the square."

I let out the relieved breath I'd been holding. "Oh. I read about that. I didn't realize it started today."

"My mom and I used to go every year. They had some pretty cool stuff. If you're not into art, they also have jewelry and ceramics, too."

"No, I love art shows. Especially local ones like this. But..."

She smiled. "Ford left me a credit card and said I can get something for my new apartment. I'm moving out of the dorms next semester. We should go do some damage."

"He left you a credit card...so he's not going with you?"

She shook her head, seeming unbothered by my asking. For that matter, she didn't seem to care about finding us dancing on the deck earlier either. "He went to the city for a meeting."

"Is he coming back?"

She shrugged. "Tomorrow, I think."

I didn't have anything to do today, so I told Bella I'd go with her. It would be a good distraction from this morning, anyway.

Since Bella drove a small car, we took my Volkswagen in case either of us found anything big we wanted to haul home. After I got over the anxiousness I felt thinking Bella might say something about Ford and me, I actually had a good time.

We walked the aisles and stopped to look at each exhibit. Our taste in art turned out to be pretty similar. Bella bought a colorful print of a surfer riding a wave at Ditch Plains, a local surf spot. It had the most amazing sunset in the background that looked color enhanced, though it wasn't.

While we were waiting in line to get a pretzel, a good-looking boy with sun-bleached blond hair struck up a conversation about the photo Bella was holding. They were still talking after we'd paid for our pretzel and waters, so I told Bella I was going to go back to a jewelry display we'd passed where I'd liked a ring.

Really I just wanted to give them some privacy because I thought there might've been a spark between her and the surfer dude.

I strolled a few aisles and heard the muffled sound of my cell ringing from inside my purse. Stopping to dig it out, I saw Mark's name flashed on the screen. Since Bella was busy, I figured I might as well answer.

"Hey, Mark."

"Hey, Valentina. What's going on?"

I sipped my water. "Not much. Stuffing my face with a pretzel and walking around an art show at the moment."

"In Montauk?"

"Yep. It's a local show in town, but there're a lot of great artists."

"Mind if I join you?"

I stopped and looked around. "You're here? In Montauk?"

"Not yet. But I will be soon. I just passed a town called Amagansett, so I don't think I'm that far. I had an appointment out in Holbrook today, and as I was parking, it got canceled. Figured what the hell? I'm halfway to Montauk already, and it's a beautiful day...so why not?"

"Oh. Wow. Amagansett is close."

He was only about ten miles away, and he'd already passed all of the spots that had heavy traffic. He'd probably be here in fifteen minutes.

I wasn't sure how I felt about Mark being in Montauk. I'd invited him out, but I'd meant it as an invitation to the study group as a whole. But it felt awkward to say I was too busy now that I'd told him I was strolling around an art show. Besides, Mark was a friend—I shouldn't feel weird about seeing him.

He must've sensed my hesitation. "If you're busy, that's okay. I just thought I'd give it a shot."

I shook my head. "No, no. I'm not busy. Of course you're welcome to join me. I'll give you a tour of Montauk, if you'd like."

"Sweet. That would be great."

Sure enough, fifteen minutes later, Mark called and asked where he should park. Bella had finished up her chat with the surfer dude, so we walked over to meet him outside of the tents.

"Hey."

We hugged.

Mark looked around. "This is really nice. I can't wait to see the whole town."

I grinned. "You pretty much just did. Well, the shopping and commercial part of it anyway. But that's not what I love about Montauk."

I introduced Bella. "This is my neighbor, Annabella. Bella, this is Mark—a friend from school. We were in a study group together, and we both just took our teaching certification exam last week. Mark has never been to Montauk."

Bella shook Mark's hand. "Did you just move to the area or something?"

He laughed. "Nope. Just never came this far east on Long Island."

We made small talk for a few minutes, and then I said, "Well, we still have a few rows of the show we haven't walked through. Do you want to check them out with us?"

Mark said sure, but Bella bowed out. "Umm...if you don't mind, I'm going to skip the rest of the show. We saw most of it anyway."

"Oh. Okay, I'll give you a ride home."

"No, enjoy yourself. I can get one from Freddie."

My brows drew down. "Freddie?"

"The guy I was talking to in line."

Oh. *The surfer dude.* My parent mode kicked in. "Do you think that's a good idea? To get into his car? You just met him."

Bella looked amused. "I'll be fine, *Mom.* He's a local."

"But..."

She looked at Mark. "Nice to meet you. I'll see you back at the house later, Val."

Before I could plead my case, she started to walk away.

Mark shook his head. "Reminds me of my daughter. She thought I was nuts for being angry that she'd skipped a concert I'd bought her tickets to for Christmas. She hung out with one of the guys from the opening band instead. She was seventeen at the time."

I had no experience with a daughter, having just Ryan, but I knew if I had one I'd want to lock her up until she was thirty.

"I was always kind of sad I never had a girl. Not so sure about that now."

Mark and I walked through the exhibit. He'd tried to insist we just check out the artists I hadn't hit yet, but I'd won that battle.

After the art show, we hopped in my car so I could give him a tour of Montauk. Our first stop was the lighthouse, followed by the fishing piers where all the commercial and party boats came in. A few had just returned from fishing trips, so we stood around and watched the mates filet their catches. After, we had a drink outside at the dockside bar. He ordered a beer, and I ordered a virgin strawberry margarita, since I was driving.

"So have you decided where you're going to apply once you're certified?" he asked.

"I'd like to find a leave-replacement job somewhere close to home, if possible."

Mark's forehead wrinkled. "You want a temp position? Not a tenure-track one?"

I sipped my frosty drink. "Yeah. I've been toying with the idea of getting a year of experience and then doing a year in Italy teaching after that."

"Wow. That'll certainly make finding a position late in the summer much easier. Most people prefer something permanent."

"It's the first time in my life that I'm able to make choices for only myself. Ryan is away at college for three more years. I want to take advantage."

Mark smiled, and his eyes roamed my face.

"What?"

He shrugged. "Nothing. I just find a woman who likes an adventure sexy."

Not sure how to respond to that, I filled my mouth with enough frosty drink to get a brain freeze.

"You ready to get going?" I asked. "I'll show you a few beaches before it gets dark. The parking is terrible by the ones the surfers frequent, but if you don't mind the walk, they're really pretty."

"That sounds fantastic." Mark stood and went behind my chair, waiting for me to stand so he could pull it out.

He was really such a nice guy, such a gentleman. When I'd pondered whether something could grow between us after he'd asked me on a date, I'd thought maybe if I saw him outside our regular setting where we studied, I might see him in a different light. But the few hours I'd spent with him today proved what I'd suspected—there was no spark. Or maybe it wasn't the last few hours that had proven anything to me, but the hours this morning with Ford where the sparks had been so strong, I still felt the burn.

I'd shown Mark around pretty much all of Montauk, and it was dark by the time I drove him back to town to where he'd parked. I pulled up behind his car and left my engine idling.

"Well, this was a really nice surprise, Mark. And I'd totally forgotten how pretty some of the beaches we stopped by today are. I tend to stay on the beach right behind my house, but I'm definitely going to be revisiting a few of the local ones we saw. I needed this little tour today."

"So your house is right on the beach, then?"

I nodded. "It's up on stilts, so the backyard is the sand."

"Wow. Would it be too much to ask to see it before I head back?"

I really wanted to just go home, shower, and climb into bed, but I felt funny saying no. "Ummm...sure. It's not too far from town. Right down Old Montauk Highway."

"I'll follow you."

"Okay."

On the short drive to my house, I started to get antsy for some reason. I knew it was stupid, because Ford and I weren't dating or anything. Yet for some reason, I didn't want him to see me pull up with Mark. Not to mention, whatever anxiousness I felt, whether right or wrong, was ridiculous because Ford wasn't even in Montauk tonight. Bella had said he planned to spend the night in the city.

Except he must've had a change of plans...

The moment my headlights turned into the driveway, they landed on a set of eyes next door. Ford was sitting on the front steps of his house drinking a beer. The looming bit of anxiousness I'd felt suddenly turned into full-blown panic.

I took a few deep breaths as I parked, telling myself I was being ridiculous and wasn't doing anything wrong. I could drag Mark back to the house to sleep with him, if I wanted to. In fact, that's probably exactly what I *should* be doing tonight.

In the rearview mirror, I could see that Mark had started to get out of his car, so I had to suck it up. My house and Ford's were only about twenty feet apart. It wasn't like I could pretend I didn't see him sitting there.

Mark met me at my car door when I got out and closed it for me. We walked a few steps toward the front stairs, and my eyes locked with Ford's. He didn't say a word, just watched me silently as he drank his beer.

"Uh, hey," I called, feeling totally awkward.

Ford nodded.

As awkward as I felt, I couldn't avoid introductions. "Um, Mark, this is my..." *Friend? Man making me take cold showers? Guy I met on Match?* "...this is Ford."

Mark walked over and extended his hand. Ford didn't get up, but shook it. It was quiet, and I tried to think of something to fill the uncomfortable silence, because it didn't seem like Ford was going to be any help.

"Ford owns the house. He's Bella's brother." I looked over at Ford, who still hadn't taken his eyes off of me. The intense look on his face made my stomach do a nervous flip. "Mark met Bella today at the art fair in town."

"Wow. Nice house for such a young guy." Mark was being his usual, friendly self. "I have a daughter I'd like to introduce you to," he chided.

I closed my eyes. I hadn't thought it could feel any more awkward, but, yup, that did the trick.

Ford's mouth was a straight line as he brought the beer to it and continued the silent treatment.

"Bella said you had a meeting in the city today and weren't back until tomorrow."

"Change of plans." His eyes darted between Mark and me. "Something came up."

I nodded.

While I felt the tension emanating from Ford, at least Mark seemed oblivious. "Nice to meet you," he said.

My eyes caught with Ford's as I started up the stairs. "Have a good night."

The antsiness I'd felt outside continued when Mark and I escaped into the house. I gave him the grand tour in record speed, showing him the inside, followed by the back deck. The moon lit the beach enough to see the ocean in the dark, and the sound of waves crashing came with a gentle breeze. He marveled over the view. It would've been a magnificent night to sit here, but I was too frazzled. I didn't even do the polite thing and offer him a drink or a cup of coffee.

Taking the not-so-subtle hint, Mark said goodbye ten minutes later. I walked him to the front door, curious to see if my neighbor was still around, but Ford had disappeared.

I should have been relieved that he wasn't hovering around anymore. But instead, his absence filled me with an overwhelming anxiety that I didn't quite know what to do with.

A good, long soak in the tub with a glass of wine helped take the edge off. Though, even after that, I still felt out of sorts and not ready for bed, so I headed down to the kitchen for a refill. I poured wine and stood staring outside the kitchen window that faced Ford and Bella's house. The lights were on, and only Ford's car was home. I knew Bella had to work tonight, so she probably wouldn't be home for a few hours. Maybe I should go over and clear the air?

I wasn't dressed, and I had no idea what the hell I'd say. There wasn't anything to discuss—because there wasn't anything between us. So instead, I sipped my wine and stared blankly out at the night.

A set of headlights turning into the driveway next to mine brought me back from deep thought. Bella must've gotten off early from the restaurant. I was glad I hadn't gone over there now. But after the car parked, I leaned closer to the window and noticed it wasn't Bella's car.

And the woman wearing a dress short enough to show her ass if she bent even slightly was certainly not Ford's sister. My emotions, which had been in turmoil for the last hour, suddenly had no conflict. The burn of jealousy rose from deep within me and heated my cheeks.

I watched the woman teeter in her stilettos and walk toward the house. When she reached the stairs, the automatic security lights flashed on, and the face I hadn't been able to see in the dark became clear.

Of course she was gorgeous.

And had a killer body.

Miles and miles of legs.

Boobs that hadn't become acquainted with gravity yet, too.

Young.

So, so young.

She had a bottle of wine in one hand, and an overnight bag in the other.

I felt sick. Yet like watching a bad car accident, I couldn't look away. As she got to the top of the stairs, Ford opened the door. He must have been waiting for her.

Anxious.

I looked away when he took her in his arms for an embrace. It shouldn't have hurt so much. But that didn't make it any easier to swallow.

I'd just drifted off to sleep when I heard a noise. Sitting up in a fog, I wasn't sure where it had come from, only that it had woken me. I waited to see if I heard it again, because I wasn't positive I hadn't imagined it.

But then I heard the noise again. It was coming from downstairs and sounded like it might be the garbage cans rolling around in the breeze. Slipping from bed, I peered out my second-floor window. Our road had no street-lights, and it was too dark to see anything without the exterior house lights. So I went downstairs to turn on the porch light and take a better look.

At the bottom of the stairs, I saw the silhouette of a person standing outside my front door. It was late, and I knew Ford had company, so it likely wouldn't be him. Maybe Mark had come back? That didn't seem probable since he'd left more than an hour ago and would be half-way home by now.

My heart sped up as I moved closer to the door. "Who is it?"

"It's Ford."

That did nothing to slow my rapid pulse.

I opened the door. "Is everything okay?"

"No. Can I come in?"

chapter eleven

Ford

"How was your *date*?" I stared out her back sliding glass doors, looking out at the darkness. Valentina stood somewhere behind me.

"It wasn't a date."

I turned and caught her eyes. "Sure looked like one."

"Well, it doesn't matter what it looked like. It wasn't. Mark is a friend from school. We belonged to a study group together."

I took a few steps toward her. "Yeah. I remember you telling me about him...the night he asked you out on a *date*."

She squared her shoulders. "How was *your* date?"

My brows drew down. *Date?* Then it dawned on me that she must've seen Nina come in—*my cousin* Nina, who came for the weekend to hang out with Bella. I wondered if she was feeling as jealous as I was—so I went with it and let her think what she'd obviously been thinking.

"Great, just great." I stuffed my hands in my pockets and shrugged. "Nina—great girl."

"She left early."

I grinned. "Nope, she's still next door. Getting all settled in for the night."

Val looked hurt, but I wanted her to be pissed. So I pushed. Her back leaned against the kitchen sink. I took a few more steps, so I stood right in front of her.

"Just came over to see if you know of any good, romantic restaurants that are open late in town."

"No." Her eyes shot daggers, and her voice was clipped. Clearly she wasn't even going to entertain my question and think about it.

I moved yet closer, just inside her personal space. She had nowhere to retreat.

"How about nude beaches? Thought maybe we'd go to a nude beach tomorrow."

Her eyes sparked. "No."

She was definitely jealous, though she did her best not to show it. But where there's a spark, there's fire, so I kept adding gasoline.

"How about lingerie shops? Nina likes to shop. I hate it, so might as well make it something we can both enjoy."

She squinted. "Maybe you should go back into the city for the weekend. Not too many shops like that in Montauk."

I clicked my mouth and grinned. "Shame. How about sex toy shops? Maybe some edible underwear and body paint? Do you think that stains sheets?"

That did it. I actually saw the spark in her eyes shoot to a flame. "You know what, Ford? I really don't want to hear about your sex life."

I put one hand on either side of the counter behind her, boxing her in. "No? Why not, Val? What's the reason you don't want to hear about me having sex with another woman?"

"I just don't. Do you want to hear about my sex life?"

My chest burned even hearing her say *sex life*. I started to get angry. "Fuck, no. But you know *why* I don't want to hear about it?"

She stared at me, steam practically coming out of her nose.

"Not going to take a guess? Let me fill you the fuck in, then. I don't want to hear about your sex life because *I'm jealous*. Because *I* want to be the one taking you out on a date and sleeping in your bed. And you feel the same goddamn way I do, but you're too afraid to admit it."

She raised her voice. "I am not!"

I leaned in so we were nose to nose. "*Liar*. Admit it."

"No!"

"Say it."

"You're crazy!"

"You know what, Val? I'd rather be crazy than a chickenshit. It must suck to finally be free to live a little and be too uptight to act on what you're feeling."

She scowled at me. "Screw you."

My mouth curved to a wicked grin. "Is that an invitation? Because I'm right here whenever you want me. And since I'm *only twenty-five*, I can pretty much fuck on demand. I doubt *old man Mark* has it in him to go all night."

Valentina's chest heaved; I could feel the heat emanating from her body. When I glanced down, I found her nipples protruding through her shirt. She was as turned on as I was, though she wouldn't budge from hiding it beneath her anger.

"You're such an asshole!" she screamed.

Fuck it. *If I'm an asshole, I might as well be a giant one.*

117

There was only one way to win this argument. I wrapped my hands around her cheeks and smashed my lips over her angry mouth. She hesitated for a half a second, but once the initial shock wore off, she opened for me and mewled into my mouth. Feeling her tits pushed up against my chest, I pressed her against the kitchen counter and tilted her head to deepen the kiss.

Whatever restraint she'd had left gave way, and all hell broke loose.

We couldn't get close enough. Grabbing the backs of her thighs, I lifted and guided her legs around my waist. The erection that had started to thicken during our argument grew painfully hard, feeling the wet heat coming from between her legs.

Valentina moaned, and anything and everything ceased to exist but the two of us. She dug her nails into my back, and I tugged at her hair. *I fucking knew it would be like this.* A physical attraction makes for intense chemistry, but a physical *and* mental connection is damn combustible.

I don't know how long we went at it, but eventually we had to come up for air, and the one-second break filled with panting was enough to allow Val to start to come to her senses. She shoved at my chest and reached to touch her swollen lips.

I caressed her face and murmured, "Thanks, Dad."

"Dad?"

I leaned my forehead against hers. "He once told me that the best thing to do when you're having an argument you can't win with a woman you care about is to kiss her—then you both win."

She smiled sadly. "You should probably go home, Ford."

I traced her bottom lip with my thumb. "Nina is my cousin. She came to spend the weekend with my sister."

Valentina's eyes narrowed. "Your cousin?"

"You thought I had a woman over, even after chasing you for a month? I'm not the kind of guy to use another woman to replace the one I want but can't have."

She looked down. I put my fingers under her chin and lifted so our eyes met again. "Tell me, Val. Did it feel as good kissing Mark as it did kissing me?"

It might've been an arrogant statement, but I knew without a doubt that kissing *anyone* did not feel like what had just happened, and I was willing to bet the feeling was mutual.

"I didn't kiss Mark. And it wasn't a date. Not that it's any of your business if it was."

I looked back and forth between her eyes. "Does *he* know it wasn't a date?"

She shook her head. "You should go. It's late."

I might've pushed my way to that kiss, but I wasn't actually an asshole. Plus, I knew her head was still fighting with her body, and it would take a while for them to be aligned, if that were even possible.

I wasn't taking the risk that I'd only ever have that one kiss with her. So I nodded and leaned in, brushing my lips with hers once more. "Goodnight, beautiful."

⌐────────✦

The kiss might have been over, but the memory was the gift that kept on giving. In the shower, I jerked off to the sounds she'd made while my lips were pressed to hers, to the feel of how wet she was, even through our clothing. I was so pathetic that I sniffed my own fucking shorts, hoping some of her juices had come through onto them.

In bed, I wondered what she was doing at this exact moment. Were her fingers inside of herself? I closed my eyes and imagined her lying spread eagle in her bed—her wild, dark hair splayed all over her pillow, and her big blue eyes glazed over as she pumped her fingers in and out of her tight pussy.

Fuck.

I really needed to jerk off again.

But instead, I reached for my phone on the nightstand. If she wasn't already regretting our kiss, she would be at some point, and I wanted to let her know I felt no remorse. In fact, I wanted her to know I was fucking *elated* the kiss had happened, and I'd come home to celebrate it.

Ford: I'm not sorry I kissed you.

I watched as the text changed from *Sent* to *Delivered* to *Read*. But no response came.

Alright, well, at least you're listening. So I continued.

Ford: I enjoyed it so much that I just came to the memory.

Sent then *Delivered* then *Read*, again.

I smiled when no return text came. I pictured her sitting in her bed, struggling with her own desire, her eager hand at the waistband of her underwear.

What was that? You want to hear more? Well, okay, then...

Ford: My cock was all lathered up and hard. I closed my eyes and imagined my hand was you. I heard the little sound you made when I yanked your hair. You liked that, didn't you? I felt your gorgeous tits pressed up against my chest. I bet you'll like it when I take your nipple between my teeth and tug hard, too.

Sent. Delivered. Read.

Ford: I came so hard...so fucking hard. But I wish it had been inside of you.

Sent. Delivered. Read.

Ford: Tell me, Val. Did you touch yourself when I left? Did you think of me? Did you use your hand? God, what I wouldn't give to suck on those fingers after they've been inside you.

Sent. Delivered. Read.

Ford: That's okay. You can tell me about it another time. I have something I need to take care of now, too. *Again*. So sweet dreams, my Valentina. I can't wait to see you tomorrow.

I'd hoped to see her before I left. But when I got up at six thirty, her car was already gone. I waited until almost eight, but when she still hadn't come back, I had to get on the road. The meeting I blew off yesterday when Bella mentioned she'd left Val at the art exhibit with some guy had been rescheduled for eleven today, and I couldn't screw this guy again. So I finished my coffee and headed out.

Though I only got about two miles before I came upon a roadside stand that sold fruit, vegetables, and fresh flowers. Sometimes my Dad and I would drive out to Montauk a day later than my mom, and he'd always stop and pick up flowers at this place. I'd passed it a half-dozen times over the last two weeks and never thought to stop.

I pulled over to the side of the road and picked out an oversized bundle of wildflowers with giant sunflowers and then drove back to the house. Valentina's car was still missing, so I left them on the mat at her front door and stepped on the gas to get to my meeting.

A few hours later, I sat in the lobby of an office, waiting for my eleven o'clock meeting to start, and I decided to send her another text.

Ford: Morning, beautiful. Hope you slept well. You were up and out early this morning. I'd been hoping to catch you before I left for the city, so we could talk.

I stopped before hitting send and smiled, deciding to add more.

Ford: Or make out some more.

After a few seconds, the text changed to *Read*. I got pumped when the dots started to jump around. But then they stopped. A minute later they started again. Then stopped again.

Stop overthinking things, Valentina.

No return text had arrived by late afternoon, so I assumed this was how it was going to be until I could get to her in person. Unfortunately, that wasn't going to be today. I needed to go into the office and do a few things after my meeting. And traffic on Friday night would be a bitch since it was the first official weekend of summer.

But I wanted to know if Val had taken off—maybe gone home to New Jersey to avoid me. I hadn't checked in with my sister all day, so I hit speakerphone and told Siri to call Bella.

"Hey. What's going on?"

"You don't have to call me just because I haven't seen you today."

I pictured Annabella's eyes rolling.

"Just checking in. I wasn't sure if you knew I wasn't going to get back out east tonight."

"Oh good. Let me plan a party. I'll make sure to put it on Instagram so a few hundred strangers crash it."

"Cute."

"I'm fine, Ford. And Nina's here for the weekend, and I have Val."

"Is Val around? Her car was gone when I left this morning."

"Yep. We're planting flowers in her deck boxes for her party this weekend right now."

"Party?"

"She's having a barbecue with her friends."

I'd forgotten she'd mentioned her best friend was coming out for a long weekend.

"Oh yeah. Alright, good."

"So...since Nina's here and Val has company this weekend, you really don't need to come back out. I'll be fine."

I knew she was right. Even though I hadn't wanted her out in Montauk by herself when we'd first talked about it, spending time out there made me feel a lot better about it. She could stay on her own for a weekend. Though...I had a party to crash on this particular one.

"I'll see you tomorrow anyway," I said. "Be good."

chapter twelve

Ford

"**M**orning." I walked out onto my back deck and nodded to the woman sitting on the adjacent one. Val's car wasn't in the driveway, but one I didn't recognize was.

The woman took off her sunglasses and smiled. "You must be Ford."

I smiled back. "And you must be Eve. Is it a good thing or a bad thing that you know my name?"

Eve got up and walked over to lean on the deck railing that faced my house. She sipped out of a mug. "You've been a hot topic of conversation lately. I was hoping I'd get to see you. Are you coming to the barbecue today?"

"I wasn't invited."

"Well, let me rectify that. Ford, would you like to come to the barbecue today? We'd love to have you."

I grinned. "Absolutely. What time?"

"Two."

"What should I bring?"

She winked. "Just your A game."

"Hey."

Valentina opened the front screen door. The look on her face told me her friend hadn't mentioned I'd be coming. I extended the bottle of wine I'd brought.

"Eve invited me."

She shook her head. "Of course she did."

"You want me to leave?"

"No. No. It's fine. Come on in. The neighbors on the other side are stopping by, too."

Not exactly a warm reception, but at least she didn't send me packing. A man came down the stairs as the two of us stood at the door. I thought it might've been her dad.

"Tom," Valentina said. "This is Ford."

Tom stuck out his hand right away. "Nice to meet you."

She finished the introduction while we shook. "Tom is Eve's husband."

I had to work at not letting the surprise show on my face. This guy was her best friend's husband, not father?

Tom held up a pair of sunglasses. "Eve needed bigger sunglasses from upstairs. Apparently the ones covering half her face already weren't cutting it."

Val smiled and nodded toward the kitchen. "She yelled for you to bring her sunscreen, too, but you were already upstairs. There's some in the cabinet next to the stove. I was about to make a batch of margaritas."

I followed the sway of her ass to the blender. Once Tom walked out the back door, I stood behind Val and whispered into her ear. "Your best friend is married to a much older man, huh?"

She poured mix into the blender. "It's different."

"How?"

Val turned to face me. "She was thirty-three when she met him. She got to experience life."

We stood in almost the same exact spot as we had two nights ago when we kissed.

"I've experienced life. Maybe we should argue about it again. I liked the way the last disagreement we had in this spot ended."

Val sighed. "Why don't you go outside? I'll be out in a minute."

I would have preferred to stay right here, but didn't want to push. So I put the wine I'd brought into the fridge and gathered the margarita glasses on the counter to carry outside with me. I almost forgot the other thing I'd brought, until I reached for the door handle.

Glancing back over my shoulder, I saw Val wasn't paying attention. I slipped the yellow sticky note I'd written from my pocket and stuck it on the back door right at her eye level before heading out. *Sleep with Ford* really should be on her to-do list anyway.

Eve pulled out the chair next to her the minute I walked out. She patted the cushion. "Come sit. I want to get to know you better."

Her husband shook his head. "That's Eve-speak for I'm about to interrogate you. Sorry, man."

I smiled and took the seat. "It's fine. Interrogate away."

A minute later, Valentina struggled to open the back door while holding a pitcher, salt container, and bag of chips. I got up to slide it open and took the pitcher from her hands.

The interrogation started before Val had even filled all the glasses.

"So, Ford, ever have a serious girlfriend?"

Valentina scolded her. "Eve…"

I waved her off. "It's fine. I don't mind at all." I looked at Eve. "One. Lasted about a year and a half."

"What happened?"

My eyes darted to Valentina's and back to Eve. *Gotta go with honesty.* "I went through a rough patch and decided I needed to make some changes in my life. She was part of those."

Valentina must've assumed the rough patch was immediately after my parents' accident. She cleared her throat and interjected, "Ford lost his parents in a car accident five years ago."

Eve's face fell. "I'm so sorry."

"Thank you." The words hung in the air for a while, so I circled back to her initial question. "The relationship I had ended two years ago."

Valentina's forehead wrinkled.

Eve sipped her margarita. "Are you still friends?"

I flashed a guilty smile. "She's not my biggest fan. No."

Eve seemed unperturbed by my answer. "Republican or Democrat?"

"Democrat."

"Last book you read?"

"*The Outsider*. Stephen King."

"Morning person or night owl?"

"Lately, morning person."

"What do you care about the most?"

"My sister. But don't tell her that."

Eve smiled. "What do you care about the least?"

I scratched my chin. "What other people think."

"Good answer." She nodded.

I snagged a chip and dipped into the guacamole. "Thank you."

"What are you obsessed with?"

My eyes jumped to meet Valentina's and then returned to Eve. I grinned. "Currently, your best friend."

Eve's smile grew wider while Valentina's blush deepened. The interrogation lasted another five minutes before Tom stood and nodded toward the beach.

"What do you say we play some volleyball?"

Eve pouted. "I'm talking to Ford."

He took her hand and tugged her up. "Yeah. That's why it's time for volleyball."

———

By nine o'clock that night, it was just Val and me on the back deck. Tom was tired, and Eve had started to slur her words. I'd had fun spending the day with everyone. Bella and Nina had come by for a while, and so did the neighbors on the other side. But I was glad to finally be alone with Valentina now.

"Sorry about the all-day inquisition. Eve's amazing, but she's not great with boundaries."

"It's fine. I really liked her."

Val sighed. "I can tell she liked you, too. Which will make her unbearable now. She wants me to get back out there."

"Smart woman." I grinned. "I concur."

"A month ago she was trying to get me to go out with a waiter who wasn't old enough to drink yet."

That wiped the grin off my face.

"She means well... She really does. She just thinks I need to get the first one under my belt."

"One?"

"Date. Sex. Relationship. Whatever."

I reached for the wine we'd just broken open and re-filled Val's glass. "You really need to start taking advice from your friend. She seems very intelligent."

Val took another deep breath. The emphasis on the exhale sounded a lot like frustration.

We were sitting next to each other, but I wanted to see her face—read every little thing it would tell me that her words wouldn't. So I pulled her chair out and moved mine so we were facing each other.

Leaning in, our knees touched, and I caught her shivering a bit—though she tried to cover it up. Her mind might've been reluctant about us, but her body was damn enthusiastic.

"I'm not sorry about the kiss the other night," I said. "Not in the least."

She closed her eyes. "It shouldn't have happened."

"Forgetting that you think that for a minute, you have to admit it was fucking phenomenal."

Val smiled sadly. "It was a good kiss, yes."

My ego felt bruised. *Good?* It was better than good. I might be younger than her, but I'd kissed my fair share of women, and that kiss... It was...addictive. We had the kind of chemistry that left us incoherent. I slipped my hands under the back of her knees and tugged her toward the edge of her seat. "If you think it was just a *good* kiss, I think you need your memory refreshed."

She put her hand on my chest, though I had a feeling if I'd leaned in and taken her mouth, her resistance wouldn't have lasted. I should've done it. But our physical connection wasn't the problem. It was her head I needed to work on.

"Fine." She sighed again. "It was a mind-blowing kiss. The kind that kept me awake for three hours afterward because my body was so revved up, it couldn't idle down enough to go to sleep. Does that make you feel better?"

I grinned. "It does. And I'm glad to know you didn't sleep either."

She rolled her eyes. "You made sure of that with your texts."

Good to know. I reached out, took one of her hands, and brought her knuckles to my lips, allowing my tongue to graze over the soft skin.

"I wasn't kidding today when I answered Eve's question about what I'm obsessed with. You're all I can think about for the last month."

"I won't insult you by trying to claim it's a one-way street. From the moment we met on Match, I've spent an inordinate amount of time thinking about you, too."

I still had her hand in mine, so I squeezed. "Doesn't that tell you something?"

Valentina looked down at her feet for a moment before she spoke. "I started dating Ryan when I was fifteen. I got pregnant at seventeen and married at eighteen. When I was thirty-four, I caught him cheating on me. Instead of leaving, I spent a year trying to make it work. I blamed myself—I'd gained a little weight, didn't put on makeup half the time. I thought if I got myself in better shape, kept the house nicer, paid more attention to him as a man, things would be okay."

She shook her head. "Obviously, they weren't. It took me a long time to accept that my failed marriage wasn't all my fault. But it's taken me even longer to figure out who I am. When you become an *us* at fifteen and then suddenly you're an *I* for the first time at thirty-five, you need to take some time to really be an *I*."

She squeezed my hand this time. "I'm incredibly attracted to you. Painfully so. But even if we were the same age, I'm not ready for a relationship yet."

My shoulders slumped. I could argue she was wrong about the age difference, but how could I argue with needing to find herself? For the first time, I felt a sense of defeat sink in.

I nodded. "Okay."

Val smiled half-heartedly. "I'm sorry."

I leaned in and kissed her cheek, knowing it was time to bow out and call it a night. "Me, too."

My dick was just as depressed as I was.

Unlike the other nights I'd come home from next door, I didn't feel the need to beat off. I took a quick shower to wash the sand and salt off and slipped on a pair of sweats.

It was Saturday night and not even ten o'clock. I should've gotten myself dressed and gone out to find someone interested in perking both my limp dick and me up. But let's face it, there was only one person either of us was interested in.

We wanted Valentina.

So instead, I fired up my laptop and started to answer some work emails. The first few were from my assistant—confirming appointments and asking what day I wanted to meet with the lawyers about converting one of the storage buildings to office space. Then I opened one from the VP of marketing. He gave me an update on our Match. com advertising campaign—the amount of the budget spent so far and which ad targets were performing the best.

Apparently, our temporary office space appealed most to divorced singles between the ages of thirty-two and forty who were not looking for a serious relationship.

I scoffed. *It must be me.*

Though it made sense. It was logical that people who had just come out of a bad marriage liked the idea of temporary office space. Their lives were in a state of flux, and the last thing they wanted to do was make a new, long-term commitment when that was happening. That's what made our office space so attractive—you could use it anytime you wanted and walk away whenever you wanted.

Use it anytime you wanted and walk away whenever you wanted.

That thought smacked me right in the face.

Jesus Christ. Am I that big of an idiot?

I'd been going about things all wrong with Valentina.

She'd told me straight out she wasn't ready for a relationship.

And what did I do? Go home to sulk.

I needed my head examined for not proposing an alternative.

Grabbing my cell, I shot off a quick text.

Ford: Can you meet me on the beach?

A minute later the dots started to jump around.

Valentina: Now?

Ford: Yeah. I need to ask you something.

Valentina: What is it?

Nope. Not happening. This was a conversation we needed to have face to face.

Ford: It will only take a minute.

Valentina: Okay. Give me a few. I just got out of the shower.

Anxious, I went outside to wait. Valentina met me at the bottom of the stairs on the sand. Her hair was wet, and she had on shorts and a tank top.

"What's going on?" she whispered.

"I was thinking about what you said—that you're not ready for a relationship."

"Okay..."

I shrugged. "Let's not have one."

Her cute button nose wrinkled up. "What are you talking about?"

"Simple. We're attracted to each other. You aren't ready for a relationship, I'm not looking to get married, and your best friend thinks you need one under your belt. We're both out here for the summer. With any luck, you'll be getting a teaching job. Bella will go back to school, and I'll go back to Manhattan. We'll both be shuttering up out here for the summer in what...eight weeks? Why not spend that time enjoying the chemistry we know is there? No strings attached. We'll part ways, and it ends. We'll enjoy what we *can be* instead of regretting what we can't be."

"That's...that's crazy."

"Why?"

"Because..." She trailed off, unable to come up with a reason.

I smirked. "Good argument."

She squinted at me. "You don't have to be an ass."

A light breeze blew, and it carried the smell of something sweet through the air. I wasn't sure if it was her shampoo, or perfume, or maybe just soap, but it definitely woke up the lazy dog between my legs who'd been pouting since I left her earlier. Slowly, I moved toward her. Valentina took a few steps back and hit the wood of the stairs behind her.

I ducked my head to align with hers and took full advantage. "What do you say? No relationship. No expectations. Just a summer of *fucking*—hard, soft, whatever you're in the mood for—whenever you're in the mood for it."

Valentina's chest heaved up and down. Why the hell hadn't I thought of this sooner? It was the perfect arrangement, really. She wanted me as much as I wanted her—we'd both be getting what we needed. Val would get a carefree summer fling, her one under the belt, and I'd get to spend the next eight weeks screwing her out of my system. I honestly wanted to kick myself in the ass for wasting the last few weeks trying to get her to go out with me when the obvious solution had been right in front of me all along.

"But..." she started to speak.

It looked like she might've finally thought of a reason my idea wasn't a good one. Whatever it was, my argument was better, though mine needed to be demonstrated. I put a finger over her mouth to stop her lips from moving.

"Screw *but*..." I wrapped my other hand around the back of her neck, and my mouth descended on hers before she could argue. Just like the first time, whatever fight she had lasted only a heartbeat. Our tongues met, and that ever-present spark ignited to a full-blown fire. Neither of us could get enough. We groped and pulled, tugged and pushed until we were both out of breath. When we came up for air, her eyes were glazed over. I pushed a piece of her wet hair behind her ear. "Think about it. We'd be good together."

She sucked her bottom lip into her mouth. "I should go inside."

I didn't want to let her, but I knew she needed to think about it.

I nodded. "Go. I'll wait until you get inside and lock up."

I followed her up the stairs so I could see from the deck that she made it safely inside. As she walked to the door, I played a mental game.

If she doesn't look back, she's going to say no.

If she looks back, she'll say yes.

She walked all the way to the door without a glance back in my direction. But at the very last second, just as she was about to shut the door behind her, she stopped, looked up one more time, and smiled.

Fuck yes!

chapter thirteen

Valentina

"So...are we going to pretend we're not going to talk about it?" Eve sipped her coffee and eyed me over the mug.

I sighed. "I was hoping I could at least get some caffeine in me first."

It was almost nine o'clock. I hadn't slept this late in years. Then again, I didn't generally stay up until three in the morning, either. But it had been impossible to fall asleep after what Ford had proposed...not to mention... *that kiss.*

Eve set her mug down and picked up a bottle of sunscreen. The sun was already strong. She squirted a glob of lotion into the palm of her hand and started to lather up. "He's ridiculously hot."

I frowned. "I know."

"Seems smart, too."

"He is."

"Has a good sense of humor."

"That's actually what first attracted me to him when he messaged me on Match.com. He's witty and made me laugh about the entire prospect of dating."

Eve finished one arm and started on the other. "Do you remember when we were ten, and I crashed my bicycle into a car that was backing out of a driveway? I steered right into it and chipped my front tooth."

"How could I forget? You flipped over the handlebars and landed sprawled out on the concrete. You were out cold, and I thought you were dead."

"Do you remember how terrified I was of riding a bicycle after that?"

I knew where she was going with her bike ride down memory lane. "You couldn't be more subtle if you tried. I get what you're trying to say, and sure—of course I'm scared to get back out there. But it's more than that. I'm just not ready."

"There are some things we never feel fully ready for. Did you feel ready to have a baby?"

"Of course not. But I was eighteen years old and still a baby myself."

"Did you feel ready to get married?"

"I was also a kid."

"Alright. Well, did you feel ready to go back to college at thirty-four? Or ready to get a divorce? Or ready for your son to move away?"

I slouched into my chair. "No."

"We're rarely ready for the big things in life, no matter how much we prepare. Sometimes *as ready as I'll ever be* has to be enough."

God, I hated when she was right. I chewed my bottom lip. "Last night he suggested we have a summer fling—no strings attached—since I don't want a relationship."

Eve held out both hands. "That's perfect!"

I'd spent half the night tossing and turning, trying to come up with an argument against his suggestion. Unfortunately, all I'd gotten out of my soul searching was dark circles under my eyes.

I sighed. "He's twenty-five...."

"My husband is *fifty*-five. Wanna trade?"

She was teasing, of course. Eve adored Tom. Besides, when the only thing "wrong" with your husband to make fun of was his age, you count your lucky stars.

Eve brought her mug to her lips and stopped before sipping. "Holy shit."

"What?"

One finger lowered her sunglasses to the bridge of her nose. Her mouth literally hung open as she stared over my shoulder down the beach. Following her line of sight, I turned around and found Ford a few houses away—shirtless and jogging along the water's edge. Even from fifty or sixty feet, we could see the flex of every muscle in his abs as he moved.

He waved while the two of us gawked like idiots.

"Seriously..." Eve fanned herself. "...if you don't take a ride on that stallion, I think you need your head examined."

Ford jogged up the beach toward the house. Eve pushed her sunglasses up. I chuckled, knowing she was hiding her eyes so she could keep ogling when he got closer.

"Morning, ladies." Ford stood with his hands on his hips, looking up at us from the sand. He wasn't even winded.

"Good morning!" Eve called down. "We were just talking about you."

I shot my best friend and her ginormous mouth the evil eye.

Ford grinned. "Oh yeah? All good, I hope."

Eve smiled broadly. "I'd say so. Our discussion was about your proposal for a few months of sex."

"*Eve!*" I looked around. I seriously wanted to kill her right now.

Ford, on the other hand, seemed amused. His brows shot up. "Good to know. How's it looking for me so far?"

Eve turned and gave me the onceover, tilting her head as if she were assessing me, then looked back down to Ford. "I'd say about fifty-fifty right now. I need a little more time to tilt the odds in your favor."

He chuckled. "Well, then, let me get out of your hair."

Ford turned to walk toward the stairs that led to his deck, and Eve called after him. "Hey, boy-toy?"

He shook his head and chuckled. "Yeah?"

"We're going to spend the day on the beach. Why don't you join us?"

His dimples appeared. "I'd love to. I have to work for a few hours, but I'll meet you down there later."

"Sounds good!"

I waited until after Ford was inside his house to lay into her. "What the hell?"

She smiled as if she hadn't just broken girl code. "You can thank me later, *after* he gives you all the orgasms I know a man with that body is capable of."

I tried to get back to relaxing, but it wasn't easy.

The water was calm today, so we'd brought out a few tube floats and tied them to an anchor on the beach with a long towrope. Slow and steady waves had started to rock me to sleep as I floated and soaked up the sun.

Until I heard his laugh.

I looked to the shoreline, though I didn't really need to confirm who it was. My body tingled an alert. Ford had just come down to the beach and planted himself in the chair I'd been sitting in next to Eve and Tom. I felt six eyes bore into me as I floated. And I was pretty sure Eve was about to start an inappropriate discussion, if she hadn't already. So I turned my face back to the sun, took a deep, cleansing breath, and concentrated on relaxing. The sound of the water breaking against the sand drowned out their voices, and after a little while, I started to drift off again.

Until suddenly I flew up in the air and splashed back down into the water.

"What the..." I pushed wet hair out of my face and spit out a mouthful of salty ocean.

Ford looked pretty damn proud of himself. He held the float I'd just been napping on in one hand. The jackass had snuck up and flipped my tube over, with me still in it.

He sported an ear-to-ear grin. "It's hot out. I thought you could use some cooling off."

I splashed water at him. "I was enjoying the peace."

"You looked bored."

I glared at him. At least I tried to, though I wasn't actually that upset. "I didn't sleep well last night. A little nap would have been nice."

Ford flashed a smug smile and moved toward me. "Why didn't you sleep well?"

I splashed more water at him as I backed up. "Go away."

His smile grew wider. "Tell me why you didn't sleep well, and I'll go away."

I splashed him again. He chuckled and lunged for me. Grabbing me by the waist, he lifted me out of the water and up into the air over his head. I screeched for him to put me down.

"Tell me."

"Put me down so I can kick your ass."

"What was that? Did you say *dunk me*?"

I tried to wiggle out of his grip. "Don't you dare!"

I'd barely finished the sentence when he plunged me into the water. Then just as fast as he'd dunked me, he lifted me back out. Only this time when he lifted me, my slippery body slid from his hands. I attempted to run out of his reach, but before I could get any momentum going, he pulled me back. His arms wrapped around my waist, and he hauled me up against his chest.

I flailed and tried to sound pissed off, but it was difficult to pull off an angry tone while smiling. "I'm seriously going to kick your ass."

"Yeah? That should be fun to watch."

I attempted to unclasp his arms from around my waist, but his fingers were too damn strong. He leaned down and rested his head on my shoulder, almost whispering he said, "Stop fighting it, Valentina."

I didn't think he was referring to our playing around in the water. "I can't believe you just tossed me off my raft and dunked me."

He bear hugged me from behind. "I'm sorry. That was wrong of me. Let's kiss and make up."

I laughed. "You're such a jerk."

As fucked up as it was, I had the strongest urge to turn around, wrap my hands around his neck, legs around his waist, and climb him like a koala bear does a tree.

I didn't. Though I allowed myself to enjoy the feeling of being wrapped in his strong arms.

I stopped struggling, and Ford whispered in my ear. "See? It's not so hard to stop fighting it."

I leaned my head back against his chest and closed my eyes. It felt so good; I honestly wasn't sure how much fight I had left in me.

———

I lay on my stomach, watching two little girls make a sandcastle twenty feet away. "I remember the first time our families met on the beach. Ryan wasn't much older than them."

Eve and Tom had gone up to the house to shower, and Ford sat in a chair next to me.

He stood. "Scoot over a little."

My blanket was big enough for two, although I'd been lying in the middle of it. I moved over, and Ford joined me on his stomach to watch the girls.

"I was twelve when my parents bought the house," he said.

"Ryan was six. He used to follow you around. You were always really sweet about it and let him hang out with you."

Ford rolled onto his side to face me. He trailed a finger along my spine. "Do you want more kids someday?"

I shielded my eyes from the sun to look over at him. "Not sure that's in the cards for me. I'm single, thirty-seven, abstinent, and about to start a new career."

"What about if you were thirty-seven and happily married?"

I smiled. "If we're pretending, could I be happily married to someone other than Ryan?"

He rested his hand on my back. "Sure. Since we're pretending, you can be married to a younger man who can't keep his hands off of you."

I rolled my eyes, but spoke honestly. "Ryan and I tried to have another child about ten years ago. We tried for more than five years, but couldn't get pregnant—which was ironic since Ryan wasn't exactly planned for my senior year of high school. Both of us got tested, and they didn't find a medical reason we couldn't conceive. It just didn't happen."

"So you want more kids, then?"

I shook my head. "I'm getting too old."

"Plenty of people have kids into their forties now. You're really hung up on numbers, aren't you? Twelve years is too much of an age difference. Thirty-seven is too old to have a baby."

There was more truth to that than he knew. Eve was the only person I'd ever admitted the truth about Ryan's cheating to.

I rolled over on the blanket and faced Ford. "Ryan cheated on me with a twenty-year-old."

Though years had passed now, it was almost as difficult to say those words today as back when it happened.

A look of understanding crossed Ford's face. He nodded. "Your ex is really a dick."

I smiled sadly. "That, he is."

We were quiet for a while, but stayed on our sides, facing each other. The beach was emptying out, though I had no desire to leave just yet, and it seemed Ford didn't either.

"How about you? Do you want kids someday?"

Ford had removed his hand from my back when I'd turned over, but now he rested it on my waist. His touch felt natural and comforting. He stroked the dip of my waistline with his thumb. "I'm not sure. I already have a nineteen-year-old, and that's not too much fun."

I smiled. "You're good with her. I think you'd be a great dad."

"Oh yeah?"

I nodded.

He skimmed his hand down from my waist, up and over my hip to my thigh. Goosebumps broke out all over my body, even lying in the warm sun.

"You know what I'm good at?"

"What?"

He leaned in and rubbed his nose with mine. "Practicing to make babies."

I grinned. "Is that so?"

He nodded. "You know what else is true?"

"What?"

"There's no better way to get back at your douche of an ex-husband for sleeping with a twenty-year-old than having a summer fling with a younger man."

chapter fourteen

Valentina

I hadn't seen Ford since Sunday evening on the beach. He'd left early the next morning for his office in the city, and we'd only exchanged a few quick texts in the days since. But when I pulled up from getting groceries an hour ago, his car had been parked in the driveway. I hated that I went right upstairs and fixed my hair, before even unpacking the bags.

And let's not even talk about how excited I got when my phone buzzed. My head had been in the refrigerator, trying to decide what to make for dinner, and I jumped and banged it on the freezer door. My damn pulse took off like a runaway train as I nabbed the phone from the counter, and that was before I'd even confirmed who sent a text.

Ford: What are you doing?
Valentina: Trying to figure out what to make for dinner. You?
Ford: Thinking about going to that tasting at the new restaurant that opened in town.

I'd seen the grand opening signs a few weeks ago. The place had a seven-course tasting menu, which was right up my alley. I acted coy, trying to pull off that I hadn't been constantly watching the window the last few days to see if he was back.

Valentina: Oh. Are you back in Montauk?

Ford: Got in about an hour ago.

More like an hour and fifteen minutes ago, but who's counting?

Before I could respond, another text arrived.

Ford: What do you say? Wanna go?

I nibbled on my bottom lip.

Valentina: Is Bella going?

Ford: Nope. Just us.

God, I wanted to. I *soooo* wanted to.

Valentina: Ford...

I laughed at his response.

Ford: Valentina...

Another text came in.

Ford: Can't two people enjoy each other's company and share a meal together?

Valentina: So it's not a date?

The tiny dots jumped around. Then stopped. Then started again.

Ford: We can call it whatever makes you happy. Just come enjoy a meal with me.

Maybe I was being ridiculous. Friends can eat together.

Valentina: Okay. Just two friends going out to eat together. I guess it's no different than Eva and me.

Ford: If you say so. I didn't know you sucked face with your best friend at the

146

end of the night. But that's cool. ;) See you in twenty minutes.

⌐⎯⎯⎯⎯⌐

Ford stood on my front porch with an enormous bouquet of flowers, similar to the ones he'd left on my doorstep not too long ago. I opened the screen door.

"Ummm. I thought this wasn't a date."

He stepped inside, stopping to lean in and kiss my cheek. Damn. He smelled good, too.

"Dating would imply a relationship, and we've already established that's out. That doesn't mean I can't buy you flowers and a nice meal before we have sex."

I arched a brow. "I didn't agree to have sex with you. I agreed to dinner."

He smirked. "Not yet. But wait until you see how charming I am on our date tonight."

I couldn't help but laugh. "I need to get my purse from upstairs. Give me a minute."

⌐⎯⎯⎯⎯⌐

Our dinner of seven, small tasting portions was delicious, and our conversation never had a moment's lull. We talked about Ford's work, how he'd decided to go forward with converting more of the self-storage business to office space, and how I'd started to look for teaching positions so I'd be ready when I got my results. We'd been sitting at a table for more than two hours, and I could have sat there for two more.

"What do you say we go over to the pub across the street and have a drink?"

I nodded. "I'd like that. Why don't we get the check? I'm sure the waiter wants to put other people in our seats by now anyway."

Ford stood and held out his hand to help me up. "Already done. I paid the bill when I went to the men's room a little while ago."

"What? Why?"

"Because otherwise you'd argue with me that we should split it so you could continue to pretend we're not on a date."

I squinted at him. "We're *not* on a date."

He gave my hand a tug, pulling me to my feet. "Right. Not a date."

"It's not."

He winked as he laced his fingers through mine. "Absolutely. And I'm not going to stare at your ass in those tight jeans when I open the restaurant door for you to walk through first, either."

I squinted. "You're an ass."

He brought our joined hands up to his lips for a kiss. "Maybe. But I'm an ass with the hottest date in the room."

My *not-a-date* date got carded.

I think that might've been a first.

Worse, the flirty bartender took one look at me and asked what I wanted to drink. *At least* pretend *we might look like we were born in the same decade if you're going to question whether my date is over twenty-one. Humor me.*

Uh. Wait. I'm not on a date.

Whatever.

The bar was packed. I'd only ever come here for lunch, so I had no idea it got this way on a Thursday night. I looked around, pretty certain I was one of the oldest, if not *the* oldest, person in the room.

"Stop overthinking shit," Ford whispered in my ear.

While we waited for our drinks, I finished scanning the bar full of twenty-somethings and turned back to Ford. "The bartender thinks I'm your mother."

Apparently, he found my anxiety amusing.

He grinned. "You think so?"

I scowled at him. "It's not funny."

"No. But if that's what they think...then *this* sure as hell is."

He hooked one of his hands around my neck and tugged me toward him. His still-grinning mouth slammed down on mine, and he kissed me until I forgot about everyone else around us. My fingers curled into his shirt as he broke our connection.

He pulled back only enough to look into my eyes. "Might as well give 'em something to talk about if they're gonna talk."

People were jockeying for standing-room-only spots at the bar to order. Ford took my hand, and we snaked through the crowd, trying to find somewhere to sit. Two people in a quieter corner were getting up, so we stood nearby to snag the table.

Just as we got seated, a burst of laughter erupted throughout the bar. It was the third time it had happened since we walked in—it sounded like everyone had just listened to the same joke, but we weren't in on it. Our table had an iPad mounted on it, and we soon realized what everyone was snickering over. There was a bar-wide game of trivia going on—*sex trivia,* to be specific.

A waitress walked over and put down two coasters and napkins. "Just drinks or would you like to see a bar menu?"

"Just drinks." Ford held up his full beer. "But we're all set for now."

"If you want in on the next game, there's a twenty-dollar entry fee. The last game just finished up, so the new one should start in a few minutes. Winner splits the kitty fifty-fifty with the bar. We do it every summer as a breast cancer fundraiser—a hundred percent of the bar's cut is donated."

Ford dug a wad of cash out of his pocket and handed her a twenty. "We're in."

When the waitress walked away, he looked at me. "Think you're better at sex trivia than me?"

Who would claim *not* to be better at such a game? "Of course."

He grinned. "How about a small side bet, then?"

"What are we betting?"

He rubbed his chin. "If I win, you go out on a real date with me—one where I take you to a nice restaurant and you don't pretend it's not a date."

"And if I win?"

"That's a hard one. A date with me could work as your prize, too."

I shook my head. "So full of yourself."

He stood to put his cash back into his front pocket. "Alright. How about this? If I win, you go out on a date with me. If you win, I'll fix your squeaky back sliding doors."

"They are squeaky, aren't they?"

"Your hardware is rusted. You need to change it out every few years. Mine needs to be done, too."

I stuck out my hand. *How could I lose?* "You have a deal. That squeak drives me nuts."

———————

What is the average length of an erect penis?

I felt my cheeks flush as I read the answers. The choices were:

A. 4.9 to 5.5 inches long
B. 5.5 to 6.2 inches long
C. 6.2 to 7.0 inches long
D. 8.7 to 9.5 inches long

Without thinking, I had spread my thumb and pointer out for a visual of what six inches looked like. When I looked up, Ford arched his brow.

"I'd offer you a measuring stick. But I'm not average."

His grin was so wicked, and he looked like he wanted to eat me alive.

I squirmed in my seat. "Ummm. I'm going to go with A."

"For manhood's sake, I'd like to say the answer is D. But I read this somewhere once, and I think it's actually B."

We'd decided to put my answers into the iPad so the computer could track one of our scores, but we kept his tally separate. So far, we were five questions in and he'd gotten three right, I'd gotten one right, and we'd both gotten one wrong.

The giant screens flashed the answer, and another point went to Ford. He flashed a smug smile.

"I got it wrong," I said. "But I'm not disappointed to find out the average male is larger than I'd guessed."

Ford winked. "You won't be disappointed when you see mine either, beautiful."

Jesus. I definitely needed another glass of wine.

A few minutes later, the next question appeared on the screen:

How many nerve endings does the clitoris have?

Oh Lord. It felt like about a gazillion at the moment. The choices were:

A. 22

B. 310

C. 1,000

D. 8,000

We were both surprised to find out the answer was D. *Well, no wonder.*

Ford caught our waitress to order me another wine and declined a refill of his half-empty beer since he was driving.

I read the next question on the screen and shook my head. "Is this a setup? Are you friends with the owner and had him put up these questions when we got here or something?"

Ford looked down to read the question.

At what age does a woman reach her sexual peak?

He looked up. "I fucking love this game."

I laughed and read the answers aloud:

A. 18

B. 25

C. 38

D. 45

Without consulting with me, Ford reached over and pressed C for our answer.

"I thought we were putting in my guesses?"

"Were you actually planning on picking something else?"

Ford's phone buzzed on the table. We looked down and found Bella's name flashing on the screen.

"I'd love to ignore it. But I can't." He groaned.

"No, of course. Get it." His relationship with his sister was one of the things I liked most about him. She drove him nuts, but he was there for her a hundred-and-ten percent.

He swiped to answer, and the simple raise of his arm caused a muscle in his bicep to flex. I lifted my wine to my lips. *That's up there pretty high on my list, too.*

"What happened?" Ford immediately stood. He dragged a hand through his hair as he listened. "I'll be right there."

One hand dug into his pocket, and he tossed a few bills on the table. "I need to go. Bella was just arrested."

Saying the tension in the air was thick on the ride home was an understatement. Ford cursed at the car in front of him for making a right without a blinker and banged his hand on the steering wheel.

"Ford?" Annabella's weak voice came from the backseat. She'd been lying down since we'd picked her up at the precinct. "I think I'm going to throw up."

Ford mumbled a string of curses and pulled down a side street. Bella struggled to work the door handle and stumbled out of the car. She took a few steps and bent her knees, leaning forward in a position ready to vomit. I reached for my door handle, but Ford stopped me.

"*Don't.*"

"But...she could choke. She'll get her hair in it."

"She'll be fine. I'll keep an eye on her from here. I'm not babying her, and I'm not letting you do it either."

"Ford..."

He turned to face me. I'd never seen him truly angry before. His jaw was hard, his lips flattened to a grim line, and his voice had all the sternness of one very pissed-off father.

"She's old enough to go to bars with a fake ID, buy weed, and get herself high and arrested, then she's old enough to hold her own hair back. I'm not an asshole. I've sat in the bathroom and held her hair plenty when she was actually sick. But she's on her own with this shit."

While I struggled with watching a teenager get sick alone on the side of the road, it also wasn't my place to decide how to parent her. I was a mom; I coddled people when they were sick or down—tough love wasn't in my genetic makeup. Though I knew my ex-husband would probably be the same way if it were our son.

Watching Ford at the police station while he'd advocated on her behalf, and now seeing him angry and disappointed in his sister, I think I realized for the first time that he truly wasn't a typical twenty-five-year-old. The life circumstances he'd been dealt had forced him to mature faster than most people his age.

He'd earned his adult card the hard way. And my treating him like he was still a boy had been insulting to him on so many levels. It was one thing to not want to date him because I wasn't ready, but another altogether to hide behind an excuse that slighted him.

I looked out the window and checked on Bella, who was still dry heaving, then reached over and put my hand on Ford's. His face softened infinitesimally, and he took a deep breath and laced his fingers with mine.

The half-hour drive home from the Hamptons took twice as long as it should've. We had to pull over three times for Bella to get sick—or at least because she thought she might get sick. As much as it pained me, I stayed in the car for all three stops. But when we got back to the house, I had to at least help her into bed. She babbled to me as I took off her shoes.

"Sometimes when I'd play at the beach all day, I'd be so tired after my bath that I'd fall asleep before Mom came in to brush my hair."

I sat down on the bed beside her and pulled up the covers. "The beach knocks us out."

"But when I woke up in the morning, my hair wasn't a mess. Mom used to brush it while I slept."

That made my heart hurt, whether she was wrong for what she did tonight or not. I smiled sadly and stroked her hair. "Moms have superpowers like that."

"I miss her. She loved it out here so much."

"It's beautiful in Montauk, but I think what your mom probably liked best was being out here with her family without the everyday distractions."

Annabella curled into the fetal position. I tucked the blanket all around her so she was wrapped like a sausage and stayed, rubbing her hair until she fell asleep.

I found Ford downstairs in the living room drinking an amber liquid from a tumbler.

"She's asleep."

He nodded and tilted the glass back to swallow the remnants in one gulp. "You want a drink?"

"Sure. But I don't think I can drink whatever it is you're having."

Ford stood and walked to a wine rack in the kitchen. "I have the cab you like."

I watched from the doorway while he pulled it out and proceeded to uncork it before filling a glass for me and refilling his own with liquor.

Returning to the living room together, he handed me the wine glass.

"You just *happen* to have the wine I like?" I bumped shoulders with him playfully.

"I also bought more of the cologne you said you liked last week." Ford sat down and leaned his head against the back of the couch, looking up at the ceiling. "I'm sure my eagerness is a sign of immaturity to you. But I just want to please you."

I shook my head. *God, I've been such a jerk.*

"Actually, I find attentiveness in a man to be incredibly attractive."

Ford lifted the glass to his mouth and drank like he was taking medicine. "Let me guess, you find attentiveness attractive, but in your mind I'm just a boy, not a man, so it doesn't apply to me."

I sighed and set my wine glass down. "I'm sorry I've been treating you the way I have."

He sat up and nodded, though his eyes were hesitant to accept my apology.

"Watching how you handled your sister tonight made me realize that you're right—age isn't what's important." I shook my head. "I know plenty of forty-year-old men who act like they're teenagers."

He still didn't look convinced that my outlook had changed. I'd never asked a man on a date in my life. Hell, I hadn't been *on* a date in more than twenty years, so who was I to judge how things should happen? I sat up taller and chugged back the rest of my wine before shifting to look directly at Ford.

"Would you...go out to dinner with me tomorrow night?"

"Can't. Have a meeting in the city in the afternoon."

"The night after?"

Ford's thumb rubbed his bottom lip as he assessed me. "Do you feel bad for me because my parents were killed and I raised my little sister?"

I was honest. "Yes, I do. But that has nothing to do with why I'm asking you out."

Usually his face was pretty easy to read, but this time I couldn't see what was going on inside his head.

He stared at me some more before speaking again. "Why?"

"Why what?"

"Why do you want to go out with me?"

"You mean why today, when I've said no before?"

He shook his head. "No. I mean, tell me the reasons you want to go out with me."

I squinted, unsure if he was screwing around. When I realized he was waiting for an actual answer, it didn't take long to think of one. "You're smart, funny, handsome, and mature."

"So you aren't just going out with me for a pity date?"

I smiled. "No. Definitely not."

Ford knocked back the rest of his second drink and slammed the empty glass down on the table. He curled a hand around my neck and pulled me toward him. His lip twitched at the corner. "Just so you know, I would have taken a pity date. I don't give a shit how I get it. But it was nice to hear you say those things."

I play-shoved at his chest, though he didn't budge.

"As long as you're asking me out, how about you come here and kiss *me* for a change?"

I smiled and leaned in to brush my lips against his. When I went to pull back, Ford wound his fingers tightly into my hair and kept me there, deepening the kiss. It was hard and needy, and before it broke, he nipped at my bottom lip, causing a sting of pain.

I found myself thinking this kiss marked the official start of my summer fling—it was hard, needy, and had the sting of pain—a lot like how things would end come Labor Day.

"It's about damn time," he growled. "We already wasted almost half the summer."

chapter fifteen

Ford

I'd made reservations for two nights later at Blue—a new, high-end restaurant overlooking Lake Montauk. The dining room had dark walls, candlelit tables, and a view that made you forget you were only a few minutes from a highway. Soft music drifted in from a piano in an adjacent room being played by a man who sounded like a young Ray Charles. I'd never taken a date to a place that had slow dancing before.

"Wow. This is really nice," Valentina said as I pulled her seat out.

Pushing her chair in, from the angle I stood, I could see right down her sexy, red dress. I leaned down, kissed her bare shoulder, and whispered in her ear. "I *really* love your dress. Especially the view from right here."

Val looked up and followed my line of sight straight down to her cleavage.

She laughed. "And here I thought you actually liked the dress."

"I do." I winked. "I can't wait to see it on your floor later."

I took my seat, and the waiter arrived to take our drink orders. We ordered a bottle of the cabernet Val loved, and I deferred to her when he offered a sample to taste before pouring. Watching her swirl the crimson liquid in her glass and raise it to her lips made me realize I probably should have taken care of business before dinner. Even the lipstick mark she left behind on the rim of the glass turned me on. I had to discreetly adjust underneath the table when I imagined what that mark might look like on my dick.

Val leaned in when the waiter disappeared. "What's going on in that head of yours? You're staring like you're deep in thought."

I swallowed and blinked a few times. "Nothing. Just thinking about a meeting I had earlier today."

She squinted. "You're full of shit."

That made me smile, because I *was* full of shit. But what I'd been thinking wasn't exactly appropriate first-date material.

"I was just thinking how gorgeous you look tonight."

She lifted her wine glass and brought it to her mouth again. I couldn't wait to taste it on her lips later.

"That's it?" She arched a brow. "You weren't thinking about anything else?"

"I don't think you really want to know."

"Of course I do. Tell me."

"You won't hold it against me if it's inappropriate?"

She smiled, and a devilish gleam sparkled from her eyes. "Of course not."

Fuck it. If you really want to know... So much for being a gentleman, then. I waited until she set her glass back down on the table and pointed my eyes to the lipstick marks on it.

I leaned in and lowered my voice. "I was imagining looking down and seeing that mark around my cock."

Val let out a nervous laugh, and I took a drink from my own glass to cool off. After that, our always-easy conversation felt off. We talked about my week in the city and what she'd been doing while I was gone, but it felt first-date awkward now and not like me and Val. I hoped I hadn't actually upset her with what I'd said.

By the time we'd finished our appetizers, I needed to say something.

"Did I...take it too far with what I said earlier about the lipstick? I didn't mean to offend you."

Val wiped the corners of her mouth with a napkin. "No. You didn't upset me. You were being a perfect gentleman. I asked you what you'd been thinking about."

"Then is something bothering you? It feels like something changed after I made that comment."

Val looked back and forth between my eyes and swallowed. "It's me. Not you."

"What's going on?"

"I'm...nervous...about...you know."

My brows furrowed. "What?"

She looked around and then leaned in and lowered her voice. "Sex."

"Why?"

"Because I haven't...it's been...I was married for..." She shook her head. "I've only ever had sex with Ryan."

Oh wow. I had no idea. But of course that made sense. She'd been with him since high school.

I tried to make light of it, calm her nerves. "I'm sure it hasn't changed much. Candlewax dripping, riding crops, all four holes."

Her eyes widened. "*Four?* What are the four?"

I laughed. "Relax. I'm kidding." I shook my head. "Nothing has to happen until you're ready. So stop thinking about it. You really need to stop overthinking everything and just take things as they come."

She took a deep breath. "Okay."

Things felt more relaxed after that. The waiter brought our dinner, and we fell back into our usual, comfortable conversation.

"How are things going between you and Bella?"

"She wasn't around when I got home today, so I still haven't seen her since that night. I texted her to check in while I was gone, but I only got one-word answers in response. *Fine. Yes. No. Okay.* Pretty sure she wanted to add *fuck you* to the end of each of them, but managed to restrain herself. I don't get it. She does something wrong, and then she acts pissed off at me, like I'm to blame."

"She's deflecting. If she's pissed off at you, she doesn't have to look inward. But Bella's a smart girl. She knows she was wrong."

"Yeah."

"I'm sure you were no angel in college."

"That's the problem. I remember what I was doing at her age."

Valentina smiled. "I skipped over the years of partying. I pretty much went from playing with dolls to having a real live one."

After dinner, Val excused herself to go to the ladies' room. While she was gone, I went over to the piano player and made a request. I guess he hadn't had many because by the time she came back, he'd started to play my song: "Lady in Red."

I stood. "Dance with me?"

"I'd love to. But I have two left feet, so I'm not responsible for any injuries."

Even though it felt completely foreign to take a woman out on a date and ask her to slow dance, I couldn't pass up the opportunity to hold Valentina close. We walked out to the dance floor, and I wrapped her tightly in my arms. She had one hand on my shoulder and the other clasped with mine.

"Did I mention how gorgeous you look tonight?"

"You did. I believe it was while you were looking down my dress."

"I can't help myself. I'm just so unbelievably attracted to you."

She blushed. "Thank you. The feeling is mutual."

I felt light—not just on my feet, but in my chest and in my mind. If someone had asked me a few months ago if I'd felt like I was in a dark place, I would have thought they were crazy. But we can adjust to almost anything— we start to be able to see in the darkness after a while, find comfort in it, even.

Val tucked her head into my chest, and we glided around the dance floor. It might've been the first time I was grateful my mother had forced me to learn how to dance. I felt content, swaying with this woman in my arms.

I knew Val needed to go slow, and even though I hadn't had sex in a while, that was perfectly fine for me— this feeling was all I needed from her right now.

Bella's car was parked in the driveway when we pulled up. She must've gotten off work early. "Do you mind if we check on Bella?"

"No, of course not. But...I'm dressed up. Maybe I should go change first?"

I shrugged. "It'll just take a minute. She might not even be up."

Val hesitated but eventually nodded. My sister was on the couch when we walked in, staring at the television. She looked back and forth between us and scowled at me.

"Hi, Val."

"Hi."

I shook my head. "You're going to give *me* an attitude? Yeah, that makes sense. I was definitely in the wrong for driving to the Hamptons and bailing your ass out of jail. And I should never have stopped a half-a-dozen times so you could puke your brains out. Not to mention, checking in on you all night to make sure you didn't choke on your own vomit. But sure, be pissed at me."

Bella rolled her eyes. "Get over yourself. It was *one time,* and you were far worse at my age. You're not Dad, and I'm over eighteen now, so you're not even my legal guardian anymore. I can do what I want." She whipped the blanket off and stomped to the bathroom. The door slam echoed through the room.

My blood was boiling. "She can't be fucking serious. If she's going to act like a ten-year-old and can't even own up to her mistakes, I'm not so sure she belongs living by herself at college. I still control her finances, and I'll drag her spoiled ass home."

Valentina rubbed my arm. "She's just embarrassed and lashing out."

"She should be embarrassed." I walked to the kitchen. "I need a beer. You want a glass of wine?"

"Sure."

I poured her wine and motioned toward the back door. "Deck?"

She nodded, and I held the door open for her.

I drank my beer while leaning over the deck in silence, thinking.

"Do you want to talk about it?" Val eventually said.

I turned. The moonlight illuminated her face, and it hit me what an idiot I was. I'd killed the mood.

"I shouldn't have stopped in to check on her."

"No. You did the right thing."

I blew out a deep breath and took Val's hand. "Let's go back to me telling you how gorgeous you look tonight."

She smiled. "We can do that."

I cupped her cheek and leaned in to kiss her, but she pulled back. "Bella's here."

I shrugged. "So?"

"What if she sees?"

"Who cares if she sees?" I thought she was being shy, so I reached for her. But she stepped back, out of my reach.

"I care."

"Why?"

"I just do..."

"Well, I don't. I'm not going to hide spending time with you all summer. You're not a dirty little secret, Val."

"It's just...inappropriate."

"Why the hell is it inappropriate?"

"It just is."

The reason hit me. "You're ashamed to be with me?"

"It's not that."

"Then what the hell is it?"

She tried to come up with some bullshit reason, but couldn't even find one.

I shook my head, pissed off. "Great. I guess you're not my dirty little secret, but I'm yours."

"Ford..."

165

I chugged the rest of my beer. "It's fine. I'm tired anyway."

Valentina looked surprised, but said nothing.

"Why don't I walk you next door?"

She'd told me it wasn't necessary, but I walked her anyway. After she unlocked the door, she opened it and turned to me. "Do you want to come in and talk?"

I shook my head. "No, thanks."

"Ford...I didn't mean to hurt your feelings. I'm sorry."

Yeah, me, too. Me, too.

I nodded. "Goodnight, Val."

chapter sixteen

Valentina

I felt awful.

Am I ashamed of him?

He's a handsome, smart, successful man. What the hell is there to be ashamed about?

Is ashamed *even the right word?*

Embarrassed?

I felt embarrassed.

The two emotions were similar but with one significant difference. *Ashamed* was what you thought of yourself. *Embarrassed* was about what others thought of you.

I was not ashamed. Yet for some reason, I *did* care what other people would think. Regardless of the distinction between the emotions, the result was the same for Ford: I'd made him feel terrible.

It was late, but I knew I'd never be able to sleep. He might be feeling the same way, so I figured it was best to clear the air. I plucked my phone from the nightstand and thought about what I wanted to say before typing.

Valentina: You were right. I am treating you like my dirty little secret. But it has nothing to do with you or what I think about you. I think you're an amazing man, and I'm still flattered and bewildered that a guy as great as you would even want me. But regardless of the reason, you do, and I want you, too. I just have this stupid sense of what's appropriate and inappropriate, and I need to get over it. I'm very sorry for the way I acted, Ford. Can you forgive me?

A minute later, my phone buzzed with an incoming message.

Ford: I'll need an in-person apology.

I blew out a breath I didn't realize I'd been holding and smiled.

Valentina: I can do that. How about I take you out to breakfast tomorrow?

Ford: How about you get your ass out of bed now instead? I've been standing at your front door for ten minutes debating on knocking.

I practically leaped out of bed and ran to the front door. Ford was leaning against the house and didn't move. He waited for me to come to him.

I walked out and stood in front of him. "I'm sorry."

He slid an arm around my waist and pulled me against him. "You need to stop giving a shit what other people think. Appropriate and inappropriate doesn't matter if you want something and you're not hurting anyone."

I nodded. "I know. I need to work on it. And if it makes you feel any better, it's not just you. I love white pants, and I still won't wear them after Labor Day because of some archaic fashion rule."

Ford's lip twitched. "Well, now I don't feel so bad."

I rested both my hands on his chest. "It's not going to happen overnight. But I'll work on it."

Ford's hand slid down to my ass. "I'd be happy to help you work on being inappropriate"

I laughed. "I bet you would."

He lowered his head and brushed his lips against mine. "I can't stay mad at you."

On that note, I needed to address what had started this whole thing. "I still don't think it's a good idea for us to be together in front of Annabella."

Ford crossed his arms, and a muscle in his jaw flexed.

"But it's not what you think. I know you're upset with her now, but you're her role model. She looks up to you. Teenagers pay attention to what people do, more than what they say. Do you really want to show her it's okay to have a summer fling? She's not going to understand why it would be okay for you and not her."

Ford thought about it for a minute. "Fine. I guess you're right. Her defense about getting herself in trouble by using a fake ID is that I used to drink when I was underage. It makes it hard to say something's wrong when you've done the same things."

"Exactly."

Ford cupped my cheek. "See? We're a good balance. I'll help you get the inappropriate stick out of your ass, and you'll help me set a good example for my pain-in-the-ass sister. Now, let's kiss and make up."

His hand slid into my hair, and he gripped the back of my neck and tilted my head up. Planting his lips over mine, his tongue dipped into my mouth and our bodies immediately melted together. The man could seriously kiss. He made my knees weak and left me panting every single time.

"Do you want to come in?" I asked when the kiss broke.

Ford looked into my eyes. "Yes, I want to. But no, I'm not going to. Another night...when you're ready for me to come in."

I was disappointed. But he was right. Though my body was definitely ready to go there, I wasn't sure *I* was.

I nodded. "Okay."

He kissed me one more time, then pressed his lips to my forehead. "Goodnight, beautiful."

In a daze, I watched him walk down my stairs. He turned back as he reached the bottom and called up to me. "You still owe me breakfast tomorrow. I'll be back to collect in the morning."

———

My phone buzzed on the vanity. Before this summer, I'd often misplaced my cell at home. Hours would go by without me checking it. Now I took it into the bathroom while I was in the shower to listen for the ping of an incoming text—talk about anxious.

Ford: Breakfast in twenty?

I wrapped my hair in a towel and texted back.

Valentina: Sounds good. Just got out of the shower. The back door is open. Let yourself in.

Ford: Will do. But do me a favor? Wear the white tank top you wore last week.

I hadn't realized he liked it. But sure. Why not?

Valentina: Okay!

Ford was leaning against my kitchen counter with a mug of coffee in his hand when I came downstairs. His eyes took their time raking down my body and snagged on my breasts on their climb back up.

I cleared my throat. "Good morning."

"That it is." He nodded.

I walked to the sink and set my empty coffee mug down.

"I didn't realize you had a thing for plain white tank tops."

I'd looked in the mirror after putting on the top he'd requested. The material hugged my curves, but not in an obscene way or anything. And the fabric was nothing special—thin, white cotton—quite plain, really. I wasn't sure what he liked so much about it. Unless perhaps it was more revealing when I was cold.

Ford caught my eyes. "Take off your bra."

I blinked a few times. "What? You mean take it off before we go to breakfast and leave it off?"

He nodded.

"I can't go to a restaurant without a bra."

"Why not?"

"Because it's inappropr..." I'd made it halfway through the word when I realized I'd walked right into his trap.

He knew what my response would be. The wiseass smirked with an arched brow.

"Okay. I get your point. But I really can't go to breakfast without a bra on."

"Is it uncomfortable to not wear one?"

"No."

"Will anyone be hurt by it?"

"I guess not. But it would feel weird. Thirty-seven-year-old women don't go out without their bras on."

He folded his arms over his chest. "Again with the age shit. Would you have gone out without one at twenty-two?"

I shrugged. "Maybe." *I totally would have.*

"You have great tits. Better than any twenty-something."

I felt uncomfortable, but *fuck it.* He was right. I did have great boobs. And if this modest act of semi-indecency made him happy, why not? I held his eyes while I reached behind my back, pushed up my shirt, and unclasped my bra. Sliding the straps down and pulling my arms out was simple—Lord knows we women are better than Houdini when it comes to taking off a bra without removing any other piece of clothing. Once my arms were out, I reached up and under my shirt and tugged the bra from my body. I was glad I'd put on something pretty this morning—nude with lace. I held it up and tossed it right at Ford's head. It landed perfectly—with a strap dangling over his face.

His eyes gleamed. They dropped to look at my boobs, and the smirk fell from his face. My nipples were standing proud, saluting him.

"*Shit,*" he groaned. "Maybe I didn't think this all the way through."

I grinned, loving how affected he was. "Ready to go?"

He mumbled something about how *he'd* be the inappropriate one walking around with a hard-on, and we left for breakfast.

———

No one seemed to notice or care.

While I'd mostly taken off my bra to prove a point to Ford, he'd actually proven one to me. John's Pancake House had a fifteen-minute wait, and no one looked at me any differently than usual. Either they didn't notice, or didn't care if they did—which had been Ford's entire argument.

Well, actually, one person certainly noticed and cared.

Ford stood from the booth and offered me his hand. He pulled me to my feet and looked down at my still-erect nipples, growling into my ear, "This lesson on inappropriate behavior is fucking phenomenal."

The sidewalk outside of John's Pancake House was packed. People filled the benches and lingered in the parking lot waiting for tables—typical for breakfast any day of the week during the summer in Montauk. Ford opened my car door, but before I could get in, he took my face in his hands and kissed me. Like the times before, it was long and passionate and left me feeling lightheaded.

"All those people probably just watched," he whispered in my ear. "Totally inappropriate."

I smiled and didn't bother to check whether anyone had paid attention, not even when I settled into the car. It felt too good to care.

"Do you have any plans for today?" Ford clicked his seatbelt in.

"No. Did you have something in mind?"

He nodded. "Yup." He started the engine and began to back up without adding anything more.

I chuckled. "Are you going to share it with me?"

"How about I give you a hint?"

"Let me guess instead. We're doing something inappropriate?"

He grinned. "Now you're catching on."

Inappropriate turned out to be a pretty long drive. We'd been on the road about forty-five minutes already. Ford wouldn't tell me where we were heading, but the minute I saw the sign up ahead, I knew he'd be turning. I wasn't wrong.

Cupid's Pleasures, as the sign read, was an adult toy store. I'd passed it a million times on the way out to Montauk myself, yet never stopped.

"I have been in an adult store before, you know."

Ford turned off the car and shifted in his seat to face me. "To shop for yourself or a gift for someone?"

"A gift. Instead of a wishing well at Eve's bridal shower, we had a dirty toy box."

"Good. Then these questions should be a piece of cake?"

My brows drew down. "Questions?"

"You're going to ask the salesperson some questions about their products."

My eyes widened.

Ford chuckled. "I'm guessing you've only ever gone in and bought something, hoping you didn't see anyone you knew."

"What kind of questions do you think I'm asking?"

He leaned forward and planted a chaste kiss on my lips. "Inappropriate ones, of course."

I didn't want to let him see I was nervous, so I walked into the store with my head held high.

Inside, two men stood behind the counter. I inwardly winced. Of course, it couldn't have been two women. Asking a strange man a question about anything to do with sex toys was totally outside my comfort zone.

Ford saw the look on my face and tried to ease me into it, saying he'd ask the first question. That prospect had me intrigued enough. Even if I was going to chicken out, I might as well stay for the entertainment.

We perused the shop for a little while. Looking at all the intimate toys made me feel an odd mix of intrigued, nervous, and turned on.

The back of the store had an open alcove section filled with videos. Ford leaned down as he thumbed through the porn. "Watch how easy it is." He cleared his throat and called over to the clerk at the counter. "Excuse me. Do you have any videos that are strictly anal?"

The clerk answered. "Yeah, sure. You looking for male-male or male-female?"

"Male-female."

The guy pointed to a wall behind us. "Check out the *Back Door is Always Open* series. I think there's about ten of them. Good quality."

"Thanks!"

Ford leaned close to me again. "*The Back Door is Always Open*? You said that to me this morning when I texted. If I'd realized what you were trying to tell me, we wouldn't be here right now."

I laughed. "I think you're going to need the movies for a while for that."

Ford walked away and came back a few minutes later holding a plastic package in his hand.

He held it out to me. *Anal balls.*

"Go ask if these come in a larger size."

My immediate reaction was *no way*. But I wanted to prove I wasn't a chickenshit—maybe I even needed to prove it to myself.

I chewed on my lip for a minute before taking the package out of his hands. "Fine."

The shocked look on Ford's face gave me enough courage to go through with it. He didn't think I had the balls. Looking down—I *literally* had the balls in my hands.

I waltzed over to the counter. "Ummm. Excuse me. Do you know if these come in a larger size?" I could feel my face starting to heat...and...I felt a sneeze coming on.

The guy answered as if I'd asked him the time. "They do. They're special order. The ones in the store are glass and go up to one inch on the last bead. But this manufacturer also has a silicone set that goes up to two inches and another that goes up to three. Would you like me to order you a set? We can have them delivered direct to the house to save you a return trip."

"Ahhhh..." I knew my face was flaming red. I covered my mouth and turned my head. "*Achoo!* Excuse me."

"God bless you."

I still had the anal balls in my hand, and the guy was waiting for an answer. "Ummm. I'll think about it. Thanks."

Before I could scurry away, Ford was at my side. He set the anal video the clerk had directed him to on the counter and took the beads from my hands. "We'll just take these for now."

The clerk rang us up, and somehow I managed to get out of the store without dying of embarrassment. In the parking lot, we started to crack up. Ford kissed me up against the car through our smiles.

I looked around. "Is there a bus full of schoolchildren I'm being inappropriate in front of or something?"

Ford pushed my hair behind my ear. "No, I just can't resist kissing you."

My heart fluttered. This man could turn me into a puddle of mush thirty seconds after embarrassing me half to death. He caused an insane array of emotions to stir alive inside of me—fear, anxiousness, lust, greed, desire.

And there was a little bit of something else sprinkled into that pool of feelings—something I knew deep down would crush me at the end of the summer.

chapter seventeen

Valentina

"**S**hit." Ford pulled into his driveway. A red convertible had parked in front of us, and two girls were removing luggage from the trunk.

"Unexpected company?"

He groaned and shook his head. "Unexpected, no. Unwanted, yes. I forgot Bella's friends were coming out for the weekend. I think she's having six of them."

Each girl had a rolling suitcase and a duffle bag. "Looks more like they're staying for the summer."

"They better not be. I should have made her cancel after the crap she pulled. But I totally forgot. And of course, she didn't remind me." Ford opened his car door. "I hope you don't mind me spending a lot of time at your place this weekend."

I smiled. "That's fine with me."

As soon as we exited the car, the girls spotted Ford.

One squealed and rushed over to greet him, her arms open wide as she approached. "Ford! I was hoping you'd be here." She pressed her young body against his. Ford did the one-arm, pat-on-the-back awkward hug.

"What's up, Sierra?" He lifted his chin to the other girl. "Hey, Holly."

The hugger looked him up and down. "You look good." Her eyes glinted with interest, and she flashed a coy smile. "Then again, you always look good."

"Yeah. Thanks. I guess my sister is in the house. I haven't seen her since last night."

The girls finally noticed another person standing next to Ford, and he made the introductions. "Valentina, these are two of my sister's pain-in-the-ass friends, Sierra and Holly."

I smiled. "Nice to meet you, girls."

Sierra tilted her head, quickly forgetting me. "Can you help me up the stairs with my suitcase, Ford?"

"I don't know what the hell you're packing so much for, but yeah, sure. I need to talk to Bella anyway." He turned to me. "You want to come over?"

I figured I'd let him deal with Bella and her friends on his own. "I have a few things to do. I'll talk to you later."

Ford nodded, though he didn't look thrilled to be going with his sister's friends.

On my way up the stairs to my front door, I tried not to notice how he looked more their age than mine. I had just been starting to forget, and seeing him with young people brought it all back.

Inside, I started a load of laundry and did a little cleaning. When my phone rang, I grimaced seeing my ex's name on the screen and considered ignoring it. But we had a son together and shared assets. It wasn't like he called me to shoot the breeze, so I reluctantly picked up.

"Hello?"

"Hey, babe."

I wanted to reach through the phone and strangle him every time he called me that. I'd corrected him at least a dozen times. Perhaps I should've argued for the return of my proper name as part of our divorce settlement.

"Valentina, please."

"Habit. Sorry. Though I don't get the big deal. I wouldn't care if you called me a pet name."

No? Which one would you like? Asshole, dickwad, cheater?

"What can I do for you, Ryan?"

"Jeez, Val. You don't have to sound so miserable every time I call."

But I was, and it took effort to hide it—effort I no longer cared to expend. "Have you talked to Ryan? Is everything okay with him?"

"No. I haven't talked to him. That's not why I'm calling. I just wanted to let you know I'll be out in Montauk tomorrow. I have a contractor meeting me to give an estimate at two o'clock for the pilings we need replaced."

He'd already had one guy come to give an estimate last week.

"Was the first one not good or something?"

"It was high. This guy's supposed to be more reasonable."

I sighed. "Okay. Fine. But I'll be here, so you don't need to come out."

"We'll get a better price if I'm there."

My brows drew down. "Do you know him or something?"

"No. But men get better prices."

Such a dick. "Who says?"

"It's a known fact."

"I don't know that to be a fact."

"That's because you're a woman."

I rolled my eyes. "I can handle it myself. I'd prefer if you didn't come out."

"You don't have to be a bitch about it. I'm coming, and that's the end of the discussion."

That sounded more like the Ryan I knew.

"Actually, *this* is the end of the discussion." I hit disconnect and tossed my phone on the table.

God, how had I stayed married to that jerk for twenty years?

I decided to go for a walk on the beach to clear my head and get some exercise. Changing into a sundress, I dug my headphones from a drawer, lubed up with sunscreen, and tied my hair in a ponytail.

On the way out, I found a new yellow sticky note stuck to the back door. *Kiss Ford more.* I peeled it off with a smile on my face. I wasn't even sure when he'd stuck this one here. That was one *to-do* item I wouldn't mind doing.

The hour-long walk did me good. I even jogged for half of it, and the rush of adrenaline left me feeling more relaxed. As I approached my house, I heard music blaring. Bodies were out on my neighbor's deck. The closer I got, the more skin I saw. It looked like Bella and her friends were starting their party early. Ford stood at the deck railing, leaning over and watching me as I walked.

"Come save me," he yelled.

I smiled. The bikinis on the women flitting around behind him were pretty small. "Doesn't look like you're being tortured."

"Looks can be pretty damn deceiving." He waved for me to come up to the deck. "Come on. You forgot to take the gift I bought you home today."

I cocked my head. *Gift?*

He smirked. "At the toy store. Don't worry, if you're too busy to come up, I'll just ask my sister to deliver the bag."

"Cute. Very cute."

However, I didn't put it past him to actually hand his sister anal beads and porn to deliver to me, so I walked up his deck stairs instead of mine.

Bella was laying out on the lounge chairs with two of her friends. She greeted me and made a face at her brother.

"Oh boy," I whispered. "Still giving you an attitude, huh?"

He nodded. "She actually had the balls to ask me to pick up alcohol for her and her friends. Can you believe that shit?"

"Ford!" the girl I'd met earlier yelled. I think her name was Sierra. "Can you help us carry these chairs down to the water's edge?"

He shook his head. "They think I'm their cabana boy, apparently."

"But if you do it, they won't be sitting up here on the deck with you."

He pointed to me. "That's very true. I'll be right back."

I watched from the deck as Ford lugged lounge chairs down the stairs to the beach. When he was done, Sierra gripped his arm and tried to pull him into the water with her. She wore a thong string bikini bottom and two small triangles up top that barely covered her nipples, and she did her best to get him to notice. The girl definitely had her eye on him.

"I think you have an admirer," I said when he returned.

"Sierra's a pain in my ass. On my sister's twelfth birthday, she had a sleepover. That one snuck into my bed while I was sleeping. I was eighteen and woke up with a twelve-year-old next to me."

I covered my mouth. "Oh my God. It's a long-running, unrequited crush then."

"Lucky me," Ford grumbled. "You want some wine or something?"

"Actually, I'll take a water, if you don't mind."

He nodded. While he went to fetch us drinks, I watched the girls on the beach. Sierra was doing cartwheels and back handsprings. She really had an incredible body. She may have been a girl when she first tried to get Ford to notice her, but she was definitely a woman now.

Ford returned with my water and leaned on the railing next to me, watching what I'd been watching.

"Your little crush is quite limber."

He turned to face me, still leaning. "Is that a hint of jealousy I detect in your tone?"

How could I not be jealous of that girl's body? "She's pretty. With the body of a nineteen-year-old." I shrugged. "I can't compete with that."

"You mean she can't compete with you."

I wasn't being insecure or jealous. I honestly didn't comprehend how Ford could say such a thing—yet I really believed he meant it.

"I don't understand, Ford. How could you want to be with me, when you could have *that*?"

He looked me up and down and shook his head. "You look in the mirror and see the woman your ex made you feel like—a thirty-seven-year-old mom. I look at you and see what you actually are—a sexy-as-fuck woman who has a killer rack, curves I want to memorize in the dark, and a laugh that's contagious. She can't hold a candle to you, Val." He cupped my cheek. "And if our summer together is all you want, I hope that at least by the end you can look in the mirror and see the woman you are."

God, this man was absolutely intoxicating. I ached for him, and I was exhausted from trying to fight it.

I leaned over to him. "How about we order takeout and you stay at my house tonight, so Blondie doesn't make a second attempt at climbing into your bed?"

Ford searched my eyes. "What if Bella asks where I slept?"

I placed a gentle kiss on his lips. "Then lie...or tell her the truth. I'm not even sure I care anymore."

chapter eighteen

Valentina

We sat on the floor in the living room eating Chinese. When I'd gone to set the table, Ford put the plates back in the cabinet and brought the bag to the living room instead. He then pulled out the coffee table to make room for us to sit and tossed two pillows on the floor.

I was never good at eating with chopsticks, but he gave me a lesson and opened his mouth wide to test my skills. Of course I bumbled the saucy Szechwan shrimp, and it splattered all over his white T-shirt. That turned out to be a good thing, because he'd tugged it off for the rest of our meal.

God, he was more delicious than the food—and Chinese was one of my favorites.

I managed to get three grains of rice into my mouth. "I spoke to Ryan this afternoon."

Ford's chopsticks were halfway to his lips, and he stopped. "Your son?"

I shook my head. "I wish. We have to get some work done on our support pilings, and he wants to be here when the contractor comes to give an estimate."

"When's he coming?"

"Tomorrow at two. I just wanted to let you know before he showed up."

He nodded. "Thank you. I appreciate that."

We talked and passed takeout boxes back and forth. I loved how at home Ford seemed in my house.

"There's a music festival coming up in a few weeks on Randall Island," he said. "I thought maybe I could get us tickets. One of the guys from Backstreet Boys is playing."

"I'd love that. I've always wanted to go to a music festival. It's actually on my list."

Ford fished a piece of cashew chicken from the container in his hands and held it out to me with his chopsticks. I opened my mouth and leaned forward to take it, but he pulled it back before I could grab it and gave me a quick kiss instead.

"Your list?"

"Eve made me a post-divorce list of things I need to do."

"Nice. What else is on it?" He fed me the piece of chicken and dug one out for himself.

"Going to Rome, getting a dog, keeping my Christmas tree up for a few months after Christmas—just stuff I always wanted to do that my ex was against."

It dawned on me that our little shopping spree touched on another item on my list. It was totally inappropriate dinner conversation, and something outside my comfort zone to talk about with a man. But today had been so much fun, and I knew Ford would appreciate my sharing, so I decided to be bold.

"And...anal."

Ford started to cough. I thought he might be choking on the piece of chicken he'd just put in his mouth. His face turned red.

"Oh my God, are you alright?"

He pounded on his chest with his palm and reached for his beer. Sucking a big gulp down, he coughed some more before speaking with a hoarse voice. "Are you kidding me? You can't say you have anal on your to-do list while I'm chewing."

"Oh. Sorry. I thought you'd appreciate that, especially with our purchases today."

His eyes darkened. "I need to see this to-do list. Better yet, I volunteer to help you check off every item this summer."

"You don't even know what else is on it."

"Don't give a shit. I'm here to serve."

I giggled, and I *really* wasn't a giggler. "Such a Boy Scout. Always prepared to lend a hand."

He shook his head. "Shit. Is that what they did in Boy Scouts? I thought they helped old ladies cross the street. If I'd have known there were anal beads and porn involved, I would have joined."

We laughed as Ford's phone rang. He glanced down to the caller ID, and his face looked torn about taking it.

"It's Devin. My CFO."

"Take it if you need to."

"You sure you don't mind?"

"Not at all. I'll clean up and open some wine."

While Ford took his phone call, I put away the leftover Chinese food and opened a bottle of wine. Pouring two glasses, I stayed in the kitchen to give him some privacy.

When he finished, he found me looking at the calendar on the refrigerator. I was holding up the July page and looking at the month of August when he snaked his arms around my waist and kissed my shoulder.

"Got plans coming up?"

"No. I just realized it's only six-and-a-half weeks until Labor Day already."

"You worried about finding a job by the time school starts? You get your results next week, right?"

Of course I was worried about finding a job. But that wasn't what was weighing on my mind at the moment. *Only six-and-a-half weeks left.* What the hell was I waiting for? I'd already missed out on almost half the summer. *Tick tock. Tick tock.* It was time—now or never. I'd invited him to stay over tonight, yet oddly, it wasn't until this very moment that I decided I wanted him *now*. *Never* was the story of my life, and I wanted to live a little.

I took a deep breath and emptied my wine glass in one big swallow before turning in Ford's arms to face him. "I'm worried that I've already wasted half the summer pushing you away."

His eyes were hesitant, and I could tell he wanted confirmation of what I was saying.

He scared the hell out of me, but I was done being afraid. "I want you, Ford."

He cupped my cheeks and pulled my face to meet his. Our lips collided in a kiss that was passionate, yet different from the others we'd shared. It was slower, less frenzied, more sensual, and deeper.

The way he held me and took his time made me feel like he treasured the moment as much as I did. Kisses between me and Ryan had always been a means to an end: step one that had to be completed before he could move on to step two. I'd never felt like he actually enjoyed kissing me. And to be honest, I didn't remember feeling that way about him either. At least not for a very long time. But I wanted to kiss Ford for hours.

He pressed me up against the refrigerator and lifted me off my feet, guiding my legs to wrap around him. He grinded down between my parted legs, and I moaned into our joined mouths, feeling how hard he already was. *God, I want him.*

I wanted him up against the refrigerator, on the kitchen floor, the table, the counters—if it were up to me, we wouldn't waste another minute of our time moving somewhere else. But Ford must've had other ideas. He gripped my ass, shifted my weight into his arms, and started moving.

"I would love nothing more than to fuck you against the wall. But it's been two years for you, and I want to take care of you right, which means you get my mouth until you're dripping wet and ready enough that my cock can glide inside of you."

Oh God.

He started up the stairs. "Even thinking that you haven't been with a man in two years makes me hard as a rock. Being near you makes me feel like some sort of Neanderthal caveman. I'm surprised I didn't club your study buddy over the head and drag you home with me when you pulled up with him."

Inside my bedroom, Ford set me down. He dug his wallet out of his pants and pulled out a strip of condoms, tossing them on my nightstand before taking a seat on the bed. My entire body zinged with the way he took his time looking over my body. His eyes filled with heat, and he licked his lips like he couldn't wait to devour me.

"Undress for me. Take off your dress."

His voice was gritty, but had a sexy edge of authority to it that turned me on.

Holding his gaze, I slipped the spaghetti straps of my sundress from one shoulder, then the other, before shimmying it down to my ankles and letting it pool on the floor. The way Ford looked at me made me feel bared in a way I hadn't expected. It was like he didn't just want to see my body—he wanted to see *me* naked.

He licked his lips. "You're beautiful. I've fantasized about being inside of you every day since we first started messaging, and I had no clue you would turn out to be a gorgeous woman inside and out."

My insides were turning to mush. This man could own me—he could ignite my body with dirty words one minute, telling me the things he wanted to do to me, and then make my heart swell with his sweet side. It was a damn dangerous combination. There wasn't much I wouldn't give him right now.

Ford lifted his chin. "Take off your bra."

Nervous, my fingers fumbled behind my back with the clasp. Though the way his eyes darkened as I slowly slipped the bra from my shoulders and revealed my breasts gave me confidence to stand tall. He took his time drinking me in, and my nipples swelled and hardened under his gaze.

"The panties."

I watched his Adam's apple bob up and down as he swallowed.

Standing before him completely naked, my heart beat out of my chest in anticipation. Ford stood and held his hand out to me. He kissed me until my knees felt too weak to hold my weight. Then he switched our places and guided me to sit at the edge of the bed.

Dropping to his knees in front of me, he put his hands on my thighs and spread my legs wide.

"I want you to watch." He lifted one leg and dropped a tender kiss on the top of my foot, looking up at me from under his thick, dark eyelashes. "Watch me lick your sweet pussy until you come in my mouth."

Oh God.

I lost that battle real quick. The minute his mouth touched between my legs, my head fell back with a moan. *So much for watching.* He licked slowly, tracing the outline of my lips before fluttering his tongue over my clit. He teased and sucked, the intensity of his movements increasing, along with my hunger.

Yet he didn't force me across the finish line. Instead, he taunted me with the threat of orgasm, and then slowed, pulling back, keeping it slightly out of reach. I wasn't sure if it was intentional or not.

Trying to gather my wits, I looked down at his face between my legs. Ford looked up, feeling my gaze on him. He flashed a wicked smile and pulled back to slowly flick my clit with his tongue. I jerked, and the gleam in his eyes flared brighter.

Oh my God. The bastard. He knew exactly what he was doing.

"Watch, and I'll make you come."

He'd been holding back until I did what he said. Frustrated and a little pissed off, I dug my fingers into his hair and yanked him harder against me. It had been *so many years* since I was this turned on, and I had the sudden urge to kick his ass for keeping my orgasm from me.

I heard a muffled chuckle, but then his tongue speared into me.

"Yes. *Yes.*"

Things turned frantic after that. Ford growled and licked, lapped and sucked. Everything inside of me built, my muscles swelling and tightening, preparing for climax to take hold.

"Ford..."

He pushed two fingers inside of me and sucked hard on my clit as he looked up at me. My body trembled while my orgasm began to pull me under. I fought to keep our gazes locked, but when the big wave hit and my muscles began to contract around his fingers, I fell back onto the bed and let it drown me.

I climaxed longer and harder than I could ever remember. It felt like years of pent-up waves of orgasm had been building and took over like a tsunami. I struggled to catch my breath as I came down.

While I was busy trying to pull myself together, apparently Ford had been busy as well. One minute I was lying on the edge of the bed, trying to collect the pieces after being shattered, and the next his pants were gone, and he hauled me up to the headboard.

"You good?" Ford kissed just above my belly button.

"No," I breathed out. "I'm mad at you, actually."

He chuckled and licked the underside of my right breast. "Oh yeah? What for?"

"You spent the last month and a half saying nice things to me and trying to get me to sleep with you...when all you had to do was *that*. You wasted so much time, damn you."

Ford sucked my nipple in and tugged it between his teeth, making my back arch off the bed. He laved attention on the other before climbing up to hover over me. "We'll just have to make up for all that lost time."

I felt how hard and hot he was, pressed up against my swollen clit. A minute ago I'd been spent and satiated, and yet now I was desperate to have him, to have the rest of him.

He pushed a piece of hair out of my face and leaned in to kiss my lips. My hands traveled down his back and slipped into his boxer briefs. I squeezed his hard ass and our kiss heated up fast. When I scraped my nails along his back, he groaned.

"*Fuck*. I need to be inside you."

He lifted and pulled off his boxers before reaching over to grab a condom. Him using his teeth to rip open the package was the sexiest thing I'd seen in a long time. Ford spit the wrapper on the floor and then took my hand and guided me to wrap around him as he sheathed himself.

When I realized how far apart my thumb and pointer were, I wasn't sure if I should be excited or worried. It had been a *really* long time.

"Spread for me, beautiful. Spread wide."

Our eyes locked, and I did as he asked, fanning my legs open to him across the bed. He lined up the thick head of his cock with my opening and pushed inside ever so slowly. I hadn't gotten a good look at how big he was; I only knew he was wide. But Ford seemed to understand he needed to take his time. He rocked his hips in and out, stretching me a little more with each thrust, going a little deeper until he was finally fully inside of me.

"*Fuck*." His arms shook, and he muttered against my lips. "You feel so incredible."

He captured my tongue and kissed me passionately as he glided in and out. I was so wet, and my body clenched around him like a fist. He broke our kiss and pulled back to look at me.

"Beautiful." He sped up his thrusts and smiled down at me. "So fucking beautiful." The room was quiet except for the sound of our bodies slapping against each other. He reached down and grabbed behind one of my legs, pulling it up at the knee. The change in position tightened my body around him even more, and he began to rub at the sensitive spot inside me.

Oh God. Here it comes again.

I dug my nails into his back, and he took the hint at what I needed—moving harder and faster, grinding down with each thrust and fucking me deep. My clit throbbed, and my heart raged out of control.

"Ford..." I called.

The veins in his neck bulged, and his breathing became uneven. I knew he was about to lose control, too.

"Come with me," he groaned. "*Feel me.*"

He slammed down so hard, it nearly knocked the wind of out me. But it was exactly what I needed. My body clenched around him and began to pulsate. Ford felt it hit, saw it on my face, and raced to his own release.

"Fuck," he roared.

I watched as his jaw tensed, and he bucked twice more before sinking into me so deeply that I gasped.

Collapsing, he buried his face in my neck and kissed me as he caught his breath. I could feel his hot cum inside of me, even through the condom. As much as I was overwhelmed and mentally and physically depleted, I couldn't help but think if it had felt that good with a condom, what the hell would it feel like skin to skin?

Ford lifted his head and looked at me. He squinted. "What are you thinking about already? My brain might not work until tomorrow after that."

I giggled. "Nothing."

"Don't even try it." He tapped one finger to my temple. "I know what it looks like when the wheels in your head are turning."

I smiled. The man had just gone down on me while I watched him and then almost fucked me into oblivion, yet I was still modest when it came to talking about sex.

But I was being silly, so I was honest. "I was thinking how good it would probably feel without the condom."

"Are you on the pill?"

Though I'd had no reason to be the last few years, I still took it to regulate my period. I nodded.

Ford jumped up from the bed so fast it startled me. I thought maybe there was a bug.

"What...what's wrong?"

"Getting rid of this damn condom."

He went to the bathroom and was back in ten seconds flat. He crawled over me. "Ready."

I laughed. "Ready for what?"

Ford gripped my hand and brought it down to feel between his legs. He was as hard as he'd been before we had sex.

Reading the confusion on my face, he smiled. "You spent the first half of the summer telling me all the reasons you didn't think twenty-five was right for you." He aligned himself, and with one firm thrust of his hips, he pushed back inside of me. "Now I get to spend the second half *showing* you all the reasons twenty-five *is* right for you."

chapter nineteen

Valentina

I woke to a prod at my rear.

Ford was wrapped around me, a sheet covering only our bottom halves as we spooned. One muscular arm kept his front tucked to my back. At first I wasn't sure if he was awake, but then the hand covering my ribcage glided up and grazed over my breast.

"Morning." His voice was raspy and so damn sexy.

"How did you know I was awake?"

His thumb and forefinger rolled my nipple. "I just did."

I smiled. We'd stayed awake until the sun came up exploring each other's bodies. I couldn't count the number of times we'd had sex...four? My body had the delicious ache to prove it. Ford's hand slid down to between my legs and cupped me.

"Sore?"

I downplayed it because I couldn't get enough of him. "A little."

He rolled us so I was suddenly on my back. "I need to jump in the shower in a few minutes. I have a meeting to prep for. And I need to eat a little before that."

"Oh. Okay. I can make you something."

He flashed a wicked grin. "I'm eating *you* for breakfast." His head disappeared under the sheet.

"That's not...*oh*. Wow. Okay, then."

Ten minutes later, I was boneless. "You're...really good at that."

He nuzzled into my neck. "I'm glad you approve. I plan to spend a fair amount of time with my head between your legs."

A few minutes later, he pushed up on his elbow. "I really don't want to get up. But I need to take a shower. I'm going to take the train into the city so I can work for the two-hour trip each way. Think you can pick me up tonight? I want to take you somewhere."

"Where?"

"It's a surprise."

I smiled. "Okay."

Ford got up from bed. I'd ogled him shirtless at the beach and felt every rippled muscle of his body last night, but seeing him stand up naked in the morning light—every ounce of gorgeous, tanned, smooth skin on display—was truly mind blowing. He had that deep-set V and each of his abdomen muscles formed their own little raised mound of deliciousness. Yet his ass was the showstopper. From behind he looked like the X-rated version of a sunscreen ad with his sun-kissed skin fading to a firm white derrière.

I lifted to my elbow to watch him walk around naked. He looked perfectly comfortable doing it, as he should be with that body.

"I need to do whatever exercise you're doing."

He laughed. "Oh yeah? We can do that. Tomorrow morning we'll go to the gym together."

I laid my head back down. "I said I *needed* to. I didn't say I was actually going to. But feel free to come over after you're done and all sweaty."

He leaned down and gave me a chaste kiss. "Care if I shower here?"

"No. Not at all. I'll drag my ass downstairs and make us some coffee while you do that."

"Great."

I wasn't ready to return to the land of reality just yet, so I picked up Ford's shirt from last night and slipped it over my head. Since it hung to nearly my knees, I didn't bother with a bra or underwear.

In the kitchen I flicked on the Bose Soundlink. The coffee pot sat right next to it and had a yellow sticky note attached.

Fondle Ford's balls

I covered my mouth and cracked up. This had become a game for him. I had no idea when he'd even come down to the kitchen. He had to have gotten up after I'd fallen asleep. I found a second note stuck to the back door.

Buy naughty schoolteacher costume.

Another was stuck to the toaster.

Paint myself with Nutella.

Then there was the one on the dishwasher.

Red lipstick.

That one was underlined with two heavy slashes.

His dirty notes had me smiling like a teenager who'd just been passed one from the cute boy in class. A Backstreet Boys song came on the radio, reminding me of the day I'd walked out on the deck and found Ford playing their album. Sighing with contentment, I grabbed the coffee beans out of the refrigerator and ground them, sporting the goofiest grin.

When the loud whirling sound stopped, a voice startled me. "Someone's happy this morning."

The smile fell from my face. *Ryan.* My ex-husband stood in the doorway of the kitchen. I hadn't heard him come in.

I crossed my arms over my braless chest. "What the hell? How did you get in here?"

He shrugged and held up a key. "I let myself in."

"You can't do that."

"I just did."

"I'm not dressed."

Ryan's eyes roamed over my bare legs. "Nothing I haven't seen before. But you're looking good, Val. Did you start exercising again?"

I hated the way he looked at me—like he was *allowed* to. I pushed past him and snatched a throw blanket from the living room couch. Wrapping it around my body, I pulled it tight to hold it closed. "You don't just walk into someone's house."

His eyes narrowed. "It's not *someone's* house...it's *my* house."

With the shock of finding someone in the house, *Ryan* of all people, I totally forgot someone *else* was also here. Ford jogged down the stairs wearing only a pair of jeans with the top button opened. His hair was wet from the shower. I watched as his smile disappeared when he saw my ex-husband standing in the kitchen.

Ryan turned, hearing someone behind him. Ford froze at the bottom of the stairs, and his eyes darted from Ryan's to mine.

I panicked and blurted out the first thing that popped into my head. "Ummm... Ford is fixing the pipe upstairs in the shower."

The minute the words left my mouth, I knew Ford wouldn't be happy. His jaw flexed, and he stared at me.

Ryan shook his head and looked disgusted. "The boy next door is fixing the pipes while you're walking around half naked? What the hell, Val? Are you trying to lure the poor kid?"

I felt the anger radiating from Ford, and I wanted to kill Ryan for creating this situation. I chose to lash out at the cause of problem. "Why are you here, Ryan? It's not even noon, and you said the contractor wasn't coming until two."

"Traffic was light, and I figured I'd check that leaky pipe in the kitchen."

"Ford already fixed it." I pulled the blanket around me even tighter. "Can you please go outside while I get dressed?"

Ryan's eyes narrowed. "This is my house."

"It's not your year. Matter of fact, neither is next year since you took the last two. You need to get out right now."

A cell started to ring. Realizing it was his, Ryan grumbled something and dug it out of his pocket as he walked toward the front door. He slammed it closed behind him. The entire floor shook in his wake.

I walked over to Ford and raised my hands to touch his chest, but he took a step back, out of my reach. "*The boy next door*? I'm fixing the pipes?"

"I'm sorry. I was just caught off guard, and...I just don't want him in my business."

Ford's jaw may have been rigid with anger, but I could see the hurt in his eyes. "Sure."

"Ford..."

He shook his head. "I gotta go."

"Wait...I didn't..."

The door slammed shut a second time, and I stood alone in the living room, wrapped in a blanket and still wearing Ford's shirt.

God, I really fucked up.

"You want to grab some lunch at the Lobster Roll?"

"No."

My ex-husband seemed genuinely confused. His forehead wrinkled. "Why not?"

"Because I have things to do."

I'd been sitting on the back deck the last twenty minutes. The contractor had come and gone, and Ryan had insisted on checking the kitchen sink to make sure the leak was fixed properly, even though I'd told him it worked fine.

"You don't look busy to me."

I glared at him. "How do you think *Kaylee* will feel about you having lunch with your ex-wife?"

"It's Kayla. And it's over. She went to India to study yoga for a few weeks and decided to stay. Met some rich tech guy."

"What a shame."

I looked up and saw a different man than I used to see. Ryan had aged and gained some weight. His hairline had started to recede, and he'd grown his hair out in a failed attempt at modern hair that wasn't thinning. Two years ago, I'd never thought the day would come when I'd look at him and not miss our life together. When he'd walked out on me, I'd thought my life was over.

But it wasn't. Turns out it was finally getting started. It had taken me a long time to get here, but I was over Ryan—like, *so* damn over.

"Come on...you love those lobster rolls. It'll be like old times."

"I do love them. But I can go enjoy them on my own... and be in better company."

Ryan rubbed the back of his neck. "Fine. Whatever. I should get on the road before rush-hour traffic anyway. I'll be in touch about scheduling the construction."

I didn't bother to walk him out. He'd helped himself in. He could figure out the way back all on his own. Once I heard his car start and pull out of the driveway, I breathed a bit easier. Though only one problem was solved.

I still hadn't heard from Ford. I'd sent a text earlier, which showed as read, but he'd never responded. I checked my phone for the tenth time, even though it hadn't vibrated. The last text was the one I'd sent him.

Valentina: I had a great time last night, and I'm sorry about what happened this morning. Let me know what train I should pick you up on later.

I sighed. He had gone into the city for a meeting, so that could be the reason he hadn't responded yet. Though, deep down, I knew that wasn't it.

Hours later, it became harder to make up an excuse and tell myself everything was fine. So I decided to send another text.

Valentina: Hey. Just checking in. Do you know what train you'll be on yet?

A few minutes later my phone buzzed.

Ford: Change of plans. Not coming back tonight.

Valentina: Oh. Okay. Everything go okay with your meeting?

Ford: Fine.

Valentina: See you Sunday, then?

Ford: Sure.

I knew we needed to talk in person, but I had to at least attempt to apologize again.

Valentina: I'm really sorry about this morning. Ryan showing up threw me for a loop.

Ford: No problem. No reason to tell your ex about your casual fucks.

He was hurt and lashing out. Taking the bait and arguing over text would only make things worse. So I tried not to.

Valentina: Dinner tomorrow night? I'll cook something for us.

Ford: Don't go to any trouble. Dinner isn't necessary. Maybe you could pencil me in to come over about eight to fuck you?

I deserve that.

Valentina: Eight sounds good. See you Sunday. I can't wait.

Not surprisingly, my sentiment wasn't returned.

chapter twenty

Ford

"**R**emember that dream I had about all the purple flowers at a funeral last week?"

Mrs. Peabody didn't even say hello. She just started talking when I answered the phone.

"Hey, Mrs. P." I tossed my pen on my desk and leaned back into my chair. "Yeah, of course I remember. You had a strong premonition during the day that someone was going to die, and then you dreamed of a funeral with tons of purple flowers."

"I threw up twice that day. But that might've been because of the tuna casserole this hellhole serves for lunch on Tuesdays. I *despise* Tuesdays. Who the heck thought it was a good idea to put mayonnaise in the oven anyway?"

I laughed for the first time today. "So what about the funeral? Did someone actually die?"

"Yep. The woman in the room next to me. Didn't wake up on Sunday. They drop like flies around here in the summer. They say more people die in the two weeks following Christmas than any other time, but not at this place. It's summer, for sure."

"Were there purple flowers at her funeral?"

"Nope. Didn't have a funeral. Just went straight to the crematory. Kids didn't want to waste any of their inheritance, I'm sure. I prepaid for mine so I wouldn't get cheated. Anyway, just wanted to tell you I was right again."

"Not for nothing, Mrs. P, but you live in an assisted living facility with senior citizens who have health problems. I'm not sure you can call this one a premonition." I reached for the coffee on my desk.

"That may be true. I suppose someone probably dies every week in this place. But the woman who kicked the bucket? Her name was *Violet*."

I was mid coffee swallow and coughed it down the wrong pipe. "The woman's name was Violet?"

"Mmmm-hmmm. So quit your doubting me, boy."

We talked for fifteen minutes. Mrs. P told me her daughter had called and was planning to come visit, though I'd heard that a few times, and she still hadn't shown up in all the years I'd been talking to her. She also complained about the physical therapist and the dentist—both of whom she swore were bilking her insurance because there was nothing really wrong with her.

"So how are things with the future Mrs. Donovan?" she finally asked.

I frowned. "Not sure you got that one right. Things aren't going like I thought they would."

"Welp. I call 'em like I see 'em. I can't control if you go and screw things up. You met the woman destined to be your wife. Lord knows it wouldn't be the first time a man threw a wrench into his own future."

"What makes you so sure it's me who's screwing things up?"

"Because you just said *things aren't going like I thought they would.*"

"So?"

"You don't sit around expecting things to happen the way you'd like. You make them happen, dumbass."

———

My afternoon meeting had been uptown.

I could've hopped in a cab afterward or even jumped on the subway located right in front of the building. But instead I decided to walk the thirty-something blocks back to my apartment. It was a nice summer evening. Going a few blocks out of my way to walk along the park wasn't that unusual.

The fact that I happened to pass a certain French bistro—that was total coincidence, too. I lingered out front for a minute before deciding to go in. Why not stop in and have a beer since I was in the neighborhood? I didn't even know if Eve would be here. Sure, she'd said she worked six days a week, but today could have been her only day off.

An older man in a suit stood at the front host area.

"Can I help you? Do you have a reservation for this evening?"

"Umm. I don't."

He used a finger to scan down a pretty full list of names and times. "I'm sorry. I don't have any tables available."

I looked around the restaurant and didn't see any sign of Eve. My shoulders slumped, but I nodded. "Thanks, anyway."

Just as I turned to walk back out, I heard my name. "Ford?"

"Hey."

Eve walked out from a door toward the rear of the restaurant. I assumed maybe it was the kitchen.

"I was just...walking by and saw the place and..."

Eve smiled and came over to hug me. She absolutely knew I was full of shit, but seemed genuinely happy to see me.

"Come in. Let's go sit at the bar."

While she went around to the other side and made us both drinks, I checked out the restaurant. The place was really nice—tons of glass along the front that showcased the park across the street. The dining room had dark wood mixed with hot pink tablecloths and at least a dozen different, ornate crystal chandeliers. Oddly, it reminded me a lot of Eve's personality.

"This place is really nice—kind of funky, yet traditional at the same time."

She hopped up on the barstool next to me. "I've been here seven years." She tilted her head toward a table in the corner. "Tom sat right over there for nineteen consecutive days until I agreed to go out with him."

"What made you finally give in?"

"That night, the hostess told me he'd requested a reservation at the same table, at the same time, for *a year*." She shrugged. "I figured any man who was that persistent was worth a date."

I lifted the drink she'd set down in front of me. "A year, huh? I only have until Labor Day."

Eve patted my hand resting on the bar. "I'm glad you *just happened* to be passing by. You know, my issues with Tom weren't all that different than what's going on in Val's head. When I met him, I was thirty, and he was fifty. I joke that he's old enough to be my father, but it was never the number that scared me. It was that we were in different places in our life. He was financially stable and thinking about retirement accounts. He'd made all of his mistakes and learned from them—he knew what he wanted. I, on the other hand, had just maxed out my credit cards buying designer waitress uniforms for a restaurant I didn't know if I'd be able to pay the next month's rent on, and I'd picked the last guy I dated because he had dimples—even though he was an unemployed, wannabe actor."

"What made you get over the differences?"

She smiled and laughed. "I'm not sure I have. I still think four thousand for a Chanel bag is a better investment in my future than an IRA. I doubt we'll ever see eye to eye on lots of things. But after our first date, he became my go-to person for stories. Silly things—I used to call my parents or Val to tell them something funny a customer did, or I'd call them to vent about my landlord raising my rent. Up until then, I'd never shared the small things that happened each day with anyone I dated. I'd get dressed up and go out on a date, have a solid time... I thought those dinners and nights out were life—but they weren't. Life is the little things that happen between the fancy outings."

I nodded. "I get it. But Val and I aren't really in that different of a place in life."

"Val *thinks* you're supposed to be in a different place. She basically missed out on dating and everything that comes with being single in your twenties because she had Ryan so young. Plus, she's gun-shy about relationships in general. Her ex-husband really burned her. She was a good wife—loyal and trusting. She didn't see it coming when he cheated on her. And the fact that the woman was a young girl—she's got to be thinking if her husband can do that...think about how things will go when she's in her fifties and you're still in your thirties."

My shoulders slumped. "Are you trying to make me feel better? Because you're doing a pretty shitty job."

Eve smiled sadly. "I'm sorry. Unfortunately, my only advice to you is to be patient. The more she enjoys each day with you, the more she'll realize what's important. She needs to figure things out on her own, and that's going to take some time. But I can promise you one thing... she's worth the wait."

———

I didn't like the way she'd handled shit.

I didn't want to be just a summer fling

I didn't like being hidden from her ex.

But Val had never been intentionally hurtful.

Unfortunately, I couldn't say the same thing.

I'd tried my hardest to make her feel like shit.

I'll be over to fuck you at eight.

And for that, I owed her an apology.

I knocked and waited, looking down at my feet.

Val's smile was hesitant when she came to the door. She also didn't fully open it to invite me in. "Hey. I didn't think you were back until later."

"I jumped on an earlier train." I looked up at her and caught her eyes. "I'm sorry for the shit I said over text, Val."

She stepped back and opened the door wide. "It's me who should be apologizing. Come in."

For the entire two-hour train ride out here, I'd thought about what Eve had said—how I needed to give Val some space to find her own way. That had been my plan...until I walked into the living room and hauled her against me.

Yeah. Great plan for space.

I buried my face in her hair and inhaled deep. "I fucking missed you."

"I'm sorry I pretended you were only here to fix the pipes when Ryan showed up, and I'm sorry I let him refer to you as the boy next door."

"I get it." I pulled back and brushed her hair behind her ear. "I hate it. But I get it. He was your husband for twenty years, and...you're still telling yourself this is just a summer fling."

"Ford..."

I pulled her against me and quieted her against my chest. "Let me finish my apology and then you can talk if you want. Okay?"

She nodded.

"People bring history into new relationships—past experiences, good or bad. You're bringing blown trust, cheating, and disappointment with you. So you're hesitant to get attached too fast. The biggest relationship influence I had in my life wasn't even my own. I grew up watching my parents—who were very much in love and had their time cut too short. So I'm anxious to move forward, afraid to let something good slip through my fingers because we never know how much time we have."

Val leaned back. She looked bewildered. "Are we sure I'm the one who's twelve years older? Because honestly, you sound a lot more mature than I've acted lately."

I pressed my lips to her forehead.

When she looked up at me, she smiled sadly. "I'm sorry about making you feel I wanted to hide what's going on between us."

I studied her eyes. "What *is* going on between us, Val?"

She shook her head. "I don't know. But is it possible to have the right feelings at the wrong time? I feel like I'm not ready for anything serious, even though I'm sort of crazy about you. There are so many things I should do for me first."

It fucking hurt to hear she thought it was the wrong time, but she'd come out of a *twenty-year* marriage and had only been with one man. I guess it was better she knew now that things with us couldn't be forever, rather than figuring it out a year down the road.

What were my choices? Take what she was capable of giving me or walking away. The way I felt, I had no choice.

I swallowed. "Let's just enjoy each other for the rest of the summer."

chapter twenty-one

Valentina

"I passed!" I covered my mouth in disbelief and stared at my name on the screen.

Valentina Di Giovanni Davis

New York State Teacher Certification Exam- *passed*

Content Specialty Test - Italian – *passed*

It was right there in black and white, yet it still felt surreal. My phone started to buzz with incoming texts. Results were posted right at eight a.m., so I knew my friends were getting theirs, too.

Ford came out from the shower in my bedroom with a towel wrapped around his waist.

"I passed!"

"Holy shit. It's eight o'clock already?"

I nodded, unable to stop smiling. He walked over to the bed and scooped me up, swinging me around in a circle.

"Congratulations. I'm fucking a teacher. That's kind of hot."

I read the flurry of texts from my friends. Mark passed. Desiree passed. Allison passed. "We all did it!"

"That's great. We need to celebrate."

I sat down on the bed and texted back to my friends. Ford sat next to me with a proud smile on his face.

"It feels surreal," I said. "Ten years ago when we had trouble getting pregnant, I decided to enroll in one Italian class. My son had just started second grade, and I needed something. Ryan told me it was a waste of money. I don't know why, but I didn't tell him I was thinking of becoming a teacher. I actually took one class a semester for a few years before telling him my plan." I shrugged. "I knew he would say I didn't need a full-time job. He saw my wanting to do something for *me* as some sort of insult to him as the financial provider. And now, ten years later, here I am, finally done—the timing couldn't be more perfect. I'm ready for a change."

Ford slid his hand up and down my bare thigh. "I'm proud of you. I know I wasn't there for the years you worked on things, but I know firsthand how difficult it can be to get caught up in the life you're in and forget about your own dreams."

I nodded. He definitely understood.

Ford got up from the bed. "I would love to stay and spend the day celebrating inside of you, but I have to be in the office. What do you say we celebrate tonight at my place? Pack a bag and stay overnight."

"Okay...but pack a bag? I can just run next door if I need something."

"I meant my place in the city. I want to show you my apartment anyway, and we need to celebrate. Take the train in, and let's stay tonight."

I loved the city and did feel like celebrating. A change of scenery would be fun. "That sounds great. I'll take the train later and meet you wherever."

―――――――

Ford had texted me to wear something sexy. Then twenty minutes before I was to leave to catch a train into the city, a black limousine pulled up in front of my house. He'd sent a stretch for me, and when I called him, he'd insisted I get in and said we were starting our celebration early.

Champagne was already open and waiting when I got in the backseat. So I asked the driver to wait a few minutes and ran back into the house to change. I'd originally considered a skimpy, royal blue, halter-top dress and stilettos, but it had felt over the top to wear it on the train. Though, wearing it in the back of a limousine made me feel like I was heading out for a special night.

The driver had been instructed not to tell me where we were going, and Ford was being coy about dinner. As we wound our way through Manhattan, excitement built within me. It was a crystal-clear night, and the city was lit up outside the tinted windows. I felt like a kid in a candy store, waiting to see what delicious treat the shop owner had for me.

But the excitement I felt about the city was totally eclipsed by the man standing at the curb when the limo slowed and pulled to the sidewalk. Ford was dressed in a suit, his feet planted wide, hands casually tucked into his pants pockets while he watched the stretch approach. He buttoned his jacket and leaned down to open the back door as we rolled to a stop. Extending a hand, he greeted me with an insanely sexy smile. It took me longer than it should have to give him my hand because I was too busy drooling.

God, Ford looked incredible. His shoulders were broad, waist narrow, and the perfection of the tailored suit contrasted so uniquely with the messiness of his hair. It looked like he didn't give a shit, and that upped the sexiness barometer to a lethal level.

I wet my dry lips and finally got out. "You look so handsome."

He wrapped his arms around my waist and pulled me close for a tender kiss. He mumbled against my lips, "Have you ever had sex in the back of a limo? Please tell me you have so I don't push you back inside and fuck up this night right from the start."

I smiled. "I haven't. But I'm not opposed to skipping dessert and having it in the car later."

He took a step back and shook his head. "You look... beautiful. Gorgeous. Sexy. And so incredibly fuckable at this moment."

I giggled, but the praise shot straight to my head to meet the two glasses of champagne I'd enjoyed on the trip in. I felt dazed and high, but so very happy.

Ford shut the limousine door and took my hand. "Come on. Let's go inside before we don't."

I distantly took in the name of the restaurant as we made our way to the door. *Osteria Isabella*—I knew it was an exclusive one. Eve had mentioned it before...the type of place where my menu wouldn't even show the prices. It was so sweet of Ford to go all out for my celebration. But I had no idea how all out he'd gone until we walked to our table.

Five smiling faces yelled "*Surprise!*" all at once. Startled, I took a step back.

"Eve? Tom?" Not only was my best friend here, but so were my three study partners. I looked at Ford. "How? When?"

"I swiped your phone when you were in the shower and took their numbers to arrange tonight. You deserve a real celebration."

I felt an ache in my chest, and my eyes started to well up. No one had ever done anything so thoughtful for me. All eyes from the table were on us. Choked up, I didn't have the words to express my gratitude, but I knew what would speak volumes. For the first time, I didn't hesitate. I reached up and took Ford's beautiful face in my hands and pulled his lips down to meet mine—in public, in front of all my friends.

After, he leaned down to my ear. "Thank you."

I smiled. "No, thank you."

"I didn't know. I'm sorry," Mark leaned across the table to me and whispered.

Seeing the confused look on my face, he clarified by pointing his eyes to Ford, who sat on the other side of me, currently engrossed in a conversation with Tom.

"In Montauk. I didn't realize you were seeing someone, and I pushed myself on you for the day."

"No. It's fine. I enjoyed showing you around."

Mark's eyes dropped to my lips for a moment. He smiled. "He's a lucky bastard. But I'm happy if you're happy. You deserve it."

"Thank you."

In my peripheral vision, I caught Ford watching my whispering session with Mark, and I turned and winked.

He smiled—definitely more comfortable with what we had now than a few weeks ago.

Throughout the night, the laughter flowed as freely as the wine. I spent time talking to my friends, celebrating our success, and enjoying good food and company. Ford and I hadn't really spoken since we walked in. He was letting me enjoy the night he'd arranged, and if I wasn't mistaken, it looked like he was having a good time, too.

We might not have spoken to each other much, but we shared plenty of intimate glances and smiles—one of which Eve had just caught.

She sipped her drink and gave me a knowing look. "I really like him."

I sighed. "Me, too."

"You look...alive again."

"Was I the walking dead before this summer?"

I'd been kidding, but Eve raised a brow.

She looked over at Ford. "He came to see me the other day."

"What? When...and *where*?"

"He passed by my restaurant and stopped in."

"He just *happened* to pass by?"

She shrugged. "He's crazy about you."

"I know. I don't understand it, but I'm finally starting to realize that for whatever reason, he really does want to be with me."

Eve shook her head. "I'd do you if I was a guy."

I laughed. "Thanks. I think."

"You don't see it, but you're a catch. You're beautiful, loving, warm, fiercely protective, loyal, smart, a great mom. Your asshole ex-husband never appreciated what he had."

"Honestly, Ford makes me feel beautiful. He watches me while I'm sleeping sometimes. That might sound creepy, but it's actually sweet. He'll just be looking at me with this reverent face you just can't fake. He's made me look at myself in the mirror and search for the beauty he sees. And you know what? Sometimes I find it."

Eve took my hand. "I know you need to do some things—hell, I was the one who bugged you about making your My Turn list. But you can have a boyfriend and still find *you*. Ryan wanted you locked up in his stingy little castle because he was weak and insecure. Ford might be younger, but he's stronger and more confident in who he is. I don't think he needs to be the center of your universe. He just wants to be part of your world."

———

I stood with my jaw hanging open.

Ford didn't have an apartment. He had an entire floor.

From the outside, the building looked like what it mostly was—a giant warehouse. But the top floor had been converted into living space. It had an industrial feel with worn steel beams, exposed ductwork, real brick walls, and polished concrete floors, yet it was also warm and homey with natural wood, a giant fireplace, and a gorgeous, modern, stainless-steel kitchen—though the best part was the open mezzanine level above half of the apartment. A rooftop terrace occupied a space twenty feet in the air, with walls of glass. Standing in the living room, you could look up and see the night sky twinkling. I was at a loss for words.

"Ford, this is...this is stunning. Absolutely incredible."

He was adorably modest. "It looks like more than it is. The area was pretty depressed when my parents bought it thirty years ago. It didn't become trendy to live down here until the last decade."

"But you *made* this?"

"Well, contractors made it. I just designed the layout and converted the space from storage to livable. It was under construction when the accident happened. My dad never got to see it completed. I finished it and moved in here after I went through that rough patch. It helped me feel like something was my own."

"I'm sure your father would be proud of this place and your choices, Ford." I walked to an open staircase toward the glass rooftop room. "Can I see up here?"

"Of course."

Ford led me to a large, outdoor space. It was partially sunken into the indoor space below to create a mezzanine level, and the interior space was viewable by looking down through a glass wall. I stood outside on the roof of the building and could see his kitchen.

"I feel like I'm in a tree house."

He smiled. On the floor, along the perimeter of the entire room, were plants in multicolored pots. "They're what's left of my mom's plants. She had a green thumb. Mine's black."

I'd never seen anything like this. "Ford, this should be in a magazine."

He pushed his hands into his pockets. "Thanks."

"So this is what you want to do to all the warehouse space, then? You can convert them all like this?"

He nodded. "Sort of. They'd all be different because I keep the commercial elements of the support structure intact, and those are different on each floor. And of course, only the top floor can have the skylight room."

I surveyed the room in awe. "I obviously know nothing about building or architecture, but I know what I like. And I'd kill to live here."

Ford walked up behind me and wrapped his arms around my waist. "Oh yeah? You know what you like?" He dropped a sweet kiss on my shoulder before moving to my neck and then up to my ear. "Tell me...do you like this?"

Uhhh...duh. I nodded. "I definitely do."

He reached down and under my dress, skimming his fingers along my thigh. "How about this?"

I shut my eyes and leaned my head back against him. "Mmm...yes."

His hands moved up to cup my breasts, and he squeezed hard. "And this?"

I let out a breathy *yes* as he pinched my nipples. My back arched as he sank his teeth into my shoulder. I'd definitely have a mark tomorrow, but I'd smile when I saw it in the mirror.

"I love the thought of fucking you out here. It's too bad we're up so high and no one will see. Because I'd like the whole world to watch."

I turned to look at him, and he took my mouth in a kiss—unhurried and drugging; he made me feel like I was floating. One hand slipped inside the halter of my dress, and he plucked and pinched my already pert nipples into stiff peaks. When I moaned into his mouth, he slid his other hand up and inside my panties.

Finding me soaked, he growled, "So fucking wet for me already."

He pressed his front deeper into my back, and I felt his erection at the top of my ass. His fingers pressed against my clit. "This—do you like this?"

I wasn't sure if he was referring to feeling him behind me or his fingers inside my panties. Since I liked both, I nodded. "*Yes.*"

"Show me how you like it." He found my hand and covered it with his, guiding us down into my panties and over my swollen bud. Applying pressure, he led me to massage slow, gentle circles.

"Ford," I whimpered.

"Tell me...tell me what you like."

"More..."

He increased the pressure over my fingers and pushed deeper into me. My eyes drifted closed, but I felt him watching me intently from the side. He steered my fingers lower, toward my opening, and then coaxed two inside of me. His hand stayed over mine as my own fingers moved in and out of my pussy.

"Does it feel good? Tell me..."

"Ford..." I opened my eyes, feeling the familiar wave start to come over me, and he pushed one of his fingers inside along with my two. He used his thumb to reach up and rub my clit at the same time our joined fingers pumped in and out. I began to shatter.

"Look at me."

My hooded eyes met his hungry ones, and I cried out.

His hand took over when my body went limp. My arms fell to my sides as he strummed every last throb of orgasm from my body. Ford scooped me up into his arms.

He kissed me while walking down the stairs. "I just want to do that to you over and over. I don't even give a shit about my own release. It's way more satisfying to watch you fall apart under my touch."

I couldn't contain my goofy smile. "I like that."

He smiled back. "That's good. Because I'm just getting started with our celebration."

chapter twenty-two

Valentina

We'd become inseparable.

During the week, when Ford had to work, I'd go into the city for a night or two. He'd spend the days in his office, and I'd go to museums and spend time hanging out with Eve at her restaurant. Sometimes I even met him for lunch. Yesterday, I'd packed us a picnic, and we ate in the park not far from his office. At night, we went out to dinner or ordered in and ate naked in bed. Weekends we spent in Montauk frolicking on different beaches.

He'd even started to teach me how to surf—another item crossed off my My Turn list. I sucked at it, but a few tumbles in the waves always ended with making out on the sand, so it was worth it. I couldn't remember being this happy in years.

But time was moving way too fast now. I'd sent out more than a hundred resumes and had a bunch of interviews already. Tomorrow I had a second interview at a school not too far from my house in New Jersey. The position would be perfect for me—a one-year leave replacement teaching Intro to Italian to middle school students. Though thinking about anything that would occur post-Labor Day made me feel a little sick to my stomach.

Tonight we were going to the music festival he'd bought tickets to—yet another item from my list. By the end of the summer, I wouldn't have many things left.

"I got an interesting email today," Ford said.

He was lying on my bed, buck naked, with his hands behind his head as he watched me try to find something appropriate to wear to a twelve-hour concert. I'd actually Googled *music festivals* earlier to see what people wore because I was that out of touch. The photos that popped up freaked me out. Not only did I not have a crocheted bikini top, micro-length denim skirt, and cowboy boots, but I wouldn't wear them if I did—even if that looked like what half the female attendees were wearing.

"Oh yeah? What was the email about?"

"A building in Chicago that's for sale."

I poked my head out of the closet. "Chicago?"

"Yeah. We used to own it. It's a long story, but my father had wanted to expand the temporary office space business outside of New York. His plan was to open an office in Chicago. He bought a building there three years before the accident. It was an old, dilapidated warehouse that needed a ton of work to convert."

"Oh. Wow. But you said it's for sale. So he owned it and sold it?"

Ford shook his head. "No. I actually sold it. When my dad bought it, there was an existing tenant that still had a few years left on their lease. We worked on the conversion plans and blueprints off and on while I was in college. It was kind of our thing. It was supposed to be the first project I'd manage after I graduated. But after the accident, being in two states was too much to deal with. It was just Bella and me, and I couldn't be running back and forth to Chicago during the construction all the time. She was only fourteen. So I sold it. Apparently it's for sale again."

"Are you thinking of buying it back?"

He shrugged. "I don't know. It's odd that it's available again so soon. Now that Bella's away at school and things run pretty smoothly again at the office here, I could probably take it on. I still have all our old plans. It feels like I should at least go check it out. I think I'm going to fly up for the day next week. I've never actually been to the property. I was in college during that time."

"Sounds almost like it might be meant to be, the way the project left your life when you needed it to and now suddenly it's back again."

He nodded. "That's sort of what I thought, too."

"I really do believe some things happen for a reason. Like how I'd been taking one class a semester for a few years, and a year and a half before my divorce, I decided to take more. I had no idea I'd be divorced and the decision would become so important to me. But the timing couldn't have been more perfect. Finishing the classes gave me something to focus on through some hard times, and when I was done, my son was off to college. Maybe you're supposed to do this project, the way the opportunity fell back into your lap."

"Yeah." He stared off to nowhere for a minute, and then his eyes returned to mine. "You might be right. Important things seem to happen for a reason, and we shouldn't walk away from them even if it wasn't how we saw things playing out originally. If something feels right, we have to make it work."

We were definitely talking about more than a building in Chicago now. And though I agreed with him, the discussion made me nervous. I broke our eye contact and reached into the closet for a cute, bright blue sundress.

Holding it up against myself, I tilted my head. "How about this?"

He frowned and held my eyes for a moment before looking at the dress. "I think any one of the sixty-three outfits you've shown me would be perfect."

I had the greatest time at the concert once I got there, once I realized no one really gave a shit about what I wore or how old I was. We arrived at the festival about three. It had been going on since noon and was scheduled to go on until at least midnight. By ten o'clock, I was definitely starting to fade. Ford and I sat in the grass, me between his legs with my back against his chest and his arms wrapped around me. Most of the audience was young, but there were also a decent amount of people my age and older.

"Did you come to a lot of these?"

Ford kissed the top of my head. "I used to when I was in college."

I looked around. "There's just such a carefree feel here. I'm not sure if it's the music or the people, or maybe both, but I'm so relaxed."

He gave me a good squeeze. "I'd like to think it's the company."

I smiled. "I'm sure that has a lot to do with it."

A high-pitched voice popped my blissful bubble. "Ford?"

His arms tightened around me. "Jess. How you doing?"

The woman didn't even try to hide her sizing me up. Her eyes started at my shoes and worked their way up to the top of my head. She made a disapproving face.

"I'm good. It's been a while."

There was an awkward silence, and I knew in my gut that he'd slept with her. Don't ask me how—women just have a sixth sense about these things. Of course, that made me examine her even closer. Her body was ridiculously perfect, tanned and thin...and *so much* of it was on display. She was basically wearing the outfit I'd seen in the festival photos I'd Googled—crocheted bikini top, tiny denim skirt and cowboy boots. She also had dozens of bracelets up her arm, a choker, and three or four different long necklaces to complete her outfit.

Ford tilted his head to me. "Valentina, this is Jessica."

"Hi," I said.

Jessica showed me her pearly white, fake smile as her eyes shifted above me. "You look good, Ford."

He shrugged. "Thanks. Must be because I'm happy."

She tilted her head. "You should give me a call sometime."

I might've been insecure about my age and whatever was going on between us, but this tart wasn't going to be disrespectful. Ford had his arms wrapped around me, for God's sake.

I answered her just as he started to speak. "Do you need office space?"

Her nose wrinkled. "No?"

I flaunted the same plastic smile she'd given to me, along with her coy tilt of the head. "So you wanted him to call for..."

I heard Ford's soft chuckle behind me.

The girl stared down at us for a few seconds, then flipped her hair and rolled her eyes. "Take care, Ford. You have my number."

I wiggled my fingers. "Bye-bye."

Jess was barely ten feet away when Ford wrangled my back to the grass. He looked thoroughly amused, grinning wide with his head hung over mine. "You're sexy as fuck when you're jealous."

"I wasn't jealous. That girl was just rude. You're sitting with your arms around me, and she asks you to what...give her a booty call?"

Ford rubbed his nose with mine. "You like me and don't want other women seeing me naked."

"I get the feeling you've already seen that particular woman naked."

"It was a long time ago."

"Glad to hear that."

"Jealousy means you give a shit."

"Well, of course I give a shit."

His face turned serious. "Do you think that's going to change in a week or two?"

God, he was right. The summer was racing to a close, and I couldn't imagine not seeing him anymore, much less walking away. He'd have plenty of women to take my place.

"No, I'm sure it won't."

"It doesn't have to."

I frowned. If only it were that easy.

He lowered his head and brushed his lips to mine. "Not too late to change your mind. Maybe you need a few Post-it reminders around the house of what this feels like."

Something told me I wouldn't need a sticky to remember how this summer made me feel. On the contrary, I might need something really potent to make me forget.

chapter twenty-three

Ford

I smiled, looking up at the old warehouse. I could definitely understand my dad's excitement over it now. My parents had bought this landmark building in an estate auction. The time Dad and I spent working on the plans to restore and renovate it were some of my best memories of him.

I knew the building so intimately from photos and drawings, yet I'd never been inside. There was always one reason or another why I couldn't make the trip to check on things out here in Chicago. But it had never felt like a rush—because we had plenty of time. Until suddenly we didn't anymore.

Selling the building a few months after my Dad died had been difficult. But when an offer for more than we'd paid for it fell into my lap, it seemed like I didn't have a choice. Still, fate had a way of bringing things that were meant to be back to you sometimes.

Like Valentina.

And this place.

A white BMW pulled up in front of the building and parked. Louise Marie Anderson had a picture on her business card in my dad's rolodex, so when the driver got out of the car, I was pretty certain it was her. She smiled as she walked toward me.

"I don't have to ask who you are. You're the spitting image of your dad." She reached out her hand. "Louise Anderson. But my friends call me Andi."

I smiled. "My dad referred to you as Andi, so I'll take that as a good sign."

After she shook my hand, she didn't let go. She wrapped her other hand around mine. "I was so sorry about the loss of your parents. They were such good people."

I nodded. "Thank you. My sister and I appreciated the flowers you sent. It was very thoughtful."

"Of course." She shook her head. "I used to melt at the way your dad looked at your mom—the way they were always holding hands. They seemed like two teenagers in love."

My brows drew down. "I didn't realize you'd met my mom. We always joked around that Dad had a girlfriend here because neither of us got to come on his trips to Chicago."

"Oh, no. She came here quite a few times. In fact, when they first came to look at this building—must've been seven years ago now—the thing they loved most was the top floor. They'd talked about making it into an apartment for themselves."

Huh. I guess my mom didn't want me to feel bad that I could never go with Dad on his trips. That would be just like my parents, though—to want to make a little love nest for themselves in a building they bought.

When they were alive, their constant touchy-feely had been sort of gross to me—they were my parents. But for some reason, after they passed away, those were among my most treasured memories.

"Well...I'm looking forward to seeing the place. I can't get over that it's back on the market in such a short time."

"Divorce." She nodded. "Hate to say it, but probably seventy-five percent of my repeat property sales are due to a breakup."

Andi and I toured the empty building. It was such an odd feeling to walk through the space Dad and I had spent so many years working on. When I'd decided to come check it out, I thought expanding to Chicago as Dad had planned to do and building our dream conversion project would bring me some sort of closure. I'd always regretted having to sell this building. But being here brought a dull ache to my chest and made my shoulders feel like I was carrying a barbell with a hundred pounds of weights.

The building was eleven stories, so it took us a while to walk through. By the time we got to the top floor, the place my parents had imagined making into theirs, I was starting to feel like I needed some fresh air.

I tugged at my tie and loosened it as I followed Andi around. She pointed to a wall of windows. "These are old, obviously. And not very heat efficient for Chicago winters. But Marie loved them. She told Michael she wanted to have them made into doors to use inside the space as room separators. I'm not sure how easy that is to do, but he seemed to love the idea."

I didn't know my dad had brought an interior designer in. "Marie? Would you happen to have her contact info? I hadn't realized he'd started working with an interior designer already. We'd only done the layout of the conversion together, not any decorating."

Andi laughed. "Your mom, Marie...not an outside designer."

"My mom's name was Athena." It wasn't a name people heard too often outside of Greek History class.

"Really?" Her brows drew down. "I could swear we had a whole conversation about how we had the same name in reverse. I'm Louise Marie, and she said she was Marie Louise."

The real estate agent looked confused, and then abruptly seemed almost flustered. She shook her head and turned to walk to the other side of the room.

"Umm... That's right. I'm...confusing her with another client. I'm so sorry about that...Athena...right."

People made mistakes with names all the time. Hell, I didn't remember most people's names thirty seconds after I met them. But something about Andi told me she hadn't made any mistake. Though, that made no sense.

My head was definitely screwing with me here—all the memories of the time Dad and I had spent together working on this building. I let the funny feeling I had pass in favor of finishing the tour. Outside, I gulped fresh air into my lungs.

"So the seller is looking to get out clean—pay what he paid and walk away. But I have a feeling there might be some wiggle room. Between us, it's not a very amicable divorce, and I think a fast sale and not dragging out separating assets might make them willing to take it at a small loss."

I nodded, but felt wiped out for some reason. I was glad I'd decided to stay in town tonight to walk through with a building engineer tomorrow because I had a feeling half of what I saw today might be a blur by morning. My emotions were really screwing with me.

"Would you like any suggestions for dinner or anything?" Andi asked after she locked the front door. She still seemed slightly off—almost standoffish or nervous.

"No, thank you. The hotel has a restaurant in it, and I'll probably just eat there."

"Okay...so...I'll see you at nine tomorrow?"

I nodded. "Nine o'clock. Thanks for the tour today."

I got into my rental car and watched as Andi pulled away. Rather than start the car, I rested my head on the headrest for a few minutes with my eyes closed. I took a few deep breaths, but couldn't shake the screwed-up feeling in my gut.

So I picked up the phone and called the accounting manager at my office. "Hey, Dan. It's Ford. Do we still have my parents' expense reports from years ago?"

"We keep six years of records in one of the storage units. IRS can generally go back and audit you for the last three years, but if they find a substantial error, they can go back six. Your dad liked to stay on the safe side, especially since he certainly had the storage space. Do you need something?"

"Think you can pull both my dad and my mom's expense reports and see if my mom ever came on any of my dad's trips to Chicago?"

"Yeah. Sure. Give me a few hours."

"Thanks, Dan."

———

Some thoughts are like a loose thread in a sweater. You can either pull it and chance unraveling the entire thing, or cut it off and move on. When Andi said my mom had come to Chicago with my dad on more than one occasion, it was a loose thread. But I cut it off and moved on, able to chalk it up to my mom not wanting me to feel badly that she got to come see the project *I* had worked on for years.

But then another thread came loose when Andi said my mother's name was Marie Louise—she'd sounded so certain. And the second time, I couldn't just cut the thread and move on. I'd pulled, and now it felt like I was waiting for my entire world to unravel.

After I'd checked into my hotel, I'd gone to the gym to work off some of my unsettled energy and then showered. Now I was sitting at the bar of the restaurant. My phone finally rang just as I got my burger.

"Hey, Dan."

"Hey, Ford."

"Did you find anything?"

"I checked all the expense reports we had, and we have no record of your mom ever taking a trip to Chicago. Their assistant made all their reservations and did their expense reports for the company—not likely she'd miss something, but I suppose it's possible."

My chest started to hurt, and I rubbed at it. "Any chance you remember if we had hired an interior designer in Chicago? I'm up here looking at the building we used to own—it came back on the market."

Dan had been with the company as long as I'd been alive and remembered everything.

"Your dad was pretty good about not spending on projects before the official construction began. You never know when you might get problems from the building department that change all your plans."

I nodded. That was definitely true. I was just about to let him off the phone. Maybe Andi was wrong about everything with my dad, and I was pulling at a thread that just needed to be snipped. It honestly seemed ridiculous to think what I'd been thinking.

I laughed. "You're right, Dan. Thanks a lot."

"No problem. If you're considering buying the building back, you might want to check in with your dad's lawyer up there. I remember there was a zoning issue she'd worked on for him before the purchase—not sure if the current owner changed zoning back. But that's something to look into if you decide to go forward."

I nodded. This is why my parents paid Dan more than the average accounting manager—his mind was a steel trap.

"Thanks, Dan. Any chance you remember the attorney's name?"

"Landsford, I think. Let me look it up in the computer. We would have cut her a check, and she'll be in our vendor list. Hang on a second."

My shoulders relaxed, and I reached down for the burger in front of me. Suddenly, my appetite had returned. Dan came back on the line just as I bit into it.

"Yeah, it was Landsford. Marie Louise Landsford, Esquire, is who we made the check out to."

Marie Louise.

I almost choked on my burger.

"You want me to email you her contact information?" he asked.

I managed to force down the mouthful of food, yet it still felt like I had a lump in my throat after I swallowed. "Yeah. That would be helpful. Thanks, Dan."

———

I didn't tend to be a nervous person.

The last time I'd felt this way was when I stood in front of the judge and told him I wanted legal custody of my fourteen-year-old sister. I wasn't nervous that I was making the wrong decision—I was nervous that he'd say I wasn't qualified or that my sister would be better off in foster care or with my aunt in Ohio.

But as I sat in my car, parked on Superior Street in front of the storefront law office of Marie Louise Landsford, Esquire, my palms were sweaty and my stomach was tied in a knot. It felt as though I could bend over and toss my breakfast, only I hadn't had anything to eat since the one bite of burger last night. My eyes also itched, though that could be from lack of sleep and not nerves. I could feel my heartbeat all over—ricocheting against my chest, swooshing through my ears, even in my throat.

My phone buzzed in my pocket—a text from Valentina. I'd exchanged a few messages with her last night, but didn't mention anything about my father or what was going on. I couldn't even admit it to myself, much less say the words out loud to someone else. I also hadn't mentioned I'd blown off the appointment I was supposed to have with the engineer this morning. The only thing she knew was that I'd pushed back my flight to meet with an attorney about zoning. Which was sort of true, I guess. At least that was what I planned to say when I walked into her office without an appointment. I had no plans beyond that. I couldn't even think about what I might say, or how I might ask her.

Valentina: Good luck with the attorney today, and have a safe flight home later. Let me know what train you're on in the morning, and I'll pick you up. I have a little surprise for you.

I stared at my cell like the words were gibberish. There was no way I could possibly text back. Instead, I shoved the phone into my pocket. I just needed to get this shit over with.

I got out of the car, took a deep breath, and headed for the door.

A woman about my age was sitting behind a reception desk. She smiled. "Hi. Can I help you?"

"Yeah. Ummm. I don't have an appointment, but I was hoping maybe I could speak to Marie."

"Can I ask what this is in reference to?"

"I'm considering buying a building in the area, and she did some work for my father on it previously."

"Oh. Okay." She motioned toward a closed door to her left. "She's with a client right now, but she should be finished any minute. As soon as she gets done, I'll ask her if she can speak with you."

"Thanks,"

"Can I have your name, please?"

"Ford. Ford Donovan."

If my last name meant anything to the receptionist, she didn't show it. She told me to take a seat, and I sat on a leather couch and pretended to thumb through a copy of *Architectural Digest*. A few minutes later, the door to Marie's office opened. My heart, which had already been beating fast, took off like a runaway train. An older man in a suit walked out first, talking to someone behind him.

"I think once we send over these last revisions, they'll finally sign the contract," a woman's voice said.

I still couldn't see her.

"Good. Good. I'm anxious to get this all behind me."

The man took a few steps, and the woman who'd been speaking appeared in the doorway.

"I'll be in touch soon."

Seeing her for the first time, I froze. *What the hell?* I knew her. But from where? I flipped through a mental rolodex of where I might've seen her before. I was absolutely positive we'd met. But I'd never come to Chicago.

The client made his way to the front door, and the attorney took a few steps toward the receptionist, who turned to speak to her.

"I didn't want to interrupt since you were almost finished with Mr. Wetson, but you have a walk-in."

Marie looked over to the seating area for the first time. I stood. The minute her eyes landed on me, her entire face changed. Her jaw dropped open, her eyes drooped with sadness, and all of her color drained away.

Completely oblivious, the receptionist kept talking. "You've done some work for his family before. He doesn't have an appointment, but you have a half hour before your next one."

That pale, sorrow-filled face—it clicked. *The funeral!* She'd come to my parents' funeral. That weekend was mostly a blur—there had been so many friends who came and went. For two days, I'd spent the majority of my time standing and shaking people's hands. I couldn't have repeated what anyone had actually said if my life depended on it.

But I remembered seeing her. She'd been sitting on a chair in the back corner all by herself, crying. She'd looked really distraught, so I'd gone over to see if she was okay. It was the first time I'd met her, but that didn't strike me as unusual. People came out of the woodwork to give their condolences at the funeral.

I walked over to where Marie stood, still staring at me. The receptionist turned as I approached. "Oh. Here he is. Marie, this is...."

239

Marie smiled sadly and shook her head. Her voice was solemn and her tone resigned. "I know who he is. Hello, Ford."

I nodded, unable to say anything.

Marie tilted her head toward her door. "Why don't we talk in my office?"

I nodded and followed her inside. She closed the door after telling the receptionist to cancel her next meeting and hold her calls.

Walking around to the other side of her desk, she held her hand out. "Please, have a seat."

I kept staring at her even as I sat.

She settled into her chair and shuffled some papers that didn't need shuffling on her desk. Speaking softly, she said, "How are you doing?"

"Fine."

She nodded. "Good. I'm glad to hear that."

I stared at her. I honestly didn't need to ask the question, the guilt and sadness on her face told me most of the answers. So I skipped over the bullshit and went to the stuff I didn't already know.

"How long were you two having an affair?"

She looked down. "About three years."

Jesus Christ. *Three fucking years*? I thought back to the last summers out in Montauk before they died. My parents had been dancing and as in love as ever. I nodded. "Why?"

She sighed. "It just happened. Neither of us planned it. I was happily married, too. At least I thought I was at the time."

"Was?"

She nodded. "I told my husband about the affair after I came home from the funeral. I couldn't hide how upset I was, and I knew our marriage was over. I'd been unfair to him for a long time. We've been divorced for a few years now."

I didn't understand. It seemed impossible to reconcile my smiling, seemingly happy parents with my dad having an affair with the woman in front of me. I thought for a long time, leaving the silence in the room to grow thick.

When I finally spoke, I looked straight into her eyes. "He loved my mother. They were happy."

I could see my words caused her pain. As fucked up as it was, that made me feel bad.

She nodded. "Of course he did. There's no excuse for what I did, what your father and I did, Ford. The only thing I can say is that we'd both been married a long time. I'd married my high school sweetheart, just like your father." She shook her head and looked out the window. "Curiosity? I don't know. I've spent a lot of time thinking about it, though, both while it was happening and over the last three years. Neither of us had much experience. We didn't date or really live adult lives outside of our spouses. So I guess maybe we reached a certain point in our lives—midlife—and wondered who we were without our spouses. You're young, so I wouldn't expect you to understand. Honestly, I'm not sure I even understand, but I think I needed validation that what I had wasn't going to be my entire life here on this Earth."

She returned her gaze to me and shook her head. There were tears pooled in her eyes. "By the time I realized what I had was enough, and I should've been thanking my lucky stars instead of thinking I was missing out on something, it was too late."

I sat in silence, trying to make sense of everything, but I couldn't seem to grasp anything in my hands. Nothing could sink in. I knew in my heart I'd never be back here, I'd never see this woman again, so I wanted to make sure to ask her what I needed to ask and say what I needed to say. Hoping things would come to me, I looked around the room, lost in thought. My eyes landed on a framed photo of a little girl. She couldn't be older than five or six.

No.

Just fucking no.

My voice was so monotone. "Is that your daughter?"

Marie smiled. "Yes. Rebecca." Her smile wilted. "The divorce was hard on her. I can't even imagine what you've been through...and now coming here and dealing with this."

I continued to stare at the photo, looking for signs of my father. I had to swallow a giant lump in my throat to ask what I needed to ask. "Is she...my father's?"

Marie's eyes grew wide. "Oh! No. God, no. That's an old picture. Rebecca is going to be ten next month." She turned around and looked at the photo. "She was about six there, so I can understand why you'd think that. But I can assure you, she was born years before I even met your father."

Thank God for one thing, I guess. I sat for another minute or two in silence, thinking about what else I need-ed to know. But really, I'd already found out too much.

I stood. "Thank you for your honesty."

She nodded and stood. "I'm sorry, Ford. About every-thing—the affair, your loss, you finding out. Everything. If I could rewind and do it all over, it would never have happened."

I walked out of Marie Louise Landsford's office with-out looking back.

Unfortunately, I didn't need to look back, because her honesty had already changed everything I saw looking forward.

chapter twenty-four

Valentina

I'd stopped listening to music over the years, and I hadn't even noticed.

I listened in the car, of course. But I didn't blast it while I was at home cleaning, showering, or cooking anymore, like I had years ago. Lately, though, that had changed. I found myself doing things I hadn't in a long time—singing along to music when in the shower, dancing while folding the laundry, planting flowers, baking without a party to bring dessert to. I felt lighter and happier than I had in a long time. And whether I wanted to admit it to myself or not, one of the big reasons for that change was the man next door, who was currently on his way back out to Montauk.

A Billy Joel song came on while I was in the shower, and I sang along, belting out "Only the Good Die Young" at the top of my lungs like I was putting on a show for a sold-out crowd. It felt good...*so damn good*. As I rinsed the last of the conditioner from my hair, I closed my eyes and joined Taylor Swift for an earsplitting performance of "Shake it Off" that culminated in my singing and shimmying the towel to dry off my back. I wrapped my hair in a towel and threw on yoga pants and a tank top. Grabbing my moisturizer, I wiped the fog from the mirror and found a face smiling at me in the reflection—my own. I felt giddy.

This morning I'd done the sunrise yoga class with Bella and then went for a long walk on the beach. Halfway back home, my cell rang. It was the school I'd had a second interview with yesterday. *I got the job!*

Since then, I hadn't stopped smiling. And I couldn't wait to tell Ford. He'd been in a rush to catch his plane home from Chicago when I'd texted him earlier, so I figured I'd save my surprise until he got back to Montauk. My plans were to go to the supermarket and pick up a few things to make his favorite dinner.

Though those plans abruptly changed the minute I opened the bathroom door.

I startled and jumped to find a man casually leaning against the top stair railing a few feet from the bathroom door. But then my eyes bulged and jaw hung open.

"Surprise." My son smiled and chuckled. "That's some show you put on. Didn't think you were ever going to come out of there. I didn't know you were such a Swiftie, Mom."

"Oh my God. Ryan! You're home!" I swamped him in a giant hug.

He laughed and hugged me back.

"What are you doing here? I thought you weren't going to be able to come home at all this summer because of the internship?"

"I finished a project I was working on a few days early, so I asked if I could take today to make it a four-day weekend for Labor Day. I need to fly back early Monday morning."

"Why didn't you call me? How did you get out here from the airport?"

He shrugged. "I wanted to surprise you. I took the train and then a cab."

"Well, you succeeded." God, I needed to squeeze him some more. I snuggled in for another hug. "I missed you."

"I figured it might be a tough summer being out here for the first time alone."

Except...*uh-oh*...I wasn't alone.

"Umm... I kept myself busy."

He looked over my face. "You look good, Mom."

I patted the towel wrapped atop my head. "Must be the turban."

Ryan smiled. "No...something's different. You look...I don't know...less stressed, maybe."

I squeezed his hand. "I am. I was going to tell you when we spoke this weekend. But I got a job."

"Wow. Congrats. That's awesome. And so quick."

"Yeah. I'm really happy about it."

His eyes crinkled at the corners, and he smiled warmly. "That's what it is. You look happy."

"I am." Though a large portion of that had nothing to do with getting a job.

"Well, come on. Go dry your hair or do whatever you do when you take it out of the towel, and let's get something to eat to celebrate. I'm starving."

"Okay! Give me fifteen minutes."

After I dried my hair, I shot off a quick text to Ford.

Valentina: My son just surprised me. He's home for the holiday weekend.

I watched for the text to show as delivered, but it never did. Checking the time on my phone, he should've been off the plane and on the train by now. Though perhaps his flight was delayed, and his phone was still off. I hit *Call*—but it went directly to voicemail. His phone was definitely off. So I shot off another text.

Valentina: I'll still pick you up from the train. Text me when you know which one you'll be on.

I tossed my phone into my purse and slipped into a pair of flip-flops. Ryan being home complicated things between Ford and me and the plans I'd had for us to celebrate this weekend, but I couldn't be upset my son had surprised me. I was happy he was home.

On my way down the stairs, I was surprised to hear two voices, but found no one in the house. "Ryan?" I yelled.

"On the back deck!"

I found Ryan leaning over the railing talking to Bella. "I didn't know Ryan was coming this weekend," she said.

"I didn't either. He surprised me."

"Awww, that's so sweet. It's been a while, huh, Rye-Rye?"

I hadn't heard that nickname in at least ten years. Bella used to call Ryan that when he was little, and he'd hated it.

But when I looked over at my son, he didn't seem to dislike it anymore. His eyes dipped down to do a quick sweep over Bella. He was checking her out. "You've changed."

She batted her eyelashes. "So did you."

Oh God. No.

I needed to get Ryan the hell out of here. I tugged at my son's arm. "We've gotta run. See you later, Bella."

Our lunch lasted two hours. We went to Lobster Roll and sat outside on the benches eating and talking, mostly about his first year of college and his internship.

"All we've done is talk about me. Tell me how your summer was. Is it weird being out here without Dad and me?"

I shook my head. "It's different, but not weird. He actually was out a few weeks ago to get an estimate on some work we need done at the house."

"How'd that go?"

I smiled. "About as well as the last few years we were together. He said something that pissed me off, and I told him to get out."

Ryan laughed. "He's been calling me a lot lately."

In my head, I thought, *Of course he is.* His toddler girlfriend moved to India, so he finally has some time to pay attention to his son. Ryan couldn't possibly have time for *two* teenagers in his busy life.

But I swallowed my real thoughts and went with something supportive. "That's good. I'm glad you two are making more of an effort to stay connected."

He shrugged. "How would you feel toward Tom if he cheated on Eve?"

I knew what he was getting at. "I adore Tom. But I'd always be on Eve's side, of course. Then again, Tom isn't my father."

He wrinkled up his napkin and tossed it on his empty plate. "He's not seeing her anymore."

I nodded. "I know. He told me."

"Is...there any way you'd ever forgive him?"

Oh God. He might look like a grown man, but inside he was still my little boy who hated to see his parents broken up.

"You know what? I sort of have forgiven him. At least I'm moving on from it. I'm not going to lie, your father and I splitting up was hard on me. I think you know that. But now that I'm on the other side of it, I realize we would have wound up here no matter what. We were kids when we got married, and I have no regrets about the decisions I made because I got you out of it, and your father and I... we had some good years. But we grew apart as we grew up, and neither of us was happy for a long time. I blamed it on what he'd done, because it was easier at the time. But our relationship was in trouble long before he did what he did. In fact, the poor state of our marriage is probably one of the main reasons he turned to someone else."

My son looked down. "I get it. It was stupid for me to even ask."

I reached out and took his hand. "No, it wasn't. It's perfectly normal for a child to want his parents to be happily married."

Ryan nodded. "That reminds me. What should I have said to Bella about her parents? I wasn't sure if I should say anything, so I didn't."

"I think you can just give your condolences if you see her again. She talks about them a lot, and she's okay with people mentioning it."

"Crazy that she lost them both." He shook his head. "And I'm sitting here selfishly asking if you and Dad might get back together. Puts things into perspective."

"Yeah. But she seems do be doing well."

My son smirked. "She looks well."

I wrinkled my nose. My son assumed it was a general icky feeling a mom might get about her son checking out a girl.

He chuckled. "Yeah. Pretty sure my face would be the same if you were telling me some guy was hot."

I winced inwardly. *Pretty sure your face would be worse if I told you the guy I thought was hot was the* brother *of the girl you thought was hot.*

———

That evening, I still hadn't heard from Ford, and my text wasn't showing as delivered yet. I was getting worried and reached out to Bella, albeit under false pretenses.

I knocked next door and she appeared in her uniform. "Hey."

"Hey, Bella. Have you heard from your brother? Umm...I wanted to ask him to look at my sink again. He fixed it for me at the beginning of the summer."

"Yeah. He's in his room. Passed out, I think."

I failed at hiding my surprise. "He's home?"

She scooped her car keys off the kitchen counter. "Got home about an hour ago. Bombed off his ass. He was swaying. I'm surprised he made it up the stairs. I have to get to work, but feel free to wake him up. Although, I doubt he's in a condition to fix anything."

"Ummm. Okay. Thanks. Maybe I'll just check on him and make sure he's okay."

She smiled. "Such a mom."

I waited downstairs until she got into her car and pulled out of the driveway, and then I went up to Ford's bedroom. Sure enough, he was out cold. Face down, his arms and legs splayed wide across the bed, he held his cell phone in one of his hands.

I walked over and whispered, "Ford?"

He didn't budge so I slipped the cell from his hand and pressed the side button. Dead. Well, at least that made me feel better about why he hadn't called. I walked over to the end table and plugged it in for him, then sat down on the edge of the bed and watched him sleep.

"Bad day, sweetheart?" I brushed a piece of his hair from his face. "You've been quiet since you went to Chicago. Probably hard to visit the building you and your dad worked on together, huh? A lot of memories."

Of course he didn't answer. After watching him sleep for a little bit, I took off his shoes, got a bottle of water and a couple of Tylenol from the bathroom, and left his hangover helper at his bedside.

I leaned down and kissed his cheek gently. I felt a tightening in my chest as I realized in a few days I wouldn't be seeing him anymore. *God, I'm not ready for this to be over.*

chapter twenty-five

Ford

My lungs burned, and I couldn't catch my breath. I wasn't even sure where I was. I'd gotten up at the ass crack of dawn with a belligerent hangover. Tylenol and two bottles of water did nothing to ease the pounding in my head. I couldn't even remember getting home. I remembered sitting at the airport bar, pounding vodka tonics and ordering more on the plane. After that, it was pretty much a blur. Somehow I'd managed to get on the right train and made it into my bed. On any other day, if I'd woken with this kind of killer headache, I'd have turned over and gone back to sleep.

But this morning, I needed to feel more pain. So I'd gone out for a run. And I'd run. And run. And kept on running. I'd run until I ran out of beach, then kept going—weaving my way through side streets and passing houses and blocks as fast as I could.

Finally, my legs gave out on me, and I fell.

So here I was, sitting in the middle of a park I'd never seen before, on some block I'd never been to, panting and bleeding from a scraped-open knee. My head still fucking hurt, but the burn in my lungs felt even better.

I sat with my elbows on my knees and my head dropped between them.

My fucking father is a cheater.

The man whose chair I sat in at work, whose daughter I'd raised for the last five years, whose relationship I'd thought was *everything*...the man who I'd looked up to since I could remember.

It fucking hurt. And I just couldn't make sense of it.

Why?

Why?

My parents had seemed so in love. They didn't fight. They didn't have financial problems. They finished each other's sentences, for Christ's sake. As I sat there, stills of them played in my head like a slideshow on fast forward.

Them dancing on the deck.

Mom reading to Dad on the beach.

Him grabbing her ass, and her giggling when they thought no one was paying attention.

All the *I love yous*.

The Mason jars.

The two of them *wrote things down* they loved about each other and exchanged them as gifts.

Who the fuck does that if you aren't in love?

And that was the part I couldn't reconcile.

Even though I'd found out he'd had a long-term relationship with another woman, I still had no doubt he loved my mother. So if he loved my mother, why would he do it?

Why?

Why?

Why?

The only answer that made sense was the one his mistress had given me. They'd gotten married so young, neither of them knew a life without the other, and my father hit a certain age and started to have an identity crisis.

A midlife crisis.

It wasn't fucking right.

That was for sure.

But it's also what had happened in Valentina's marriage.

Fuck.

I was pissed as hell at my father, but that wasn't what had my chest feeling hollow at the moment.

Valentina had been right all along.

I didn't see it because I didn't want to see it.

She'd been with her husband since she was sixteen—the same age my parents got together.

I wanted her to choose to be with me, but how could she decide what she wanted when she didn't even know what was out there.

———

Shit.

This morning I'd read Val's texts from yesterday, so I knew her son Ryan was in town. But I had no idea what she'd told him. I assumed nothing. Yet I couldn't be sure, so I played it close to the vest. The two of them were out on the back deck, leaning over the railing looking at the beach when I walked up on the sand—hours after I'd left for my run.

"Hey." I lifted my chin up at them.

"What's up, man? Long time no see." Ryan smiled.

"Hey." Valentina's voice was laced with hesitance.

I figured it was a good sign that he didn't run down the stairs and punch me in the face for banging his mother. But while Ryan seemed chipper and relaxed, Val looked anything but. Seeing the veins pop from her neck as she stressed made me smile for the first time in two days. Why did seeing her freak out about someone finding out about us bring me such joy? Perhaps I was just a dick.

I walked up the stairs to their deck instead of mine and shook Ryan's hand. The last time I saw him, he was only fourteen. Now he was almost as tall as I was. "All grown up. I take it you're not going to want me to make sandcastles with you this year?"

Ryan smiled. "I've moved on to searching for mermaids. Maybe we can go find some tail together later."

My eyes flickered to Val and then back, and I coughed. "You're at University of North Carolina, right? How do you like it?"

"It's great. My first year was a blast."

He looked over at his mom and his face fell serious. *Shit*. Maybe I'd misjudged the situation and she had told him.

"Listen...I just wanted to say I'm really sorry about your parents."

I nodded. "Thank you."

The simple reminder of my father swept away any momentary levity that had crept in. My shoulders went back to holding boulders.

"I'm gonna head home to shower." I glanced at Val and then nodded to Ryan. "Good to see you."

When I got out of the shower, I wasn't surprised to find a text from Val.

Valentina: Everything okay? I came by last night but you were out cold.

I hadn't even known she'd been here. But my phone was charged and there had been water and Tylenol on the end table. That made sense now.

Ford: Sorry about that. Just a long trip. I hadn't eaten and had a few.

Valentina: No problem. I figured the trip might have been difficult. ☹

You could say that again.

She typed more before I could respond.

Valentina: Ryan surprised me. I know it sort of puts a damper on us spending time together this last weekend...

Yesterday, I would have said her son showing up on the last weekend I had to convince her what we had was more than a fling was the universe conspiring to rip my heart out. But today, without my brain swimming in alcohol, I was starting to think maybe fate had intervened.

Chicago had taught me a lesson. I needed to step back and allow Valentina to move on. She deserved an easy break. It's what she wanted, and I would have just made it harder on her. Her son's surprise trip would keep us from spending an entire weekend in bed—it sucked, though it was probably for the best.

Ford: It's fine. Enjoy your time with him. I have a lot of work to do, anyway. Bella's flight is Sunday. I'll probably just drop her off and stay in the city.

Valentina: Ryan's going to go surfing later. Maybe we could talk then?

Ford: Sure.

A few hours later, the only actual work I'd accomplished was to send an email to the real estate agent in Chicago, thanking her for her time, but letting her know

I'd decided against moving forward with the repurchase. All the reasons for wanting that property had vanished the moment I left Marie's office. She wrote back and didn't seem surprised.

Bella spent the afternoon starting to pack and then went in to work for her final shift. I was cleaning out the fridge—tossing things we weren't going to use over the next two days—when Val knocked at the back door.

"Hey."

I slid the screen door open. She took one look at what I was doing and her smile fell. "I can't believe the summer is really almost over."

This afternoon, I'd decided not to mention what I'd found out in Chicago to Val. I wasn't planning on telling my sister—why ruin her memory of our asshole father, too? So it didn't seem fair to tell anyone else. That, and what good would it do? Val had lost enough faith in men with her own marriage. There was no reason to completely obliterate whatever hope she clung to that maybe not every guy out there was a total asshole.

But she knew something was off.

"Ryan decided to skip surfing because it was too flat. He went for a run, so I figured I'd stop over." She looked around me into the living room. "Is Bella home? I thought I saw her car pull out."

"She went to work. Left a few minutes ago."

She nodded, and it took me a few seconds to realize why that seemed to make her feel badly. It was probably the first time she'd been in my presence alone that I didn't try to maul her.

I pulled her to me and wrapped her in my arms. Inhaling deep, I took in the smell that would forever remind me of this summer—faded floral perfume, coconut suntan lotion, and the beach. I wanted to bottle the scent and call it Valentina.

I felt her shoulders relax as she snuggled into me. "What happened in Chicago?"

I swallowed. "Building just needs too much work."

She looked at me. "I'm sorry. I know the project meant a lot to you."

"It's fine. It is what it is."

"I had this big weekend planned for us. I was going to make your favorite dinner and be your favorite dessert. But with Ryan here..."

"I'm assuming you didn't tell him about us."

She shook her head. "I just couldn't. And it has nothing to do with us. It's just the first time I've seen him in months and...well, he's barely accepted that his father and I aren't getting back together. Yesterday, he actually asked me if there was a chance I could forgive his father."

We'd talked about her ex before, but my interest in how she felt about him had definitely changed after my trip to Chicago.

I looked into her eyes. "You said the infidelity wasn't the only issue, that it was the catalyst that caused you to step back and re-examine your marriage, and then you realized how broken things were. But what if you'd stepped back and seen a happy marriage?"

"I don't know. It's hard to say. But I think I'd be more apt to be able to move past a one-night stand, a drunken mistake he regretted. But not a relationship. Ryan had been seeing the woman he cheated with for months and had feelings for her. They stayed together through our divorce. I guess I just can't see stepping back from more than a one-night stand and finding a happy marriage, because while mistakes can happen, having a relationship with someone else isn't a mistake. It's a choice."

VI KEELAND

I nodded. "Ryan's asking if you might get back together. Did he not see that your marriage wasn't happy?"

She smiled sadly. "*I* didn't even see that my marriage wasn't happy."

I guess you really never know what's going on behind closed doors. This conversation had taken a depressing turn, and I needed to lighten it up. I reached around and slipped my hands into the back of her shorts. "So how light of a sleeper is your son? Are we sneaking to your place tonight or mine?"

She wrapped her hands around my neck. "How about if we sneak out and take a walk down the beach where the dunes get high. We can take along a blanket?"

"Nice. Finally having sand in the crack of my ass this summer will be worth it." I brushed my lips to hers. "That sounds like a plan."

chapter twenty-six

Valentina

It was now or never.

Ryan had just turned in for the night, and I'd taken a shower.

This was it. The moment of truth had finally come. *A summer fling.*

That's what it was supposed to be. Get my *one under the belt*, stick my toe into the pool to feel the water before diving in. But somewhere along the way, it had turned into more. I tried to pretend it hadn't, that the smile on my face was from just a good time—but that wasn't the truth, was it?

I'd started falling for Ford before we even met. We'd connected with just text exchanges. He'd made me laugh, made me be myself—a person I'd oddly forgotten how to be. And that was before the physical connection, which had been undeniably intense from the first touch. The man could light up my body in a way I didn't even realize I could shine. But he did more than that—he lit up my *insides*. I hadn't felt as alive as I had this summer in... well, forever.

For weeks I'd been questioning how I was going to walk away at the end of the summer. But as the last days ticked away, I'd started to wonder if I *could* walk away. Of course I physically could, but if I did, would I be leaving a piece of my heart behind?

I looked in the mirror as I swiped on some lipstick and had a little heart-to-heart with myself. "What are you so afraid of? You've already fallen for him."

I closed my eyes, realizing the answer. *You're afraid to get hurt again.*

That was the truth in a nutshell. I'd made every excuse in the book: *You're too young for me. I'm not ready for a relationship. I need to find myself.* But they were all defenses I'd put up to avoid being smacked in the face with the truth.

I'm terrified.

Then there was the fact that Ford seemed to have stopped pushing for anything more lately. I suppose a person can only take so much rejection. Perhaps he'd warmed to the idea of a summer fling and no longer wanted anything more.

There was only one way to find out. It wasn't like I could put it off any longer. This was it.

Now or never.

He could go back home and jump into the dating world in a few weeks. I couldn't imagine he'd stay celibate for two years like me.

And maybe he'd meet someone he liked.

Sometimes you don't get a second chance.

So what if it didn't work out? Maybe he isn't my forever. I might get hurt. But I could also regret not taking a chance.

And I'd rather have memories than regrets.

I suddenly felt a little out of breath. I wasn't ready for things to be over, and I needed to let him know that tonight.

I smiled at my reflection in the mirror. *Oh my God. You're really going to take a chance.*

Making my decision, the feeling of impending doom I'd had the last few days turned to giddy anticipation. I grabbed my phone, still smiling, and sent off a text.

Valentina: Meet soon?

It felt like the longest wait in my life.

Shit. What if he fell asleep?

What if I don't get to talk to him.

What if...

The tiny dots started to jump around, and my pulse raced.

Ford: Ready when you are.

Thump-thump-thump.

God, my heart was pounding.

Valentina: Meet you on the beach in five!

I found a blanket in my bedroom closet and gently opened the door. Ryan's bedroom was right next to mine. Not hearing a sound, I tiptoed down the stairs, thankful I'd decided to put a carpet runner over the stairs so they wouldn't creak. In the kitchen, I left the lights off while I grabbed a bottle of wine and swiped two glasses from the cabinet before sliding the back door open. I'd have to remember to thank Ford again for ridding the door of the loud squeak the other morning while I was sleeping.

The moon was bright tonight. It lit the beach enough to see and made the water, which was unusually calm, glisten majestically. At the bottom of the stairs, Ford held up a blanket, a bottle of wine, and two wine glasses.

I laughed. "Great minds think alike."

He reached around to his back pocket and pulled something out. Holding up a bottle opener, he smiled. "Where's your opener?"

I hadn't thought of that. I chuckled. "Okay, you win."

We left my supplies under the stairs and took Ford's with us for our walk. He took my hand in his, and it felt so natural. "There's a dune about a quarter mile up ahead and no houses in the area."

"Are you planning on something happening that we need privacy for?" I bumped my shoulder to his.

"It's our last night together. I'm planning on something happening *at least three times.*"

He'd been teasing, but hearing him say it was our last night together made me feel anxious. My fears all came rushing back. What if he'd changed his mind? He'd been so persistent up until recently. Had he decided a summer fling was all he wanted? My nerves got the best of me as we walked, and I grew quiet.

When we arrived at the tall section of the dunes, Ford stopped, brushed some sticks out of the way, and spread out the blanket. He uncorked the wine, poured two glasses, and we sat side by side, facing the ocean.

It was such a serene night. The water washed against the shore fifty feet away, and the sound was almost hypnotic. The moon illuminated the ocean, casting a wide streak of light across the sparkling, dark water. We both stared. We'd just gotten here, and I already wanted this night to never end.

With that thought, I took a deep breath.

"Val, I...." Ford spoke at the same exact moment, I said, "Ford, I..."

We both laughed.

"You first," he said.

"No, go ahead. Really," I stalled. "I was only going to comment about how we should've done this earlier in the summer. Come down to the beach, I mean."

Ford nodded. He picked up a twig—a small one, a few inches long—and broke it in half, tossing part of it. Then he broke the small piece a second time and did the same.

"Is everything okay?" I turned from the water to face him, tilting my head.

"Yeah. I'm just tired from my trip."

"Oh. Okay."

He shifted to face me and spent the longest time just studying my face. Finally, he brushed a piece of hair from my shoulder and began to speak. "This summer has been incredible. When we first met, you were looking to find yourself. But something happened over the last few months. You stopped trying to find the person you were, and let yourself be who you are now." He swallowed. "I'll never forget this summer."

That sounded an awful lot like goodbye. A lump in my throat made it difficult to speak. "I feel different than I did when I came out here. I'm not mad at my ex-husband anymore. I'm not as worried about what people I don't even know think." I smiled. "Though I don't think I'll be shopping for anal beads by myself again in the near future."

He smirked. "That's a shame."

"But seriously. You're right. I feel like I've started to find who I am. And a lot of that is because of you. You made me stop looking back, stop clinging to my fears, and just *be*. It has been a really long time since I just lived in the moment."

I took a deep breath and looked down, gathering the strength to say what I'd been thinking about for a while.

"I know I said this couldn't be more than a summer fling. But it was. It is. And...I don't want it to end, Ford."

Our eyes locked, and I saw so much turmoil swimming in his. He broke our gaze to look out over the ocean for a long time, and when he looked back at me, a pool of tears had built in his eyes.

Oh my God. Those don't look like tears of happiness.

He took my hand and squeezed it. "You were the one who was right. I was wrong. You need to go live a little and experience things. I'm happy we had this summer—but that's all it could ever be."

It felt like an elephant sat on my chest. My heart snapped in half like that twig he'd so easily broken a few moments ago. Even though I'd known this was a distinct possibility, I wasn't ready for how much it hurt.

I'd opened myself up for this, and it made it that much more painful to be rejected. I don't know how I held in the sobbing, but I definitely couldn't speak. So I simply nodded.

Ford took that to mean I agreed and pulled me to him for a hug. Silent tears ran down my cheeks as I clung to him. We rocked back and forth and held on tight. The way he held me so close, if he hadn't just said what he'd said, I might've thought that he was holding on because he didn't want it to end, either.

After the longest time, I discreetly wiped away my tears and pulled my head back to look at him. I was glad we were in moonlight and not daylight so he couldn't see the color of my face—I knew it had to be red and blotchy.

"Make love to me, Ford."

I wanted to get lost in him at least one more time. He looked into my eyes, as if making sure that was what I really wanted. And in that moment, it hit me hard. God, I'd fallen in love with him.

I nodded, even though he hadn't asked a question, and whispered, "Please."

Ever so slowly, Ford wrapped his hands around my cheeks and started to kiss me. I poured everything I was feeling from my mouth into his—sadness, longing, love, *desire*. I wanted to show him with my touch how I felt about him, because I knew I'd never get the chance to say the words now.

The kiss was so passionate and tender, and my heart beat so fast in my chest. When he guided me to lie down on the blanket, our lips separated, and we stared into each other's eyes. It felt...I don't know...monumental somehow. Like my life was going to change after this night in some major way, and I wasn't so sure it was for the better anymore.

But I needed him inside of me. I needed to feel the connection one last time. Reaching up, I cradled his neck and pulled his lips back down to mine. The feel of his weight on top of me was almost crushing, but it was exactly what I needed.

Ford took it slow, kissing down my neck and across my collarbone. He kissed along my jaw and up to my ear. "You're so incredibly beautiful, Valentina. I'll remember this summer forever."

I was never so lost in a moment. I heard nothing else, saw nothing else, felt only him. Somehow we shed our clothes and then he was at my entrance, once again looking down at me.

He pushed inside with a tenderness that made my tears begin to flow once more. He kissed me again in the nick of time. We'd always been connected, but this time was different—it felt like our minds, bodies, and souls were all in alignment as he began to move in and out of me. Nothing had ever felt so incredible. I'd heard people say when they made love they became one—yet, until this moment, I'd never actually experienced it myself. But we were one, connected in every way we could be—even if just for those brief moments. It was a heartbreaking yet magical experience.

I wrapped my arms and legs around him and held on for dear life. Though I felt my orgasm building, I couldn't have prepared myself for the intensity when it hit. Earth-shattering. Or maybe it wasn't so much the earth breaking to pieces, but my own heart inside my chest. I cried out, letting Ford's name sing from my lips like a hymn. He tensed and groaned into my mouth as he released inside of me.

We lay panting for a long time, his head hanging over my shoulder with his face in the blanket.

When he finally lifted it, his voice was raspy. "I'm going to miss you."

I couldn't return the sentiment because I was too terrified that if I opened my mouth, uncontrolled blubbering and an affirmation of love might spill out.

So instead, I hugged him and thought to myself...

I'm going to miss you, too. More than you'll ever know.

We made love twice more that night. And the intensity and passion never dulled one bit. After round three, my head rested on his chest, and I heard Ford's breathing become slower and deeper. He'd drifted off, but I couldn't. I wanted to savor every last minute we had left together.

chapter twenty-seven

Ford

I wasn't good with goodbyes.

The last time I had to say one of any significance had been when I said goodbye to my parents. The wake had just ended, and the funeral director had asked me if I wanted to take a few moments in private to say farewell. My sister was too young and waited outside with my aunt while they shut me in the room with two caskets, lying side by side.

While most of those days were a blur, I remember sitting there all by myself so clearly. The priest had said something that stuck with me: *Goodbyes are not forever and aren't the end; they are only until we meet again.*

Maybe I just needed to believe that was true that day, but those words gave me the strength to walk out of that room without actually feeling like it was the last time I'd see them.

Today felt a lot like that. I knew in my heart that letting Valentina go was what I had to do—yet that didn't make it any damn easier. Especially since I was pretty certain if I hadn't made a clean break last night, she would have given a shot to continuing things.

That made it so much harder. It killed me to know she was hurting, and it pained me to be the cause of it. But I also knew in my heart it had to be like this. She *needed* this time. She'd said it all along, and I was too selfish to believe it. I guess I have dear old Dad to thank for making me see the realities of a relationship.

That was pretty ironic to think about right now.

I carried my sister's bags out to the car. Somehow she'd come with two suitcases and now, eight weeks later, had four, in addition to some artwork she wanted me to ship to her at school. Her flight wasn't until tonight—almost seven hours from now. But she needed to stop at my apartment to pick up a few things she'd left behind and then had to be at the airport two hours before departure. Traffic this time of the year could be three hours—or even five—from Montauk to Manhattan, so that seven hours didn't actually have too much padding built into it.

My sister tossed a backpack in the passenger seat of my car. "I'm going to go next door and say goodbye to Valentina. You want to come?" she said.

Is skipping saying goodbye and taking her home with me an option instead? I shook my head. "You go ahead. I have to grab a few things from the house still. I'll stop over in a minute."

Bella went next door, and I took a seat on the couch. I'd been up since we walked home at dawn, so all of my shit was packed and in the car already. I looked around the living room. Everything was back in its place, just like when we'd arrived at the start of the summer. Yet nothing was the same. I leaned my elbows on my knees, and my head dropped into my hands. My mind had been spinning for the better part of a week, but this morning was the worst. I felt dizzy as I went back and forth, debating with myself nonstop.

Maybe this didn't have to be the end? Maybe we'd both be back out here next summer?

Goodbyes are not forever and aren't the end; they are only until we meet again.

Or maybe I was fucking fooling myself just to make today easier, like I did at the funeral.

A part of me wanted to propose *same time next year if we're both single?* But that wouldn't be fair. I knew Val cared about me, had feelings for me. She needed to be free to experience and figure out what she really wanted. As much as it made me want to punch the wall at the thought—she needed to date. So I couldn't *say* same time next year. But that couldn't stop me from thinking it. When you loved someone, it was easier to go on day after day if you believed it wasn't truly over.

Jesus Christ.

When you love someone...

Did I love her?

I thought about the way I could stare at her for hours while she slept. How I felt calmer and less stressed than I had in years. How I had zero interest in other women. How she's the first person I wanted to call if anything good or bad happened.

I tugged at my hair.

Fuck.

When the hell did that happen?

A knock at the front screen door ripped me from my pity party. Val smiled sadly on the other side before letting herself in.

"Bella went to town to get junk food for the long day of travel. Ryan was going to get breakfast, so they went together." She looked around the empty room. "Looks like you're all ready to close up."

I nodded.

She came and sat down next to me on the couch. Her face was free of all makeup, and it looked like she might be a little puffy from crying. Though we were up all night, so it could've been that, too.

I put my arm around her shoulder and pulled her to me. I didn't have the strength to look directly at her and do this.

"I suck at goodbyes, Val." I shook my head and looked down.

Her voice was soft. "So do I."

We were quiet for a long time. I didn't want to walk out that door without letting her know what she meant to me, but I also needed to make sure I cut the cord. Town was only a few minutes away, so we didn't have very long before Bella and Ryan were back.

I racked my brain to come up with the right words, but then realized I didn't have to figure out how to summarize everything I was feeling. A wise woman had once done that for me.

I turned and cupped her cheek, allowing my thumb to stroke her soft skin one last time. "A while back you asked me if it was possible to have the right feelings at the wrong time. I didn't understand how that was possible. But I do now."

A tear leaked from one eye. But then she raised her chin, swallowed, and forced a smile through her sadness. And God, her strength made me fall a little bit harder. I heard the crunch of gravel next door and pulled her to me for one last kiss.

We stared into each other's eyes until Bella opened the front door. "You ready to go, pain-in-the-ass big brother?"

She was completely oblivious at what she'd walked in on. I took one last, long look at Valentina's face and nodded. "I guess so."

Val and I stood. "Take care of yourself, Val."

"You, too, Ford."

Valentina walked out first, then Bella, then me. By the time I locked the house up, Bella was already getting into the passenger seat. Val stood at the bottom of her stairs, holding onto the banister. I had to fight myself with every step I took down the stairs and to the car not to run back and grab her—scream what she meant to me and fuck letting her go.

But I wasn't walking away for me. I was doing it for her, and somehow that gave me the strength—though just barely.

I started the car and looked up from behind the wheel one last time before backing out of the driveway. Our eyes met. Inwardly, I said what I needed to believe was possible, but on the outside I only waved.

Same time next year, maybe?

chapter
twenty-eight

Ford

Two weeks dragged by.

I had no contact with Valentina after I left with Bella. Our only connection had been Montauk and Match, and the summer was over. Though I had taken to stalking Match.com once or twice a day—checking to see if her profile had changed to active. Logically, I understood that I hadn't fought for her because she needed to see other people—so her profile *should* change to active. But it was going to slice my heart in two when it did.

In a fucked-up way, I wanted that to happen. I wanted the pain, wanted to know she'd moved on. Maybe being jealous and pissed off would make it easier for me to do just that.

Tonight I'd made plans with Logan, even though I hadn't been in the mood to go out. He'd busted my balls about being scarce all summer until I agreed to meet for drinks. I figured one drink wouldn't kill me. We sat at the bar bullshitting for two hours. I'd intentionally picked a place I knew wasn't a hookup hotspot. I wasn't in the mood to spend the night talking to a bunch of women I had no interest in.

But I guess that didn't work out too well.

"Are these seats taken?" a tall blonde said.

I looked around the bar. There were plenty of other open seats. But Logan beat me to the answer.

He pulled out the stool next to him. "We were holding them, just waiting for the two of you to get here."

I rolled my eyes.

The women giggled.

"I'm Gianna," the blonde said. She had on a low-cut red shirt, and her tits were spilling out of it.

"I'm Amber." The brunette offered me her hand.

"Logan Flint." He lifted Gianna's hand and brought it to his lips.

No one flirted more than Logan. He didn't know how to turn it off. It either got him laid or got him smacked—it was fifty-fifty, odds he did pretty damn well with.

"Ford." I nodded and shook Barbie Number One's hand.

I might not have been in the mood for company, but there was nothing wrong with my eyesight. They were both pretty. Sexy, actually. Though, I found myself comparing them to Valentina.

Val had a natural beauty, a girl-next-door look that let you see who she was right away. Most women wore masks. I'd never understood why they put so much make-up on, especially when they were young. They painted their entire faces—eyebrows, eyelids, cheekbones, noses, lips—until their skin looked artificial. They thought it hid their flaws, but to me it hid their beauty.

Logan called the bartender over and told him to put whatever the ladies were drinking on his tab. While they were ordering, he leaned over to me. "Dibs on the blonde."

"You can have both, buddy."

He squinted at me like I had two heads. As fucked up as it was, it felt wrong to be talking to women in a bar.

I was single and hadn't spoken to Valentina in two weeks, yet my heart felt like it was cheating. I had to force myself to stick around and finish my beer while making conversation. Despite my mood, the ladies turned out to be pretty nice. I'd judged them because they cared about their appearances and approached men in a bar. But Amber turned out to be an attorney, and Gianna was a teacher. I found myself asking Gianna questions about her job—what she'd thought of her first year teaching and what time she got out in the afternoons.

Basically, I was desperate to know how Valentina was enjoying her first few weeks and used this woman as a substitute.

The bar had gotten busier, and they'd turned up the music, which made it difficult to hold a conversation.

Gianna held one hand to her ear. "Would you guys want to get out of here? I only live a few blocks away, and it's so loud."

Logan jumped at the offer. "Absolutely." He lifted his hand for the bartender to close out the tab. I might've been substituting Gianna for Val in a conversation about teaching, but there was no way I was substituting her for anything else.

I leaned in to Gianna so she could hear me. "Thank you for the offer. But I have an early day tomorrow, so I'm gonna head out."

She pouted. "You sure? Maybe just one drink?"

"Yeah. I'm sure." I stood and reached into my pocket to pull out my billfold. Dropping a hundred on the bar, I turned to Logan, "I'm gonna head out, buddy."

His brows drew down. "What? Why?"

"I have a meeting first thing in the morning."

"So? You're the boss. Push it back to the afternoon."

"Can't," I said.

Though, that wasn't exactly true. I could push back my morning marketing meeting if I wanted to. I just didn't want to. It was probably against bro code to duck out as Logan's wingman, but I was confident he'd still be going home with them both.

Logan attempted to object. But I'd already said good-night to the ladies. I slapped my buddy on the back. "Talk to you later."

He shook his head and mumbled so only I could hear him. "You're crazy."

Yeah, crazy about a woman I *might* get to see next year.

I took the long way home.

It wasn't the fastest route, but it was only about seven blocks out of my way. Logan and I had met at a bar up-town, not too far from Eve's restaurant. If I walked two blocks north and five blocks east, I could jump on the R train, and that would let me off a block from my building. So what if I'd passed the N train five blocks ago and that dropped me just as close? I was still, technically, on my way home.

I told myself I was just going to pass by, not stop, and definitely not go inside. With that agenda, I wasn't even sure what the hell the point was; yet I was compelled to at least walk past.

Unfortunately, even though I'd slowed to a snail's pace a building before the restaurant, when I walked past

Eve's bistro, the only thing I'd accomplished was taking twelve more steps. No one happened to be coming in or out, and Eve was nowhere in sight. Deflated—though, not sure what I'd expected to happen—I kept walking. But by the time I made it to the corner, my mind had started to reel.

It's Friday night. It wouldn't be out of the ordinary for Val to have dinner at her friend's restaurant.

She might be inside.

Maybe I could just look in the window and see.

Yeah, I'll just go back and take one quick look.

Turning around, I started back toward the restaurant.

Fuck. What am I doing?

What if Val's in there with a date?

What if they walk out the door laughing and smiling just as I pass by?

I think I'm losing it.

I grumbled to myself, yet slowed as I arrived back at the restaurant door. When I was almost all the way to the other end of the long windows, I attempted to look casual. Stopping, I took out my phone and played with it. My back was to the window, so I turned around to look inside. Only there was too much glare, and all I could see was a reflection of myself. I let out a sigh of frustration, shoved my phone in my pocket, and turned to walk away once again.

But I only made it three steps.

"Fuck this," I groaned. I had to know. Backing up to the window once again, I cupped my hands to peer inside, my nose pressed to the glass. I could see inside now, but there wasn't too much going on. A few tables were filled, but the restaurant was half empty—which I suppose made sense, since it was getting pretty late. I surveyed the room, scanning each table. At one point, I saw a flash of dark, curly hair, and for half a second I got excited... though, it turned out not to be her.

My shoulders slumped. I'd been looking into the room and not directly in front of me, so a knock on the glass startled me. I finally looked at the couple sitting literally right on the other side of where my face was pressed. The guy held up his hands in the universal *what the fuck are you doing* gesture. *Shit.*

I waved an apology and took off.

Perfect. Now I'm not just watching her Match account, Instagram, and Facebook. I'm turning into a full-fledged stalker. I needed to go the hell home.

At least one relationship from Match.com had worked out.

A few weeks later, I sat in the conference room with my marketing team going through the first two months of results from our advertising campaign. It turned out to be the best bang for our buck we'd ever had—more successful than billboards, newspaper ads, and advertising in commercial real estate mags.

The marketing team had come up with a few new advertisements to run—four video ads—each one targeting a different demographic. So far, we'd only used static graphics. Each twenty-second video featured a different couple who'd met on Match.com and also used shared office space. Apparently, people ate up those short vignettes where the happy couple tells their bullshit love story, so the click rates are through the roof.

Though today, I fucking hated them. *Screw these happy people when I have to be miserable.*

The spots were shot in our offices, and the couples mentioned why they loved using our shared workspace. They seemed more like Match.com success stories than advertising, but I guessed that was the point. I was able to stomach two, anxious to be done with the happy couples projected onto the whiteboard.

The third couple came on the screen, and a woman who was probably in her mid-thirties said, "My parents are divorced. I'm divorced. Ron was the first person I met on Match.com."

Ron piped in, smiling at her. "We hit it off, but *she* didn't want a relationship."

The camera zoomed down to the man's knee, where the woman laid her hand. "I went out with a bunch of men because it felt like I was supposed to." She shrugged. "But I just kept thinking about Ron."

The dude laughed. "She was in denial, but I knew right away."

The camera moved in close to their faces, and they looked into each other's eyes. Then it zoomed down to her belly—her pregnant belly—and her hand, adorned with a wedding ring, rubbed her stomach. "Sometimes you just have to take a chance."

The video then moved on to how he also took a chance and started his own business and needed impressive office space without the commitment and price tag. But I'd stopped listening.

I stood abruptly before they could even show the last video. "Good job. Run with it."

I saw the confusion on my team's faces as I walked toward the door. They looked at each other, silently asking what the hell was wrong with me. I just didn't give a shit.

Later that night, my office phone rang. The caller ID said it was Logan. I didn't feel like talking, but he'd called my cell earlier, so I figured I'd make sure everything was alright. Tossing my pen on the desk, I leaned back into my chair.

He started talking before I even said hello. "Remember the twins from Chi Omega? The gymnasts who had those juicy lips?"

I nodded. "Jenna and Justine. Jenna was a business major and Justine pre-med."

"Whatever. I saw them in the elevator of my building today at work. Haven't seen them in a few years."

"How are they doing?"

"They're fucking hotter than ever. That's how they're doing."

"Are you calling to tell me you hooked up with them both? Because I really don't want to hear the details."

"No. I'm calling to tell you Jenna asked about you. She said she had the biggest crush on you back in college."

"Oh yeah? That must've bruised your ego."

"Not at all. I'll take either one. I still can't tell the difference anyway. We have plans with them Friday night."

"We?"

"Yeah. The four of us."

"No, thanks."

"Dude...do you know how flexible they are?"

I still had no interest. I rubbed my eyes with one hand. "I'm not up for it."

"They'll get you up for it. Come on. What are you going to do? Spend the next year abstinent, only to drive out to Montauk with your hopes up on Memorial Day and have Valerie's new, forty-year-old boyfriend answer the fucking door when you knock?"

My jaw flexed. "It's Valentina."

I should've never told him about what was going on with me, what went down this summer. But the day after

I left him alone with the two women who'd tried to pick us up at the bar, he showed up at my office to ask what the hell was going on. And like a pussy, I unloaded my tale of woe on him.

But the thing was, I knew Logan—he could be relentless, and believe it or not, he was concerned about me. He just thought getting me laid was the way to make me feel better. I had no doubt that if I said no, he'd be standing in my office at some point tomorrow. I wouldn't even put it past him to show up with the twins at my place Friday night.

"Fine."

"Excellent." I could hear the smile in his voice. "You won't regret it, buddy. I'm telling you, that Janna had a twinkle in her eye when she said your name."

"It's Jenna."

"Whatever. Meet us at seven at Boggs for dinner."

Dinner wasn't terrible, mostly because it felt like four old friends from college catching up, rather than a double date. Though, that was despite Logan's constant flirting with Justine. Actually, he'd been flirting with Justine at the bar while we waited for our table. But when we were seated for dinner, he started flirting with Jenna, too. The bonehead still couldn't tell them apart—even though I'd pointed out that one was wearing red and the other black.

After we finished eating, Logan suggested we go over to the bar across the street. I'd ditched him last time, so I went along with it, even though I would have rather gone home. At one point he and Justine went to dance, leaving Jenna and me alone to talk.

"So...are you seeing anyone?" She sipped her vodka and cranberry through a skinny red straw.

I tried to hide my flinch. "No."

"Me either. I've been so busy with work that I haven't gone out on a date in months." She smiled and tilted her head. "What's your excuse?"

I didn't want to be rude, but I also didn't want to explain anything. Luckily, the bartender came by and saved me from answering.

"Can I get you two another round?"

I looked to Jenna.

"Sure," she said. "I'd love another."

"Just for her, please. I'm good."

The bartender walked away.

"You're not joining me for another drink?" She smiled.

"I have a lot of work to do in the morning."

"Oh. Okay." She reached for her purse. "Can you excuse me for just a minute? I need to run to the ladies' room."

"Of course." I stood and waited for her to get out of her seat.

While she was in the ladies' room, I took out my phone and started to scroll through email. Nothing caught my attention, so I opened up Instagram.

The first photo that popped up was a picture on Eve's account. We'd followed each other over the summer. *Fuck.* I shouldn't have taken out my phone. It felt like someone kicked me in the stomach. Eve and her husband Tom were smiling wide for the camera on one side of a table, and sitting across from them, looking just as happy, was Val and some douchebag. How did I know the guy was a douchebag? Simple. He was sitting next to my girl. The picture was like a bad car accident. I knew it was stupid to look, but I couldn't stop staring. After way too long, I managed to drop my eyes down to read the caption.

Shenanigans are overdue.

Logically, I knew I had zero right to get pissed. She's supposed to move on, go on dates, experience life—that's the fucking reason we weren't together. But did it have to be so easy for her?

I looked down at her face again. Over the summer, I'd learned her smiles—the nervous one, the fake one she put on when she was trying to be polite, and the real one she'd given me so often. And that there, that was the real damn thing. I wanted to hurl my phone across the room in the worst way.

But because I'm a glutton for punishment, I instead clicked from Instagram over to Match.com. I only had to type in V and her name auto populated, probably because I'd searched it so many times. Her profile popped up on my screen, and I got the wind knocked out of me. Val's profile status had been changed sometime over the past twenty-four hours—from *Inactive* to *Active*.

Fuck.

Fuck.

Fuck.

I'd left it up to fate, and it looked like fate had fucked me.

Jenna returned from the bathroom while I was still staring at my phone.

"Did you miss me?" She batted her eyelashes, and her newly glossed lips shimmered.

I should get out of here with her. If Val could move on so easily, so could I.

But...God, I was such a pussy.

I stood and dug into my pocket for cash. Tossing enough on the bar to cover three times what we drank, I looked at Jenna and held up my phone. "I'm sorry. Something's come up. I need to run."

"Oh no. Is everything okay?"

"Yeah. No. Yeah. I just...need to call it a night. I'm really sorry. It was nice seeing you, Jenna."

"Do you...want my number?"

I didn't want to insult her more than I already had by not calling. "I was honest earlier when I said I wasn't seeing anyone. But I did meet someone this summer, and I'm just not over her yet."

Jenna smiled sadly. "Lucky girl." She opened her purse and dug something out. Handing me a business card, she said, "If you want help getting over her, give me a call. Not many men would have admitted what you just did, and I really appreciate that. I like you. It doesn't need to be more than it is. Call if you just want some company one night."

I leaned in and kissed her cheek, taking the card from her hand. "Thanks, Jenna. Take care of yourself."

chapter twenty-nine

Valentina

"So...any interesting men at work?" Eve poured wine into her glass, but I held my hand over mine, stopping her from refilling.

"You asked me that a week ago when we went to lunch."

"I know. But you were sulking still. I was hoping you'd notice some once you started smiling again. And why don't you want more wine?"

I shrugged. "The smile is still fake. I'm getting good at it. And I don't want more wine because I just feel worse after I have too much to drink."

Tonight was movie night. Eve and I hadn't had our regular monthly get-together in a while. First I'd been in Montauk all summer, and then when I was finally back home, I'd had a ton going on the first few weeks of work. Between open school night, preparing lesson plans, and settling back at home, the only thing I seemed to find time to do was pout.

It had been my turn to pick the movie, so I'd rented some sappy, sad drama about a dog dying.

"My mother used to have a saying. *Pain makes us strong. Tears make us brave. A broken heart makes us wise. But wine makes us forget all that crap.*"

I'd attempted to shake off the heavy feeling of melancholy, but I just couldn't get past it, no matter how hard I tried.

"When Ryan and I split up, I felt lost. I wasn't sure how to be just me when we'd been a couple for so long. But thinking back, I never really longed for Ryan as a man. I longed for the comfort of who we were. It was almost like quitting smoking—you know it's not good for you...but yet when you stop, you feel like you're missing a big part of your life. It's just hard to get over the habit. It's different with Ford. I miss *him*...not a routine or couple-dom. I miss sitting around talking at 2 a.m. I miss the way he looked at me—like I was something special, the way he cupped my cheeks before he kissed me. The way he made me laugh. When we were together, everything just felt super easy and natural, and he made me feel...I don't know...safe. Even though I'd been cheated on and hurt, I felt like I could trust him. You know?"

The hopeful spark in Eve's eyes fizzled out. "You're really in love with him."

I nodded. "I don't even know when it happened. One minute I was minding my own business and getting by each day, and the next I couldn't wait to wake up in the morning. I thought it was safe to have a good time with him because I never expected it to be more than just that. You know? I just didn't expect it to *be* him."

"I get it. I really do. I didn't expect the love of my life to be a man in his fifties who wears a Mister Rogers sweater and goes to bed at nine o'clock. But that's how it happens—with the most unexpected person, at the most unexpected time. When we looked forward, we couldn't see anything. But all of a sudden we look back and shake our heads—how did we miss seeing this is what would happen when we looked at him the first time, because suddenly it's as clear as day."

I sighed. "I need to move on."

"Are you sure that's what you need, Val? Maybe you should talk to him. Maybe there's a reason you can't move on. Sometimes you need to follow your gut and fight for what feels right. He might be feeling the same way."

"No. It was only supposed to be a summer fling. I'm being silly."

"You're not being silly. You should have time to grieve the loss of someone you care so much about. Just don't let it be two years, like after the divorce. Okay?"

I nodded. "Anyway, to get back to your original question, there is a nice-looking guy at work. He's in my department. Italian is his first language, so he has a sexy accent."

Eve sipped her wine. "Go on. Tell me more."

I shrugged. "He's been a teacher for fifteen years, but just started this year because he moved to New Jersey from Connecticut. He's a widower at only forty."

"Wow. How did his wife die?"

"I'm not sure. He hasn't said. He just mentioned that his wife died three years ago, and he moved back to New York to be closer to some family. He has a teenage daughter."

"How's his ass?"

I chuckled. "I didn't notice."

"What's he look like?"

"I don't know. Italian—dark skin, dark eyes, dark hair. He's nice looking."

"*Nice looking*. So is my dad. He's not hot?"

"What can I tell you? It's hard to compare to the last man I saw naked."

"Oh, God. Sweetheart, you can't compare anything to Ford. He's gorgeous and young. If you let that be your standard, you'll die an old maid. Comparison is the thief of joy. Don't do it."

"I know. I really do. It's just going to take some time." I got up and refilled the chip bowl, setting it down on the coffee table in front of Eve. "Mark called me last week."

"Oh yeah? I liked him. He seemed like a nice guy."

"He is. We actually talked on the phone for over an hour. He said he'd been going back and forth for two weeks on whether to call or not. But he wanted to check in and see how I liked teaching. It was really good to hear from him. He had some pretty funny stories to share about his first few weeks. He's teaching in a tough neighborhood in Brooklyn."

"And..."

"He asked how things were going with Ford and me. I said it had ended. He suggested we get together to catch up soon. But I think he knows things between us are only ever going to be platonic."

"Why? You should go out with him. Get back out there."

"Oh my God. The last time you pushed me to go out with someone, I got my heart broken."

"Yes, but you got yourself back out there. It had been twenty years since you spent time with a man. Actually, you'd *never* spent time with a man because back then they were just boys. This was just a summer. It will be easier to get back out there this time than it was after a two-decade marriage."

I wasn't so sure Eve was right about that. "I'll think about it."

She smiled. "That's my girl."

———

"Hey, babe."

Ugh. Does he ever listen to anything I say? I should've gone with my first instinct when I'd seen my ex-husband's name flash on my cell.

"If we're going to call each other nicknames, I'm going to use the one I favored *after* you moved out."

He ignored my comment. "Listen, about the summer place."

Great. I get to talk to you and *be reminded about my summer with Ford all in one conversation.* "What about it?"

"The piling fix will cost about thirty grand. But that's just a Band-Aid. We need all the stilts replaced in the next five to seven years to repair it correctly, and that's almost twice the price."

Wonderful. And I'm responsible for half of that, according to our divorce settlement. "I don't have that kind of money. You know I just went back to work."

"Yeah. I don't have it either. That's why I think we should dump the place."

"What? *No!*"

"The market out there is hot right now. We could get almost five times what we paid for it fifteen years ago."

"Yes, but then what? Neither of us would be able to afford a replacement."

"You might be able to pick up a small place up toward the lighthouse that isn't on the beach. I don't really even like it out there anymore, so I wouldn't rebuy."

"I love our house. We can't sell it."

"Well, if we don't do something, it will fall into the water within the next few years. That'll solve our problem."

God, he really was always a jerk. "We *do* need to do something—pay for the repair."

"So you're gonna come up with sixty grand, then?"

"Sixty? Thirty would be my half."

"Told you I don't have the thirty either."

"But our divorce agreement requires us to each pay half."

"Can't pay what I don't have."

Ryan made a good salary. Although, he was paying me alimony and paying college tuition and still had to foot the bill for his own house. I wanted to argue with him and say that was his problem, but it was actually *our* problem, and it became *my* problem if I wanted to keep the summer place.

"What if we take a mortgage on the Montauk house to pay for the repair?"

"I can't afford another payment, Val."

"I'll pay it. I have a job now. You only have two more years of alimony. When that's done, you can help me pay it off."

"See if you can even get a mortgage, and we'll talk about it. Otherwise, I don't think we have a choice but to sell it."

Great. I'm sure the bank will love my one month of employment history.

chapter thirty

Ford

"**F**ord? Is that you?"

Shit.

I'd started passing by Eve's restaurant pretty much every day, but it was the first time in four weeks that I'd run into her. I'd made it a few steps past the door when she opened it and called after me.

"Oh, hey. I was just passing by. I have an appointment a few blocks away or I would have stopped in to say hi." *Yeah, right.*

Eve gave me a suspect smile, but I wasn't sure which part of my bullshit she wasn't buying. She thumbed toward the restaurant behind her. "I was setting the table, getting ready for dinner reservations, when I saw you walk by."

I nodded and shoved my hands into my pockets. I really was a shit liar. "How's it going?"

She tilted her head. "Good. Busy. You?"

"Good. Good." I had to ask. It would have been rude not to. "How's Valentina doing?"

She seemed to think about the answer before speaking. "She's doing amazing. Loves her job. Met an Italian teacher. Getting back into the swing of things."

"An Italian teacher?" Apparently, I needed it spelled out for me.

Eve shrugged as if the next words weren't going to make me feel like she'd kicked me square in the nuts. "She's taking it slow, of course. The whole dating scene is new for her."

I swallowed and nodded, but my expression went from bullshit happy to wounded. "I gotta run."

"Right." Eve smiled like she'd enjoyed delivering the blow. "Your meeting nearby. I guess you have a lot of those. You should get to that. Take care of yourself, Ford."

The entire night and next morning, I was fucking useless. I sat in on a meeting and read a few emails, but I couldn't tell you what the hell either was about. Thankfully, it was Friday. I walked out of my office at only two o'clock.

My assistant looked up. "Late lunch today?"

I shook my head. "I'm going to take a ride over to the Long Island City property, just to check in. I won't be back. If you need me, you can reach me on my cell."

"Okay. Have a great weekend.'"

"Yeah. You, too, Esmée."

I walked to work, but kept my car parked in a garage a few blocks from the office. Since it was still early, I managed to navigate through the city and out the tunnel in less than a half hour. My mind was stuck replaying everything about Valentina over and over again...from the time we spent together to what Eve had said last night. The only good thing was that being so sorry for myself about what I'd lost kept me from thinking about my father and all the shit that had gone down in Chicago.

It was a beautiful, warm day—we wouldn't have too many of those left now that it was almost mid October. So I decided to get off the Expressway at the next exit and pull over to put the top down on my car. Some fresh air might help to clear my head on the half-hour drive. But as the roof lifted off the top of my car, instead of blue sky, all I saw was a billboard.

A giant damn Match.com advertisement that had to be three-stories tall.

I laughed sardonically and shook my head. *Forget fate*, it read. *Take your future into your own hands. Join Match.com today. She's waiting for you.*

The universe is really fucking with me today.

"Yeah," I grumbled. "She's not waiting for me."

I took a deep breath, put the car into drive, and turned on the radio—only to have the song end and a new one come on. One by the Backstreet Boys. I reached down to turn it off but couldn't bring myself to push the damn button.

Forget fate? It was pretty hard to when it was busy throwing shit in your face.

Long Island Expressway West—Manhattan.

The large, green road sign up ahead showed an arrow pointing to the two left lanes. The sign next to it had an arrow pointing right.

Long Island Expressway East—Eastern Long Island.

Home was left. Yet when I came to the fork in the road, at the last second I jerked the car right and took the turn to get on heading east.

Why? I had no fucking idea. It just felt like I needed to go out to Montauk, for some reason. Maybe I needed to clear my head...I wasn't sure. Though, going to the place that reminded me of my parents sham of a happy marriage *and* the woman I loved who'd just started dating another man probably wasn't the best place to find clarity.

But once I got on the road, there was no turning back. For some reason, it was where I needed to be today.

The fall traffic wasn't too bad, and I pulled down Old Montauk Highway just as the sun started to go down. I still had the top down, and the air temperature seemed to drop twenty degrees between the loss of daylight and the breeze blowing off the ocean. Montauk was a ghost town this time of year. Most of the driveways were empty as I passed, including the one next to mine—not that I'd expected anyone to be around. I pulled into our adjoining driveways, the sound of gravel crunching under my tires reminding me so much of summer.

With no suitcase or any bags at all, I parked and took a deep breath of the fresh air before getting out. Closing my eyes, I smelled the ocean and summer. Maybe this really was what I needed to feel better.

Though, that fleeting thought didn't last long. In fact, it disappeared the moment I opened my eyes and started to get out of the car.

What the fuck?

What the actual fuck?

How had I not noticed that when I pulled into the driveway?

I'd come out here searching for something—maybe a sign that it was time to move on. But what I hadn't expected was that sign to be literal.

Greeting me from the lawn next door was just that.

Sotheby's

For Sale

Exclusive Listing

I felt like I was sitting in someone else's house—like I'd walked into an Airbnb I'd rented for the weekend, rather than the back deck of a place where I'd pretty much felt at home my whole life. It was fucked up to feel like I didn't belong here anymore when this summer it had felt like the *only* place I belonged. What a difference in a short period of time.

I'd considered going into town and picking up a bottle of, well, anything, in order to forget the sign outside. But I'd come out here for clarity, and drowning my sorrows would only make things blurrier.

So instead, I sat on the back deck and finished watching the sun go down. I looked over at the empty deck next door and then back to the spot where we'd first danced to her favorite music. She'd smelled so good that day. I took a deep breath in and closed my eyes. I might've been nuts, but I could actually smell her scent, see her laughing as I took her in my arms, feel the way her soft body felt pressed up against mine. That's what felt like home now. Without her, everything felt empty. It wasn't the house or the place—it was me, inside.

I opened my eyes, and the most fucked-up thing happened. Right where I'd imagined myself dancing with Valentina, I saw my parents dancing—the same way they used to. My mother wore that white flowy dress she used to put on after she got out of the shower, and my dad had on navy blue swim trunks. They looked so goddamned happy. What a farce.

I sat outside, seeing things that weren't really there for a long time, until it was so dark I couldn't see the deck next door anymore. Then I went inside. I figured I'd crash here for the night since it was late. The end-of-season cleaning crew had stripped all the beds, so I went up to my parents' room where the spare blankets were kept and planned to just sleep on the couch. But when I pulled a blanket down, something came tumbling down along with it—straight to the floor and smashed all over the place.

My parents' Mason jars.

One of them, anyway. The other I saw tucked into the back of the closet behind the rest of the blankets.

Great. Just what I needed. Shattered glass to clean up and more memories of a life that was built on a lie.

I went to the kitchen closet to grab the broom and dustpan, and then back upstairs to the bedroom to sweep up the glass. God knows why, but I picked the folded little strips of paper out of the glass pile and set them aside on the dresser. Without looking at them, I wasn't even sure whose they were—my mother's or father's.

After I finished cleaning up, I scooped up the papers and opened the top drawer to put them in there for the time being.

But as I went to close the drawer, I couldn't do it.

I picked up one of the little slips and stared down at it in my hand. It felt like an invasion of privacy to read them, but it also felt like I was here for a reason and maybe this was part of it. Fate had been drawing me to this place all day, so why stop now. Wary, I slowly unfolded the first one and read.

Because I told you you've been hogging the sheet at night lately, and today you made the bed with two sheets so we could each have one.

I smiled. That sounded like something my mother would do for sure. Apparently, I'd gotten my father's jar.

That made it feel a little less intrusive—or I gave a shit about intruding on his privacy a hell of a lot less. I took another one from the drawer and unfolded it.

Because you swam with Annabella for an hour this afternoon, when all you really wanted to do was sit on the beach and read your book.

That was nice. Although it didn't make me any less angry with him for what he'd done.

Because when I went into the bathroom to get ready for bed, you'd already put the toothpaste on my tooth-brush for me.

I kept going.

Because you drove all the way to the Hamptons to get the book I'd been dying to read the day it came out and surprised me.

I started to get pissed at all the reminders of how good my mother was to my father. How the hell could he step out on her with how thoughtful she was? My jaw set tight as I continued to open them.

Because you forgave me when I didn't deserve for-giveness.

I froze. Did she know? I'd just assumed since they stayed together that she had no idea. I knew couples got past cheating sometimes, but it had to be a struggle, and I'd never seen any signs of hard times. From the outside, my parents had a picture-perfect marriage. I picked up another slip...there were still a dozen or so left.

Because you watch The Bachelor *just because I love it, even though you hate it.*

My brows drew together. My father hated that show, yet he sat with my mother while she watched it every week. I went back and re-read all of the slips of paper I'd opened already. I'd assumed these were my father's notes, but the closer I looked at the handwriting, the more I realized I'd been reading from my mother's jar all along.

But what the hell did he have to forgive her for?

I kept going, feeling more wary than ever. The rest shed no more light on what had gone on between the two of them, until I came to the very last one.

Because while fate decided we came into each other's lives, sometimes we have to fight to stay. And every day, you remind me we're worth the fight.

———————

I couldn't sleep. The blood in my veins seemed to be pumping so fast that it made it impossible to even lie down. I paced back and forth in the living room. Everything was just so fucked up. My father cheated on my mother, maybe my mother cheated on my father, or maybe she'd done something else to hurt him. Maybe she knew about his affair and chose to stay anyway. Maybe she'd even had her own. I'd never know, and at this point, I didn't want to know.

The most fucked-up part of it all was that I was looking at them to figure out how to live my own life. Before I'd gone to Chicago, I'd been so sure of things between Valentina and me. *She'd* been the one who wasn't sure. And when I'd come back, she'd obviously decided we should give pursuing things after the summer a try—exactly what I'd wanted. And I was the idiot who pushed her away. *Pushed her back into dating*. I shook my head thinking of the photo of her and that guy on Instagram.

Great fucking job, Ford.

Nice work!

If you love something, set it free, and if it doesn't come back, it was never yours.

That was a crock of shit.

If you love something and set it free—it serves you fucking right. You should've held on to that shit.

If she's here next year—that will be a sign.

Yeah. I got a sign out here, alright.

For. Fucking. Sale.

I raked my hands through my hair and tugged at the roots.

What the hell was I thinking?

When you love someone, you don't walk away. *Ever.*

Fuck.

Fuck.

Fuuuck.

I needed to see her.

Before it was too late.

If it wasn't already.

chapter
thirty-one

Valentina

You can't force feelings to exist any more than you can
force them to go away.

My study group get-together tonight was fun, and I
was glad I'd decided to stop sulking long enough to go
after all.

Allison hadn't been able to find a full-time, tenure-track position, so she took a job as a district-wide
permanent sub. Basically, she played sit-down-and-shut-
up for six, forty-two-minute periods a day. She wasn't
thrilled, but supposedly an Italian teacher in her district
was retiring at the end of the year, and she'd have a foot
in the door for that. Desiree had taken a three-month ma-
ternity leave replacement. It seemed Mark and I had been
lucky to get full-time spots with benefits for the year.

I'd taken the train to the restaurant so I could have
a glass of wine or two, and after dinner, Mark offered to
give me a lift home. My house was pretty much on his
way, so it felt weird to say no.

When we pulled up in front of my house, he put the car into park and turned to face me. "Tonight was fun. I'm glad you decided to come."

I smiled. "Me, too."

He caught my gaze. "So...things with you and young blood ended?

I swallowed. "Yeah."

Mark's nodded. "You seemed happy with him."

"I was."

He nodded and looked away for a minute. "If things don't work out with him, I'd love to take you out...as friends...or more."

It seemed like an odd way to phrase it...if things don't work out with him...after I'd just acknowledged we broke up. Mark saw the confusion on my face.

He lifted his chin toward my house. "Not sure he got the memo you broke up."

I didn't understand, but turned to look where Mark had been motioning. My heart skipped a beat.

Oh my God.

Ford.

He was sitting on my front porch in the dark.

"I...I...wasn't expecting him."

"I can see that. Are you going to be okay?"

Physically, yes. Mentally, probably not. "Umm... yeah...sure."

I wanted to get out of the car, but I couldn't seem to figure out how to move.

Luckily, Mark was a gentleman. While I sat there staring at the man sitting in front of my house, he got out and walked around to the passenger side and opened my door. Extending a hand, he helped me out of the car. Though my feet still didn't move.

Mark smiled sadly. "I'd give you a kiss on the cheek, but I have a feeling that might get my teeth knocked out. So I'm going to just say goodnight. Do you want me to walk you to the door?"

"Ummm... No. I'm good." I took a few hesitant steps and turned back. "Mark?"

He looked up.

"Thank you for being such a good friend."

He gave a resigned nod. "Anytime, Val. Anytime."

Somehow I managed to put one foot in front of the other while Mark pulled away. Ford stood when I got to the steps.

"Hey." His voice was raspy, and he looked a little disheveled, but God, he was so damn handsome. Any waning emotions I felt over losing him came barreling back. My pulse started to race full speed ahead just being near him, yet my mind was screaming *Run the other way*! He had such an intense, magnetic pull over me that it was like fighting gravity.

"What are you doing here?"

He looked down, and I thought it was an act of shame. *Oh my God. Is this a booty call?*

"Can we...go inside?"

My emotions were jumping all over the place. One minute I felt hope and warmth, and the next I was angry and cold.

I walked up the stairs, brushing past him. "Go to a bar, Ford. I'm sure you'll have no problem finding someone to go home with for the night."

"What? No." He reached out and grabbed my arm. "That's...that's not why I'm here." He raked a hand through his hair. "I meant, could we go inside to talk?"

I looked into his eyes and saw nothing but sincerity. And maybe a little fear. I nodded. "Okay. Come on in."

My keys jingled in my hand, shaking as I dug them out of my purse and opened the lock. Ford followed me in.

I pointed to the living room. "Just give me a minute. I'll be right out."

I took off my coat and hung it up, then headed straight to the bathroom. I needed a minute to get my head screwed on straight. Though five solid minutes didn't even begin to do that, so I went back out just as discombobulated as I'd been when I walked in.

"Do you want something to drink?" I certainly needed something.

Ford shook his head. "No, thanks."

I went to the kitchen and poured a very full glass of wine.

"Your house is really nice. I like the lampshades."

That made me smile. He'd picked the one thing Ryan hated most. "Thank you. I forgot you've never been here."

Ford was sitting on the chair, so I took a seat across from him on the couch. His elbows were on his knees, and his head was in his hands. I'd initially thought the disheveled look was because he was drunk, but now I could see it was stress.

"Is everything okay?"

He shook his head. "No."

Oh God. I felt that freeze of panic. "Is Bella okay?"

He nodded. "Yeah, yeah. She's fine. Everyone is fine."

"Okay..."

He continued to stare down at the floor for the longest time before looking up into my eyes. "Actually, that's a lie. Everyone isn't fine. I'm a fucking disaster."

I set my wine on the table. "What's going on? You're making me nervous."

He shook his head. "I'm sorry." After a minute, he got up and moved to the couch next to me. He took one of my hands in his.

I attempted to hide the jolt his touch sent through my body by staring down at our joined hands.

Eventually, Ford put two fingers under my chin and lifted so our eyes met. "I don't know where to start."

"Just say whatever is on your mind."

The two fingers he'd used to lift my chin were still resting beneath it. His thumb reached up and stroked my cheek, tenderly. "I've missed you so much."

I closed my eyes. I wanted to hear those words more than anything, but I was afraid to believe they meant more than they did. The last month had been so hard, and I didn't want to go backwards.

Ford squeezed my hand. "When I went to Chicago, I found out my father had been having an affair."

"What? How?"

"It's a long story, but basically, the real estate agent mentioned a few things that didn't add up—like meeting my mom a few times when I knew she'd never been to Chicago." He shrugged. "I followed a trail and wound up face to face with a woman my father had been with for years."

My forehead wrinkled. "But that doesn't make any sense. Your parents were the happiest people I knew. They were so in love."

He nodded and let out a hefty sigh. "That's what I thought, too. But apparently, my father had some sort of midlife crisis—thought he was missing out on something better since he didn't know what else was out there. He'd been with my mom since high school."

We fell silent. I needed to let what he'd said sink in. It seemed unimaginable that either of his happy parents had cheated. But I suppose some people would have said the same thing about my marriage.

"Are you sure?"

He shrugged. "She admitted it. It went on for years."

While the news was mind-blowing, I had to wonder why he hadn't told me before now. Of course Ryan had been home when Ford returned from his trip, but we'd spent that last night together and had plenty of time to talk.

Then it hit me, the words he'd used. Things started to click into place.

My dad thought he was missing out on something better since he didn't know what else was out there. They'd been together since high school.

I'd been telling Ford all summer how I needed to experience life because I didn't know what else was out there. Finding out about his father must've made him think the same thing would happen between us if we didn't separate.

I looked up into his sad eyes. "I didn't want things to end. I tried to tell you that on our last night together."

He nodded. "I know. But I thought that was how it had to be. Thought maybe next summer...after you'd had some time."

"You wanted me to date until next summer?"

He scoffed. "*Fuck, no.* But I thought that was the way it had to be...what was best for you."

I shook my head, afraid to ask the question. "And now? Do you still think that's the way it has to be?"

"It probably should be." He paused for a long time and then looked so deeply into my eyes, I felt him inside of me. "But I'm so damn in love with you, I just can't."

Tears filled my eyes. "You love me?"

"I loved you almost from the beginning. It just took me a while to admit it to myself because you were so sure we shouldn't be together."

"I was afraid to get hurt again. I thought if we physically stayed apart, my heart wouldn't get broken. But being physically separated doesn't mean your heart can let go."

Ford took a deep breath in and seemed to brace himself. "Are you and Mark...together?"

I shook my head. "No. Not at all. I went to dinner with him, Allison, and Desiree. He just gave me a ride home."

"And the guy the other night?"

"What guy?"

"The one Eve posted on Instagram?"

"That's her weekend manager. It was taken a year or two ago on his birthday, and we'd just sung to him after the restaurant closed. He's happily married with four daughters. I don't even know why she posted it the other day. It was so random."

Ford let out a long whoosh of air and ran his fingers through his hair. "I've been a wreck ever since you reactivated your Match.com profile."

I furrowed my brow. "I didn't reactivate my profile."

"No?"

"I haven't signed on since before the summer."

It hit me that I wasn't the only one with access to that account. Eve had set it up. A reactivated profile, posting a picture of me on Instagram smiling while sitting next to another man...something told me those weren't a coincidence. I started to laugh.

"What's so funny?"

"You, jealous."

His brows rose. "You think me going out of my mind is funny?"

"I do. It serves you right for dumping me. I'm thinking I should go out on a few dates and post a pictorial on Instagram just for you."

Ford's jaw clenched, but he also had to work to hide a smirk. He leaned forward, bent me over his shoulder, and lifted, flipping me onto my back in some stealth move.

Hovering over me, he pushed a stray hair from my face. "Can we pick up where we left off?"

"You mean sneaking around like teenagers and hiding from my son and your sister?"

He rubbed his nose with mine. "No, I mean falling more in love."

I shook my head. "I don't think I can, Ford."

His face dropped, and the pain in his eyes was truly real. I couldn't hurt him like that, even after what he'd put me through.

Reaching up, I stroked his cheek. "I can't because I'm not sure it's possible to fall more in love with you."

His chin dropped to his chest, and he let out a deep, low chuckle. "You're going to make me pay for a long time, aren't you?"

I grinned. "Oh yeah."

Ford pressed his lips to mine. A warmth that had been missing since the summer immediately spread through my body. God, I'd missed him so much.

"I'm sorry," he whispered. "I should have never walked away. I thought if I let you go, if you came back, you would be mine for good."

"When someone is already inside of you, you can't just let go of their heart. The only way to disconnect is to break it."

"Yeah. I know that now. Do you remember when you asked me if it was possible to have the right feelings at the wrong time?"

I nodded. "I was terrified back then."

"We both were, just at different times. The truth is, you can never have the right feelings at the wrong time, because there is never a wrong time for the right person."

I looked into his eyes. "Let's stop running away from each other."

Ford rested his forehead to mine. "I freaking love you, Valentina. I love how you have no rhythm, but it doesn't stop you from dancing. I love how you sneeze when you're nervous and still try to hide that you are. I love the little sound you make when you come, and that you give yourself so completely to me that you don't even know you make it. I love that you went back to school and want to go after all the things you didn't get to do. But most of all, I love you because I *have to*...I can't *not* love you. I tried, and it's physically impossible."

"God, Ford. I love you, too. And I want the whole world to know it. Including my son."

"Good. I'll give you a hand in passing out the message." He took hold of my waist, and suddenly I was in the air and plopped back down on his lap, straddling him. "I'll start by telling the guy who dropped you off."

chapter thirty-two

Ford

I tossed my keys on the table and yelled, "Val?"

"I'm upstairs! Getting changed."

"Our reservations are for eight thirty. Don't take too long."

I'd had a late meeting this afternoon, and tonight had been the winter parent-teacher night at her school, so we were going out to eat. It had been one long-ass week, and it wasn't even Friday yet.

Val had been a nervous wreck about meeting with parents, especially with the few students who weren't doing so hot in her class. It didn't help that last weekend, when she'd planned to prepare a little summary of notes on each student, she'd had an unexpected visitor who took up the majority of her free time.

Her son had again surprised her, coming home early for winter recess. Well, he'd surprised both of us, actually. Valentina hadn't yet told him about us. She'd wanted to tell him in person when he came home on break, instead of over the phone. Her plan had been to talk to him by herself one night and then the three of us would go out to dinner a night or two later. But just like all things between Val and me, it didn't exactly go as planned.

Ryan's flight was due to land at eight in the evening last Saturday night. For the last couple of months, we'd been taking turns staying at each other's places. With Bella back at school and her son not around, the two of us had grown pretty comfortable with walking around half dressed and occasionally fucking on the kitchen floor, if the mood struck. I was as crazy about her as ever, and the mood struck *a lot*. So it wasn't unusual that I'd woken Val by going down on her and then had my junk swinging in the wind while I made two cups of coffee in her kitchen an hour later.

But it *was* unusual for someone to unlock the front door at nine in the morning and walk in while said junk was on full display.

Ryan's early flight home surprised both of us, alright. I still had the fading remnants of a black eye to show exactly what a damn surprise it had been. Her son punched first and asked questions later. I couldn't say I blamed him. Needless to say, the visual had been a lot harder to swallow than the way his mother had planned to tell him she had a boyfriend now—especially since it was me.

I took off my jacket and tossed it over a chair at the kitchen table. The whoosh of air caused a folded piece of mail from the top of a stack to fly off the table and onto the floor. Thinking nothing of it, I bent to pick it up, only the colors of the logo at the top of the letter caught my eye—green, white, and red.

Collocamento internazionale di Roma

My Italian was rusty, but I knew what it was. My heart sank reading the first line.

Dear Ms. Di Giovanni,

Congratulations! We're excited to inform you that we've received your application and one of our consortium member schools has invited you to join their staff for the upcoming school year.

I heard the sound of heels clicking down the stairs, and then Val's happy voice. "I survived, and I'm ready to celebrate that I didn't sneeze on any of the parents!"

I turned with the letter still in my hand, and the smile fell from Val's face. "Oh. Yeah. That came today. The directions said it could take up to twelve weeks to find out if you get a placement. I hadn't expected it after only two."

It wasn't like it was a surprise that she'd applied. I'd been the one to encourage her not to change her plans. But this made it a reality.

I forced a smile. "Congratulations. That's great."

She walked to me and took the letter from my hands, pressing a kiss to my lips. "You're so full of shit."

"No." I shook my head. "It's good news. I just didn't expect it today, I guess, so it caught me off guard."

Val sighed. "I haven't decided if I'm going yet. I just had to apply by the year-end deadline."

"*You're going.*"

She frowned. "Sounds like you can't wait to get rid of me."

I wrapped my hands around her waist and locked them behind her back. "Not a chance. I'm going to be living for school vacations more than I did in high school. I told you, it's gonna take more than an ocean of distance to separate us." I squeezed her to me. "This is good. You're going to have a great time, and I'm gonna be busy while you're gone, too."

Val's eyes widened. "You got the building?"

I nodded. "I did. They accepted my offer. I'll soon be the proud owner of one rundown pile of steel."

She smiled. "That you'll turn into something amazing."

After I passed on the building in Chicago, I hadn't really been planning on looking for another project to expand. But one fell right into my lap. I'd picked up Val for lunch at school one day, and we went to a pizza place a few blocks away. After, I'd pulled into a parking lot nearby so I could kiss her and cop a cheap feel before dropping her back off. The parking lot just happened to be attached to an old, rundown warehouse on the outskirts of a nice, up-and-coming area.

I'd kissed my girl until she made that noise I loved so much, and then when I put the car in reverse with a big-ass smile on my face, I looked up and found myself staring at a giant notice of public auction on the building in front of me. I drove back after dropping Val at school, and one thing led to another.

"I hope so. Because right now the place should be condemned."

Things between Val and me were serious. Probably more serious than they should've been after six months. As fucked up as it was, I'd marry her tomorrow and never look back. But I still thought it was important that she have the experiences she'd wanted to have, that she found herself. Teaching in Rome for a year was a big part of that. Did I want her four-thousand miles away? *Fuck, no.* But I wanted her to be happy more than I hated the thought of her being so far away. She needed to finish off her My Turn list. Well, not all of them—there was no damn way she'd be dating seven different men in seven nights. But I'd been encouraging her to keep up on the important ones—like teaching in Rome and *trying anal.*

And pushing her to follow her dreams had made me realize it was okay to have my own, too—like expanding the temporary office space business into a new area. It wouldn't be Chicago, but something on my own terms.

"Since we're on the subject of real estate and travel..." Val's face turned gloomy. "...I signed the contract for the sale of the beach house today."

"Oh yeah? You don't look happy about that."

"It's hard. I'm thrilled they offered full asking price, yet it's difficult to be happy about selling it, in general. I just have so many memories there of Ryan growing up."

Val hadn't wanted to sell the beach house at all, but her asshole ex-husband had forced her hand. According to her divorce settlement, they had to split the cost of all major repairs. She didn't have the money to fund the major piling replacement that needed to be done, and she also couldn't get a loan since she didn't have a steady work history yet. The beach house meant a lot to her, and I'd offered to give her the money or even lend it to her, but she wouldn't go for it. Which was why...I'd had to buy it under a corporate name and not tell her.

"I know. But if it's any consolation, I'm sure the new owner will make great memories, too."

"I guess..."

"I'm sure they'll fuck all over the house."

Val cringed. "That's not exactly making me feel better."

"Why? The new owner is entitled to make new memories. It shouldn't taint yours in any way."

She shrugged. "I guess. It's just hard to think of someone else inside my house. You know?"

I pulled her close and whispered in her ear. "I know. That's why I bought the house."

Valentina's head pulled back abruptly. "What did you say?"

"I bought the house. For us."

"What are you talking about? A corporation bought the house."

"And what's the name of that corporation?"

"BJ Cummings, Inc."

I raised a brow. I'd been waiting for her to tell me about the name of the corporation, but she never did. And now I knew why—she'd totally missed the joke.

Her eyes grew wide. "Oh my God. You're kidding me? BJ Cummings? What the hell?"

I laughed. "There was no way I was letting you get rid of that place, not when I have big plans for it."

Her brows furrowed. "What plans?"

I pushed a lock of hair behind her ear. "I'm going to give it to my wife as a wedding gift someday. That's still a few years away...because she's stubborn and needs to go slow. But that's my plan."

Valentina's face melted. Her eyes filled with tears. "That's the sweetest thing anyone's ever done for me. But the fact that you wanted to do it is more than enough, Ford. I can't let you spend that kind of money on a house next door to the one you own. It makes no sense."

"My sister really loves my parents' house. And while I enjoyed being out there this summer, it was only because of you. I don't want their family home. I want to make my own family with you. Besides, you don't have any choice but to finish the sale. Money is already in escrow, and we have a binding contract."

"You're unbelievable. I want to at least pay you for half of the house, so we own it jointly."

"BJ Cummings doesn't accept cash."

"Oh no?"

I shook my head. "He only takes sex for payment."

"Is that so?" Her eyes twinkled with mischief, and she wrapped her arms back around my neck. "Well, then, I'd like to make a down payment right now."

"We have dinner reservations in fifteen minutes."

She pushed up on her toes and spoke with her lips against mine. "Fuck dinner."

Now she was talking. I backed her up to the wall and pinned her against it. Hiding what I'd been up to with her house had been weighing on my shoulders. Secrets had no place in a relationship, and getting it off my chest was a huge relief.

It had only been four days since I'd been inside of her, but it felt like a year. I buried my face in her neck and started to suck along the delicate skin leading up to her ear. "God, I missed you."

She panted. "I missed you, too. No time to undress. I took off my panties before I came downstairs and slipped them into my purse so I could give them to you during dinner."

I immediately reached under the hem of her dress and slid my hand up between her legs. Sure enough, she was bare. *And wet.* I groaned. "You're soaked for me already."

Val slipped her hands between us and started to unbuckle my pants. There was no sexier sight in the world than my girl shaking in a frenzy to get to my cock. Later, when it hit her that I'd really bought her house and told her she'd be getting it as a wedding present some day, I'd make love to her when doubt started to creep in. But right now? Right now was all about fucking. Fucking my woman who was going to leave me for months to teach in Rome. And her fucking me because a part of her was scared and angry at what I'd done.

I used my hips to keep her pinned to the wall while I helped push down my pants. Val wrapped her legs around my waist. The minute my throbbing cock felt the hot wetness between her open legs, I was done for. I needed to be inside.

I gripped my shaft and guided myself inside her. Our groans blended into an achingly erotic song as I simultaneously pulled her onto me and lifted until I sank balls-deep inside of her. Then, I stilled to take in the feeling. Nothing had ever felt so damn good.

I tried to start slow, easing in and out in a smooth rhythm, but it didn't last. Before long, I was pounding into her. But she was right there with me, begging for more, telling me to go harder, faster...*more.*

That word...*more*...it was everything about how I felt about her. I wanted more—more of her heart, more of her body, just more.

I pulled my head back to look at her, and our gazes caught. Val's voice shook. "I love you, Ford."

"I love you *more.*"

As I came, her body shook, and I mumbled her name over and over.

"Thank you, Ford. And if what we just did is the payment BJ Cummings wants, he'll be getting plenty of those in the future."

"BJ plans to collect every one of those payments—but this is a fifty-year mortgage."

"Fifty years?" Her eyebrows raised. "I don't even want to do the math on how old I'll be by then."

"Good. Because age is just a number to use to count all the years I'm going to love you."

epilogue

Valentina – Almost two years later

Go commando under my dress.

I peeled the sticky note off the coffee pot and smiled from ear to ear. Ford must've snuck in during the middle of the night to put this here. Considering the girls and I didn't go to bed until after one in the morning, he had to have been up pretty late. I laughed to myself—Tom definitely didn't keep him company next door. He conks out by nine. At least he had Ryan over there.

After a rocky start, my two guys had grown close. Lately, Ryan had even been talking about changing his major to architecture. He'd spent all last summer working with Ford on a building renovation, and it seemed to have given him some direction for his career path.

"Good morning, almost-Mrs. Donovan." I turned to find my almost-sister-in-law rubbing the sandman from her eyes as she padded into the kitchen.

"You're up early." I reached up and took two mugs out of the cabinet over the coffee pot.

"My brother is still a pain in the ass."

"What did he do now?"

Bella squinted and leaned in to read a sticky note on to the refrigerator. Her face twisted like she'd smelled something bad. "Ugh. Really? It's too early to read *that* from my brother. "

I hadn't noticed the other one. I quickly snatched it down.

Bend over naked in mirror and send Ford an ass selfie.

I chuckled but then glanced around the room and swiped three other sticky notes. I couldn't have my future husband's sister going blind on our wedding day. Which she might have, considering the other to-do tasks included *Sneak next door and blow my boyfriend one last time*, and *Insert butt plug to prepare for wedding night festivities.* Though, the last one confused me a little: *Get licked by wedding gift.*

Bella poured half and half into our coffees and lifted a mug to her lips. "You guys are really gross. You're going to make me toss my cookies."

"Did someone say cookies?" Eve wandered into the kitchen.

She had on a T-shirt that barely covered half her round belly and a pair of sweatpants rolled underneath it. She scratched her very pregnant tummy.

I walked over and dipped my head to talk to my future goddaughter. "Good morning, my little princess."

"Or prince."

"There's no way my goddaughter is a boy."

Eve and Tom had been pretty shocked to discover they were pregnant eight months ago. When they first got together, they'd decided to leave having children up to fate. With Eve almost forty and nothing having happened, she'd pretty much concluded they wouldn't have a family. So it was a shocker when Eve's stomach virus had turned out to be that she was two months pregnant.

I myself had thought I might be pregnant last week, but I'd taken a test, and it was negative. The stress of the wedding and moving into Ford's place must've just thrown off my cycle. Like Eve and Tom, Ford and I had agreed to leave adding more members to the family up to fate. Though, I'll admit, I was a little sad when a minus sign appeared on the stick last week.

"Oh shit. I almost forgot. My brother woke me up for a reason."

"What?"

"He called and said to go to the front door. Apparently he left a wedding gift for you there, and I'm supposed to bring it to you."

My brows furrowed, and Eve and I followed Bella to the door.

I shrieked, finding a cage. "Oh my God! A puppy!"

The adorable little pug started to bark and jump up and down. He was so excited, he kept banging his head on the top of the plastic carrier. "Bring him in. Bring him in." I laughed. "He's going to get hurt doing that."

Bella carried the cage inside, and I sat on the living room floor and unlatched the metal door. The little guy sprinted out and right onto my lap. He actually knocked me over and started to lick my face.

"Well, look at that," Eve said. "He reminds me of your fiancé when he first saw you."

Ah. That last sticky note makes more sense now.

I'd been bugging Ford about getting a puppy for a few months now—one of the last few items left on my My Turn list. At first, we'd put it off because of the year I taught in Rome. Then I'd gotten a new tenure-track position at my school, and Ford was busy getting the new temp office space building ready for the grand opening. Life had just been busy the last two years. But this summer, our plan was to slow down, and the timing was perfect to train this little guy. Our Memorial Day weekend clambake wedding was only the start of a long and lazy summer back in Montauk.

"I cannot believe he did this. He's so adorable." I scratched behind his ears, and the puppy's left hind leg started to spasm. "Bella, would you mind getting my cell so I can text Ford? I don't want to let go of this little guy. It's on the kitchen counter."

Bella found my phone and snapped a picture of my new puppy licking my face while I smiled. She showed it to me, and I told her to send it to her brother.

A minute later, my phone buzzed with an incoming text.

Ford: I'm jealous of a dog. How do I get me some of that?

I smiled and texted back. My sweet little pup had knocked himself out in less than two minutes and was now snuggled in my lap.

Valentina: I'll let you lick my face after you say I do.

Ford: It's not your face I'll be licking tonight, sweetheart.

Bella groaned. "You two should get a room. I can't even look at you texting each other. You get that..." She waved her hand around in front of my face. "...that look that says you're sexting with my brother. Gross."

I laughed.

Valentina: BTW...your sister found one of your sticky notes this morning.

Ford: What the hell was she doing up before you?

Valentina: We were up late, and I slept in. The Montauk air must've wiped me out.

Ford: Well, you better relax and save all your energy for tonight.

Valentina: I will. And thank you for the puppy! He's so adorable. Though now I have a child out of wedlock for the second time. You couldn't have waited a few hours to give him to me? ;)

Ford: I can come take him back?

Valentina: Too late. I love him already. Does he have a name?

Ford: Nope. That's all you. Pick something good.

Valentina: Are you nervous about today?

Ford: Not at all. You're already my forever. This is just a formality.

Oh my God.

I covered my mouth and stared down at the stick. The plus sign was a deep, dark blue. I must've taken the first test too early. My hand shook, and I just kept whispering *Oh my God, Oh my God* over and over. I think I was in more shock than I'd been at seventeen the first time it happened.

"Everything okay in there?" Eve knocked on the bathroom door.

The sound made me jump.

"Ummm. Yeah." *Achoo!* "Everything is fine. I'll be out in a few minutes."

"Alright. Fifteen minutes to show time. Don't take too long."

I'm pregnant.

Oh my God.

My son is twenty-one.

And I'm pregnant again.

My ex-husband and I had tried for years after we had Ryan, so I'd just assumed it couldn't happen. Then again, Ryan and I never practiced getting pregnant anywhere near as much as Ford and I do. I had my doubts about lots of things with my future husband, but his desire for me was never one of them. The man was insatiable, so I really shouldn't be surprised he'd knocked me up.

Oh my God.

I need to tell him.

I'd gotten him an antique pocket watch for a wedding gift. This was so much better.

Still shaking, I tossed the stick in the wastebasket and unlocked the bathroom door. My maid of honor and bridesmaid were downstairs waiting for me. In the excitement, I'd forgotten that this was the first time they were seeing me in my wedding gown. I'd picked a simple, lace dress with a mermaid silhouette and slight train. It had a beachy vibe to it and was perfect for a barefoot wedding in the sand.

I walked slowly down the stairs.

"You look..." Eve wiped her eyes. "Gorgeous. You're glowing, Val. I've never seen you so happy."

Glowing. Good choice of words.

I hugged my best friend and almost-sister-in-law. "Thank you. You both look beautiful."

"You ready to get married?"

"Actually, no."

Eve's smile fell. "What's the matter?"

"Nothing. Nothing. But I need to talk to Ford before the ceremony."

"He's already outside on the beach, waiting for you."

"Can you...go out and ask him to come over? It'll just be a minute."

"Sure. Of course." She hesitated. "Are you sure everything is okay? I heard you sneezing in the bathroom."

I smiled. "It's just pollen. I'm good."

Eve and Bella went out the back, and a few minutes later, Ford knocked on the door.

"I thought you didn't want to see me before the wedding because of the silly superstition?"

My feet were frozen to the living room floor. Ford had to walk to me. I couldn't even meet him halfway. The minute he got a good look at my face, his grew pale.

"What's going on, babe? Are you nervous?"

I nodded.

He immediately wrapped me in his arms. "It's okay. That's normal. Just take a few deep breaths."

I did, but it didn't make me any calmer. After a minute, Ford pulled his head back to look at me. "You're shaking."

I nodded. "Ford... I..." I choked up, and a fat tear spilled out and ran down my cheek.

He wiped it away with his thumb. "Don't cry, baby. Everything is going to be okay. We don't have to do this if you're not ready."

Oh my God, no. That's what he thought? I couldn't pull my head together enough to explain, so instead, I just blurted, "I'm pregnant."

He froze. "What?"

I nodded. "When I went to put on my lipstick, a wave of nausea came over me from the smell of it. I still haven't gotten my period, and I just got a funny feeling. The test I bought last week had two tests, so I did the second one. It was positive. I'm pregnant. *We're* pregnant."

Ford's head dropped. "Jesus Christ, Val. I thought you were having cold feet. You scared the shit out of me."

"I'm sorry. I didn't mean to."

He lifted me up off my feet into the air. "You're really freaking pregnant? We're going to have a kid?"

I laughed. "We are."

He spun me around twice and yelled louder, "We're going to have a baby! We're going to have a baby!"

"Ummm...Ford, if you keep spinning me like that, you're going to be getting married with puke all over your shoulder. I've been queasy ever since I tried to put on the lipstick. I thought it was just my nerves, but apparently not."

"Oh shit. Sorry." He set me down and wrapped me in his arms—so tight, I could barely breathe. "I didn't think..." He shook his head. "I just didn't think it would happen. And I would've been fine with that. But now... holy shit, I guess I really wanted this."

I smiled and sniffled back tears. "Me, too. I didn't actually realize how much so until I saw that plus sign a few minutes ago. I couldn't even wait until after the ceremony to tell you."

Ford took my cheeks into his hands and spoke with his lips pressed to mine. "My wife is going to have my baby."

"Well, technically, I'm not your wife yet. We do have to go outside and get that part over with. There are fifty or so people out there that we're keeping from a clambake."

He kissed me hard. "Let 'em wait."

After a long, emotional kiss, Ford leaned his forehead against mine. "You know what I just thought of?"

"That I can't seem to get married *before* getting pregnant?"

He chuckled. "No. But that is pretty funny."

"What did you just think of then?"

"Do you remember when we first met, I told you Mrs. Peabody had a dream that I'd met my future wife?"

I nodded. "I do."

"Do you remember what else she said?"

I thought back. He'd said something about her throwing up. "She got sick after the premonition, right?"

"She woke up and smelled cinnamon buns cooking in the oven, and then threw up. *Bun in the oven.*"

I covered my mouth. "Oh wow. That's crazy."

"Well, that's not the half of it. This morning she called and asked me if I had two little girls in our wedding party. I said no. She said she'd dreamed twin girls were at our wedding."

I got goosebumps down my arms, and my eyes widened. "Oh my God. You don't think…"

Ford shook his head and his smile fell. "Fuck me. *Two girls.*"

I laughed. "We don't know that's true."

"Yes, I do. *We're having twin girls.* And I'm gonna need a shotgun if they look anything like their mother." He kissed me again. "Come on, I need to go marry my baby momma so I can at least qualify for some conjugal visits while I'm in prison."

We laughed and walked out onto the back deck together. Down below were all of our friends and family, casually milling around, waiting for the ceremony to start. We stopped at the railing to take it all in. Two big, white party tents were set up right on the beach, and a wooden walkway led from the bottom of the stairs of both houses, down to a flower-filled archway. White chairs had been set up on both sides of the wooden path. This little summer town held so many old memories for both of us. And now, we would make new ones of our own as a family.

I looked around at all of the people waiting to share our day. It was pretty amazing, really. We go through life picking up puzzle pieces, and we never really know where they'll fit or how they'll come together to form the big picture. I'd spent years trying to fit pieces into places they didn't belong, but never really felt complete. Until today. All of my puzzle pieces finally clicked into place, and I could see the beautiful picture.

I took a deep breath and seared the moment into my memory before turning around in Ford's arms. "You ready to marry me, Mr. Donovan?"

He brushed his lips with mine. "I've been waiting my whole life to marry you, Mrs. Donovan. Let's do this."

acknowledgements

To you – the *readers*. Whether this was your first book of mine, or your twenty-fifth, I am so grateful that you've allowed Ford and Valentina in to your hearts and homes. I hope you enjoyed the escape to Montauk and you'll come back in the fall to see where we'll travel to next!

To Penelope – Things keep getting tougher in booklandia, which only makes our friendship even more important to me. Our partnership is so valuable, but knowing that if it all went away tomorrow, I'd still have the dearest friend, is invaluable.

To Cheri – Thank you for always being up for a crazy trip! Signings would be no fun without you. I've said it before, but it still holds true today: Books brought us together, but friendship made us forever.

To Julie – Thank you for being one of the most dependable friends I've been lucky enough to cross paths with.

To Luna – Thank you for your friendship and love. And for making my books come alive with your beautiful graphics—every single time!

To my amazing Facebook reader group, Vi's Violets – This group is a gift. You not only celebrate my successes, but you bring me the encouragement and support I sometimes need when things get difficult. Your love and kindness is my daily motivation!

To Sommer – Once again, you wrapped my book in the perfect cover. Thank you for your attention to every detail and for not firing me as a client when I drive you nuts.

To my agent and friend, Kimberly Brower – Thank you for all of your hard work and always going above and beyond what is expected. There is no agent who works as hard as you do!

To Jessica, Elaine, and Eda – Thank you for being the dream team of editing! You smooth out the all the rough edges and make me shine!

To Mindy –Thank you for pulling things together for *All Grown Up!*

To all of the bloggers – Once again, thank you for all of your support. Your passion is contagious and your thoughtful reviews inspire potential readers to try my stories. Thank you for everything you do—taking time out of your busy lives to read my stories, sharing your love of books, and always supporting my work.

Much love
Vi

about the author

Vi Keeland is a #1 *New York Times*, #1 *Wall Street Journal*, and *USA Today* Bestselling author. With millions of books sold, her titles have appeared in over a hundred Bestseller lists and are currently translated in twenty-five languages. She resides in New York with her husband and their three children where she is living out her own happily ever after with the boy she met at age six.

other books by vi keeland

Standalone novels
We Shouldn't
The Naked Truth
Sex, Not Love
Beautiful Mistake
EgoManiac
Bossman
The Baller
Hate Notes (Co-written with Penelope Ward)
British Bedmate (Co-written with Penelope Ward)
Mister Moneybags (Co-written with Penelope Ward)
Playboy Pilot (Co-written with Penelope Ward)
Stuck-Up Suit (Co-written with Penelope Ward)
Cocky Bastard (Co-written with Penelope Ward)
Left Behind (A Young Adult Novel)
First Thing I See

The Rush Series
Rebel Heir (Co-written with Penelope Ward)
Rebel Heart (Co-written with Penelope Ward)

Life on Stage series (2 standalone books)
Beat
Throb

MMA Fighter series (3 standalone books)
Worth the Fight
Worth the Chance
Worth Forgiving

The Cole Series (2 book serial)
Belong to You
Made for You